THE POOL IN THE DESERT

THE POOL IN THE DESERT

Sara Jeannette Duncan

edited by Gillian Siddall
with an introduction by Rosemary Sullivan

broadview literary texts

Canadian Cataloguing in Publication Data

Duncan, Sara Jeannette, 1861-1922
     The pool in the desert

(Broadview literary texts)
Contents: The pool in the desert – A mother in India – An impossible ideal –
The hesitation of Miss Anderson.
ISBN 1-55111-153-5

I. Siddall, Gillian H. (Gillian Heather)   II. Title.   III. Series.

PS8455.O85P6 2000   C813'.4   C00-932876-9
PR9199.2.C68P6 2000

Broadview Press Ltd. is an independent, international publishing house, incor-
porated in 1985

North America
Post Office Box 1243, Peterborough, Ontario, Canada K9J 7H5
3576 California Road, Orchard Park, NY 14127
Tel: (705) 743-8990; Fax: (705) 743-8353;
e-mail: customerservice@broadviewpress.com

United Kingdom:
Thomas Lyster, Ltd.,
Unit 9, Ormskirk Industrial Park, Old Boundary Way, Burscough Rd,
Ormskirk, Lancashire L39 2YW Tel: (1695) 575112; Fax: (1695) 570120;
E-Mail: books@tlyster.co.uk

Australia:
St. Clair Press, P.O. Box 287, Rozelle, NSW 2039
Tel: (02) 818-1942; Fax: (02) 418-1923

www.broadviewpress.com

Broadview Press is grateful to Professor Eugene Benson for advice on editorial
matters for the Broadview Literary Texts series.

Broadview Press gratefully acknowledges the financial support of the Book
Publishing Industry Development Program, Ministry of Canadian Heritage,
Government of Canada.

Typesetting and assembly: True to Type Inc., Mississauga, Canada.
PRINTED IN CANADA

Contents

Acknowledgements

I would like to extend my thanks to Tom Tausky, Ajay Heble, and Judy Barton, and to my colleagues at Lakehead University for their assistance with this project. I also gratefully acknowledge the librarians at Lakehead University for their co-operation and assistance. I would also like to thank the people at Broadview Press, especially Barbara Conolly and Don LePan. Finally, many thanks to Eugene Benson for his ongoing encouragement and patience.

Abbreviations

OED: *Oxford English Dictionary*

OF: *Oxford French-English Dictionary*

EN: *Microsoft Encarta Encyclopedia Deluxe*, 1999

RT: David Barton, *The Raj at the Table*, London: Faber and Faber, 1994

HJ: Hobson Jobson, *A Glossary of Colloquial Anglo-Indian Words Phrases*, London, 1903

TH: Sinharaja Tammita-Delgoda, *A Traveller's History of India.* New York: Interlink Books, 1995

Introduction

Rosemary Sullivan

Often we condescend to history, particularly where the historical experience of women is concerned. We assume that the social and economic constraints on the lives of women in the past meant that they could never be as independent and ambitious as modern women are. When we find a woman who achieved a significant professional career with singlemindedness and intelligence, we are surprised. We should not be. There were more of them than we realize.

Sara Jeannette Duncan was such a woman. How she surfaced from the hinterland of nineteenth-century colonial Canada to become a well-known journalist and novelist with over twenty books to her credit is a fascinating and edifying story. And how her books, for the most part, were lost to public memory is also instructive. One novel, *The Imperialist*, focusing on the imperial debate in Canada at the turn of the century, has long been considered a Canadian classic, and has been available in paperback since 1961. But no other books by Duncan are generally available beyond academic circles. We reprint here one of her best: *The Pool in the Desert*, first published in 1903. It is a fine collection of stories set in India. Reading it, one enters the world of a gifted woman of wit and insight, capable of discriminating attention to human motivation. After almost a century, the stories are still fresh.

Duncan was born in Brantford, Canada West (later Ontario) in 1861. At that time Brantford was a small provincial city of ten thousand, rather smug in the way that only a colonial town can be, confident in its newness and assured of its own brilliant future. It was not necessarily a bad beginning for a young novelist. Coming from the right class, Duncan inherited the town's pioneer confidence, without being seduced by its complacency.

At nine, Duncan wanted to be a novelist: "I remember once entertaining, and unguardedly expressing, at the age of nine, a wild desire to write a novel. 'Put it out of your mind, my dear,' nodded a placid old lady of the last century over her knitting. 'Novel-making women always come to some bad end.'" (The *Globe*, November 12, 1986). But against the conventionalities of her class and sex, she persisted in her eccentricities. After a brief stint as a teacher, the safe career preferred by her parents, Duncan decided to become a journalist. She devised a scheme to attend the New Orleans Cotton Centennial, a World's Fair opening in December 1884, and presented her plan to the editor of the Toronto *Globe*, John Cameron.

Perhaps it was her charm and self-assurance that convinced him to buy her articles at "five dollars each, with the option of refusing any he did not like." She set off by train alone to New Orleans on the trip that launched her journalistic career. She was twenty-three.

On the strength of her New Orleans copy, she was hired by the *Globe* as a weekly columnist. Then in October 1885 she went to Washington to assume an editorial position as the columnist of "Current Literature" for the Washington *Post*, writing book reviews, editorials on cultural subjects, and, occasionally, lead articles. The *Post* was one of the most prestigious American papers, and Duncan had made it to the inner sanctum, the editorial office. Rather than being a handicap, being female was an asset at this time when American women were beginning to make a name for themselves in journalism. And there was already a long-standing tradition of women making successful careers as writers.

Duncan returned to Canada and, in July 1886, resumed her position with the *Globe*, writing the "Women's World" daily column, thus becoming the first woman to work in the editorial department of a leading Canadian newspaper. She proved to be an intelligent and reflective journalist. Writing what was nominally a society column, she found scope for her political and cultural interests, namely Canadian national identity, Canadian culture, and contemporary feminism. Her position as a nationalist was unambiguous; Canada would need its own literature if it was to have a complete national existence. As a feminist Duncan was neither a suffragette nor a political activist, believing that women would achieve equality through individual effort and education. And perhaps, like many attractive women, she was afraid that feminist "stridency" would compromise the impact of her own feminine charm, which she used to good effect.

She stayed with the *Globe* only until April, thereby establishing a pattern. She never stayed long with any particular paper. It may have been that she was simply restless for new experience. Or perhaps journalism could only momentarily hold the attention of a woman whose real talent was for fiction.

Her next post was in Montreal with the *Star*. After four months she moved to Ottawa as one of the *Star's* parliamentary correspondents, and stayed three months covering the political beat. Although Duncan continued to work as a freelance journalist, this was her last formal post. At the age of twenty-seven, edging her way towards her first book, she set off on a world tour with fellow journalist Lily Lewis. Their travels became the subject of *A Social Departure* (1890), which proved to be a best selling book in Canada and England.

It was decidedly unorthodox for two young women to travel alone, and with characteristic zest Duncan wrote that she deliberately went "round the world the wrong way." She and Lily Lewis left for the west coast on the Canadian Pacific, completed just three years previously, "You may choose to be dragged along in an inlaid box upholstered in silk plush all the days of your earthly pilgrimage if you like, but for me, I would ride on the engine always." Their itinerary was exotic: from Vancouver to Japan, Ceylon, India, Suez, Cairo, and back to England via Brindisi, Malta, and Gibraltar. They travelled from November 1888 to May 1889, and Duncan sent her travelogues back to the *Star* in installments. Her enthusiasm is infectious: "There is a satisfaction that is difficult to parallel in getting as far as you can go."

While in India she met her future husband, Everard Cotes, an entomologist who had come out from England four years earlier as assistant to the Superintendent of Calcutta's India Museum. Cotes was to prove a solicitous and generous husband. He proposed to Duncan at the Taj Mahal (an interesting context for her story "A Mother in India") and she accepted. Leaving her fiancé in India, Duncan continued her travels with Lily Lewis as far as England. She returned to Canada in the summer of 1890, after an absence of two years, and in October set out once again for India. She had not seen Everard Cotes for a year and a half, and her knowledge of him was based on a brief encounter that spanned a few weeks. It says much for her intuition that he proved to be an admirable man. But she found the Anglo-Indian set of Calcutta and Simla, where she later lived, impossibly stuffy, provincial, and dedicated to an official decorum that was entirely stultifying. Duncan was an elitist and a monarchist. She had no difficulty with the lot of the Indians and the ethics of imperialism (in fact, the social context of Indian poverty and suffering is virtually absent from her stories). What she did question was the cost to the individual Anglo of sustaining the sterile and artificial facade of British order on the reaches of Empire. In sum, she found herself on the periphery of the cultured world at whose centre she wanted to be, the world where a writer could matter. This disgruntlement provided the satiric edge to her writing and identified its controlling theme: the moral and creative costs of the failure to live to the full stretch of one's talent and emotional needs. Marriage, too, Duncan found constraining, for while the man was admirable, the social institution forced her to live in a context that suffocated her. Yet, these are powerful themes for fiction, as her novels and stories were to prove.

After a second book with a travelogue theme, *An American Girl in London* (1891), she began to write of colonial life in India, and here she found a rich vein. Works like *The Simple Adventures of a Memsahib* (1893) or *His Honour and a Lady* (1896) are good books, and among her best. Duncan had a very successful career, earning reputation and enough money to finance her many escapes to England. Yet it must be admitted that her work after 1904 is thin at best. Perhaps she couldn't sustain herself (who can?) in an environment that didn't meet the needs of her particular imagination, and by disposition and training she wasn't able to leave the British compound to find in India a world that might have challenged her.

Duncan left India permanently in 1915, and her husband did not join her until 1919. They finally bought a house outside London in 1922, but by this time Duncan was already ill, having suffered for years from chest ailments. She died at the age of sixty-one on June 22, 1922, after a five-week bout with pneumonia. On her gravestone is a somewhat ambiguous epitaph: "This leaf was blown far."

The Pool in the Desert is a remarkable synthesis of Duncan's experiences of India. Not only are the stories very well crafted, but they also show that she could write with a shrewd social intelligence and from a decidedly feminine perspective. She found her literary model in Henry James, from whom she took the clue that a story is generated from *a donné* or what she would call a "situation." Each of her stories poses a situation that must work itself out through the circuitous route of social etiquette or convention. She is interested in the psyches of her female characters as mothers, wives, lovers, and even as failed artists, and in all cases the women find the conventional world a tight fit, though one to which they generally acquiesce.

In "A Mother in India" the situation is simple. A mother is reunited with her daughter whom she has seen only twice in twenty-one years. The focus of the story is the mother's discovery of her own ambivalence toward her straight-laced, provincial daughter. Not only does she discover that the daughter is a stranger, and blood ties do not guarantee temperamental affinity, but she also begins to understand that conventional ideas about maternity are, in some ways, a male invention. "Men are very slow in changing their philosophy about women. I fancy their idea of the maternal relation is firmest fixed of all." When she is candid enough to convey her ambivalence to a young male friend, she describes his response: "The primitive man in him rose up as Pope of nature and excommunicated me as a creature recusant to her functions." The young man decides to court the daughter as an "office of consolation" in order to castigate the mother for her failure of feeling. The story is neither polemical nor strident. It is a witty, subtle, and extremely intelligent study of a woman who discovers that her notions of her own independent being are in conflict with her maternal role, which in her case has no roots in a history of feeling, but is rather a masquerade imposed by social demands.

The fact that Duncan herself had given birth, in 1900, to a child who lived only a few days adds a particular poignancy to her reference to the tragedy of the barren woman. And it must have taken courage to attempt the subject of maternal ambivalence in a character whom she clearly intends to be attractive.

"An Impossible Ideal" is Duncan's effort to explore the artist's need for freedom. It is interesting that she chooses to make the artist a young man and that the woman in the story achieves the height of her own creativity only vicariously through him. The temptation for the artist is "the possibilities of marriage, social position, assured income, support in old age, the strands in the bond that held him, the bond that holds us all." Will he make his terrified escape? The impossible ideal is to remain uncompromised, to be finally unbiddable: the price of escape would seem to be to abandon the social ideal of a life with others. Duncan's ambivalence in the judgment of her characters is fascinating. It seems for her so hard to choose.

In "The Hesitation of Miss Anderson," Duncan's portrait of Simla is decidedly bitter. It is a superficial world of trivial scandals, devoted to a "cult of official dignity." Using a rather sentimental plot with a complicated coincidence, she works with a theme that must have been close to the bone. This time her female character seeks to secure freedom and fulfilment without violating the moral norms of conventional honour and good taste. She wishes to act with conscience and only at moments is drawn "by something stronger than her sense of honesty and humanity, a determination to see, to know, that swept these things away." For modern readers, this story appears somewhat dated in that Duncan's horror of vulgarity is exaggerated and fastidious. And yet the longing for freedom, for impulsive action, the temptation for a life "without boundaries" is poignant in this world of the hesitant, scrupulous conscience. Duncan is so anxious to make a careful distinction between the trivial and the tragic, between self-indulgent and righteous action, that the story seems to ring with labyrinthine confusions about freedom that may have been her own.

The first story, "The Pool in the Desert," is again an exploration in minute detail of the motivations of a powerful and emotional woman, filtered through the perspective of a third party, a sympathetic and yet objective female friend. Here Duncan presents a model of female friendship in which women are capable of deeper intellectual bonds than their rather superficial husbands. The plot is "high comedy with the proximity of tears": Judy, a woman of thirty-seven, falls in love with a friend's twenty-six-year-old son. British India is bitterly caricatured: in the foreground "the tinsel vision of India"; in reality "the arid stretch beyond." "People in India were sepulchers of themselves, but ... now and then one came who could roll away another's stone." Judy is married to an inadequate husband who had the temerity to "interfere between [this] woman and what she was entitled to live for." For years she has been feeding on herself, and is therefore the kind of woman capable of "sacrificing everything ... of gathering her life into an hour." Duncan has posed the possibility for her character of a blessed "Second Chance," and now the choice is framed not in terms of moral scruples, but rather in terms of a complicated and paradoxical tension between pride and humility.

While Duncan may rehearse in her female characters the problem of frustration and unfulfillment, she is nowhere strident. Her stories are not simply displacements of some personal confusion, nor are they written in a way that implies self-pity. In fact, she is a master ironist, and the failure to live one's true potential is seen as the general human lot. Her stories are fused with an elegiac sense of diminishment, an ironic resignation to the human capacity for self-deception, and a longing for the self to be deeply moved.

Sara Jeannette Duncan: A Brief Chronology

1861   Born Sarah Janet in Brantford, Ontario (then Canada West) on December 22 to Charles Duncan and Jane Duncan, née Bell.

1879   Attends County Model School to obtain 3rd class teaching certificate. Drops "h" from Sarah.

1880   First poem published in the Toronto *Globe*. Other poems that year printed in the *Canadian Illustrated News* and *The Canada Monthly*.

1881   First essay appears in *Rose-Belford's Canadian Monthly and National Review*.

1882   Attends Toronto Normal School to obtain 2nd class teaching certificate.

1884   Does some supply teaching; begins writing for a Brantford newspaper, probably the *Courier*; goes to New Orleans to cover the Cotton Centennial for the Toronto *Globe* and the London *Advertiser*; while in New Orleans, she also writes for the *Memphis Appeal*, the *New Orleans Times-Democrat* and the *Washington Post*, all under the name "Garth."

1885   Hired to write a weekly column for the Toronto *Globe*; she writes under the pen-name of "Garth Grafton"; some of these columns also printed in the *Washington Post* and the *Memphis Daily Appeal*; leaves for Washington to work as an editorial writer for the *Washington Post*.

1886   Becomes a regular contributor to the Toronto *The Week* in addition to her work at the *Post*; writes columns for *The Week* under names "Sara Jeannette Duncan" and "Garth Grafton"; begins long friendship with William Dean Howells; attends Woman Suffrage Convention in Washington with featured speaker Susan B. Anthony; returns to Brantford; hired by the Toronto *Globe* (first woman in Canada to work on a regular basis for a leading newspaper).

1887   Moves to Montreal to become a regular columnist for the Montreal *Star*.

1888   In February moves to Ottawa to become a parliamentary reporter for the *Star*; in September departs for round-the-world tour with friend Lily Lewis, including stops in Japan, Hong Kong, Singapore, Ceylon, India, and England.

1889   Meets Everard Cotes in Calcutta; he proposes to her at the Taj Mahal in Agra; she and Lily continue on their journey; they part in May. Duncan goes to Wallingford, England, to meet Everard's family and then on to London.

1890   Presented to Queen Victoria at St James Palace; publication of *A Social Departure: How Orthodocia and I Went Round the World by Ourselves*. London: Chatto & Windus; New York: D. Appleton; in the summer returns to Brantford; October returns to India; marries Everard in Calcutta, December 6. They settle in Calcutta.

1891   Publication of *An American Girl in London*. Chatto & Windus; New York: D. Appleton; Toronto: Williamson & Company; and *Two Girls on a Barge*. London: Chatto & Windus; New York: D. Appleton.

1892   First of many lengthy visits to London after her marriage.

1893   Publication of *The Simple Adventures of a Memsahib*. London: Chatto & Windus; New York: D. Appleton.

1894   Everard takes position as editor of the *Indian Daily News*; Duncan also joins the editorial staff ; publication of *A Daughter of To-day*. London: Chatto & Windus; New York: D. Appleton; Toronto: Toronto New Company; *Vernon's Aunt*. London: Chatto & Windus; New York: D. Appleton (1895) and *The Story of Sonny Sahib*. London: Chatto & Windus; New York: D. Appleton (1895); London: Henry Frowde, Hodder & Stoughton, n.d.

1896   Publication of *His Honor, and a Lady*. London: Macmillan; New York: D. Appleton; Toronto: G.M. Rose.

1897   Duncan and Everard move to Simla, India, where Everard takes position as a government press correspondent.

1898   Publication of *A Voyage of Consolation*. London: Methuen; New York: D. Appleton.

1899   Publication of *The Path of a Star*. London: Methuen. American title: *Hilda: A Story of Calcutta*. New York: Frederick A. Stokes.

1900   Birth of the Cotes' only child, who lives only a few days (the birth is not confirmed in any public record); Duncan contracts tuberculosis and is ordered to spend the summer resting outside in her garden; during that time she writes *On the Other Side of the Latch*.

1901   Publication of *On the Other Side of the Latch*. London: Methuen; American title: *The Crow's Nest*. New York: Dodd, Mead; Duncan and Everard move back to Calcutta so Everard can recruit for the Boer War.

1902   Publication of *Those Delightful Americans*. London: Methuen. New York: D. Appleton.

1903   Honoured by the Canadian Society of Authors in Toronto; publication of *The Pool in the Desert*. London: Methuen; New York: D. Appleton.

1904   Publication of *The Imperialist*. London: Constable; New York: D. Appleton; Toronto: Copp Clark.

1906   Publication of *Set in Authority*. London: Constable; New York: Doubleday, Page.

1908   Publication of *Cousin Cinderella*; London: Methuen; New York: Macmillan.

1909   Publication of *The Burnt Offering*. London: Methuen; New York: John Lane (1910).

1912   Publication of *The Consort*. London: Stanley Paul; E.M. Forster visits the Cotes in Simla.

1914   Publication of *His Royal Happiness*. New York: D. Appleton; London: Stodder & Staughton (1915).

1915   *His Royal Happiness* produced as a play in Toronto; *The Convalescents* produced by the Simla Amateur Dramatic Club; Duncan moves to London, England.

1916   *Beauchamp and Beecham* (the new title for *The Convalescents*) produced at the Lyric Theatre, London.

1917   *Julyann* produced at the Globe Theatre, London.

1919   Everard joins Duncan in London.

1922   Publication of *Title Clear*. London: Hutchinson; Duncan dies
        of pneumonia, July 22; she is buried at St Giles
        Anglican church in Ashtead, England.

1924   Publication of *The Gold Cure*. London: Hutchinson.

A Note on the Text

The Pool in the Desert was published in the summer of 1903 by D. Appleton and Co. in New York and by Methuen and Co. in London. The two editions are virtually identical, with the exception of American and English spellings and different pagination. In the few instances of substantive variants, the Appleton edition offers the more credible alternative, and it is this text that has been used for this edition. For example, in "An Impossible Ideal," the Appleton edition tells us that Ingersoll Amour, an artist who has come to Simla, is making a "little wooden 'pochade'" whereas the Methuen edition tells us that he is making a "little wooden 'pochard.'" A pochade is a sketch; a pochard is a type of duck; it seems more likely that Duncan was referring generically to sketching rather than specifically to a particular subject matter that does not seem to be in keeping with the kind of work Ingersoll Armour creates.

Two of the stories from *The Pool in the Desert* appeared in magazines prior to the publication of the book. "The Pool in the Desert" appeared in its entirety in *Century Magazine* in May 1903. "A Mother in India" appeared in the June and July editions of *Scribner's Magazine* in 1903. Substantive changes have been made to both stories in the Appleton and Methuen editions. The changes to "A Mother in India" are fairly inconsequential; they seem to have been made with an eye to clarification of plot or to enhance the aesthetic quality of particular sentences. Most of the changes to the *Century Magazine* edition of "A Pool in the Desert" are of a similar nature, but, in addition, some fairly major changes have been made to this story that appear to be motivated by a desire to enhance and refine characterization. For example, a long section has been added in which Judy Harbottle explains more fully than in the *Century Magazine* edition the history of her romance with her best friend's young adult son.

In addition, a substantial change to the conclusion of the story changes a comic ending to a more wistful one, and again alters and complicates the way in which we are invited to understand and judge Judy Harbottle. In *Century Magazine*, the last word is given to Judy's best friend, the mother of the young man with whom Judy claims to have fallen in love: "'Dear Judy!' she said with sentiment. 'She could n't exchange me for a mother-in-law.'" The Appleton (and Methuen) gives the final word to the narrator who states:

It was like her to abandon in pride a happiness that asked so much less humiliation; I don't know why, but it was like her. And of course, when one thought of it, she had consulted all sorts of high expediencies. But I sat silent with remembrance, quieting a pang in my heart, trying not to calculate how much it had cost Judy Harbottle to take her second chance.

A facsimile edition of the Appleton text of *The Pool in the Desert* was published by the University of Toronto Press in 1978. *The Pool in the Desert* was also published by Penguin Books in 1984. The Appleton edition was used as the text for this edition, but the order of the stories was altered so that "The Pool in the Desert" appeared last instead of first, perhaps to feature "A Mother in India," arguably the collection's strongest story, as the starting story. The original ordering of the stories has been retained in this edition.

THE POOL IN THE DESERT

BY

MRS. EVERARD COTES

(SARA JEANNETTE DUNCAN)

NEW YORK

D. APPLETON AND COMPANY

MCMIII

Part I

The Pool in the Desert

I KNEW Anna Chichele and Judy Harbottle so well, and they figured so vividly at one time against the rather empty landscape of life in a frontier station,[1] that my affection for one of them used to seem little more, or less, than a variant upon my affection for the other. That recollection, however, bears examination badly; Judy was much the better sort, and it is Judy's part in it that draws me into telling the story. Conveying Judy is what I tremble at: her part was simple. Looking back — and not so very far — her part has the relief of high comedy with the proximity of tears; but looking close, I find that it is mostly Judy, and that what she did is entirely second, in my untarnished picture, to what she was. Still I do not think I can dissuade myself from putting it down.

They would, of course, inevitably have found each other sooner or later, Mrs. Harbottle and Mrs. Chichele, but it was I who actually introduced them; my palmy veranda in Rawul Pindi,[2] where the tea-cups used to assemble, was the scene of it. I presided behind my samovar[3] over the early formalities that were almost at once to drop from their friendship, like the sheath of some bursting flower. I deliberately brought them together, so the birth was not accidental, and my interest in it quite legitimately maternal. We always had tea in the veranda in Rawul Pindi, the drawing-room was painted blue, blue for thirty feet up to the whitewashed cotton ceiling; nothing of any value in the way of a human relation, I am sure, could have originated there. The veranda was spacious and open, their mutual observation had room and freedom; I watched it to and fro. I had not long to wait for my reward; the beautiful candor I expected between them was not ten minutes in coming. For the sake of it I had taken some trouble, but when I perceived it revealing I went and sat down beside Judy's husband, Robert Harbottle, and talked about Pharaoh's split hoof. It was only fair; and when next day I got their impressions of one another, I felt single-minded and deserving.

I knew it would be a satisfactory sort of thing to do, but perhaps it was rather more for Judy's sake than for Anna's that I did it.

---

1   frontier station: a reference to the military stations built by the British throughout the subcontinent. These communities were self-contained living quarters, designed to preserve a British way of life and to segregate the British and the Indians. TH

2   Rawul Pindi: a city in what is now Northern Pakistan, in Punjab province. EN

3   samovar: a Russian urn for making tea. OED

Mrs. Harbottle was only twenty-seven then and Robert a major, but he had brought her to India out of an episode too color-flushed to tone with English hedges; their marriage had come, in short, of his divorce, and as too natural a consequence. In India it is well known that the eye becomes accustomed to primitive pigments[1] and high lights; the esthetic consideration, if nothing else, demanded Robert's exchange. He was lucky to get a Piffer[2] regiment, and the Twelfth were lucky to get him; we were all lucky, I thought, to get Judy. It was an opinion, of course, a good deal challenged, even in Rawul Pindi, where it was thought, especially in the beginning, that acquiescence was the most the Harbottles could hope for. That is not enough in India; cordiality is the common right. I could not have Judy preserving her atmosphere at our tea-parties and gymkhanas.[3] Not that there were two minds among us about "the case"; it was a preposterous case, sentimentally undignified, from some points of view deplorable. I chose to reserve my point of view, from which I saw it, on Judy's behalf, merely quixotic, preferring on Robert's just to close my eyes. There is no doubt that his first wife was odious to a degree which it is simply pleasanter not to recount, but her malignity must almost have amounted to a sense of humor. Her detestation of her cousin Judy Thynne dated much further back than Robert's attachment. That began in Paris, where Judy, a young widow, was developing a real vein at Julian's. I am entirely convinced that there was nothing, as people say, "in it," Judy had not a thought at that time that was not based on Chinese white[4] and permeated with good-fellowship; but there was a good deal of it, and no doubt the turgid imagination of the first Mrs. Harbottle dealt with it honestly enough. At all events, she saw her opportunity, and the depths of her indifference to Robert bubbled up venomously into the suit. That it was undefended was the senseless mystery; decency ordained that he and Judy should have made a fight, even in the hope that it would be a losing one. The reason it had to be a losing one — the reason

---

1   primitive pigments: probably a reference to the natural local colours in the rock, soil, and flora.
2   Piffer: Punjab Frontier Force.
3   gymkhanas: a meeting for competition or display in sport, especially horse-riding. OED
4   Chinese white: white oxide of zinc — a valuable pigment. OED. Presumably here a reference to the purity of Judy's thoughts.

so immensely criticized — was that the petitioning lady obstinately refused to bring her action against any other set of circumstances than those to which, I have no doubt, Judy contributed every indiscretion. It is hard to imagine Robert Harbottle refusing her any sort of justification that the law demands short of beating her, but her malice would accept nothing of which the account did not go for final settlement to Judy Thynne. If her husband wanted his liberty, he should have it, she declared, at that price and no other. Major Harbottle did indeed deeply long for his liberty, and his interesting friend, Mrs. Thynne, had, one can only say, the most vivid commiseration for his bondage. Whatever chance they had of winning, to win would be, for the end they had at heart, to lose, so they simply abstained, as it were, from comment upon the detestable procedure which terminated in the rule absolute. I have often wondered whether the whole business would not have been more defensible if there had been on Judy's part any emotional spring for the leap they made. I offer my conviction that there was none, that she was only extravagantly affected by the ideals of the Quarter[1] — it is a transporting atmosphere — and held a view of comradeship which permitted the reversal of the modern situation filled by a blameless co-respondent. Robert, of course, was tremendously in love with her; but my theory is that she married him as the logical outcome of her sacrifice and by no means the smallest part of it.

It was all quite unimaginable, as so many things are, but the upshot of it brought Judy to Rawul Pindi, as I have said, where I for one thought her mistake insignificant compared with her value. It would have been great, her value, anywhere; in the middle of the Punjab[2] it was incalculable. To explain why would be to explain British India, but I hope it will appear; and I am quite willing, remember, to take the responsibility if it does not.

Somers Chichele, Anna's son, it is absurd to think, must have been about fifteen then, reflecting at Winchester[3] with the other "men" upon the comparative merits of tinned sardines and jam roll, and whether a packet of real Egyptians[4] was not worth the sacrifice of either. His father was colonel of the Twelfth; his moth-

---

1 the Quarter: presumably the Latin Quarter in Paris.
2 the Punjab: a northern state in India.
3 Winchester: a famous private boarding school in England.
4 real Egyptians: Egyptian cigarettes.

er was still charming. It was the year before Dick Forsyth came down from the neighborhood of Sheik-budin with a brevet[1] and a good deal of personal damage. I mention him because he proved Anna's charm in the only conclusive way before the eyes of us all; and the station, I remember, was edified to observe that if Mrs. Chichele came out of the matter "straight" — one relapses so easily into the simple definitions of those parts — which she undoubtedly did, she owed it in no small degree to Judy Harbottle. This one feels to be hardly a legitimate reference, but it is something tangible to lay hold upon in trying to describe the web of volitions which began to weave itself between the two that afternoon on my veranda and which afterward became so strong a bond. I was delighted with the thing; its simplicity and sincerity stood out among our conventional little compromises at friendship like an ideal. She and Judy had the assurance of one another; they made upon one another the finest and often the most unconscionable demands. One met them walking at odd hours in queer places, of which I imagine they were not much aware. They would turn deliberately off the Maidan[2] and away from the band-stand to be rid of our irrelevant bows; they did their duty by the rest of us, but the most egregious among us, the Deputy-Commissioner for selection, could see that he hardly counted. I thought I understood, but that may have been my fatuity; certainly when their husbands inquired what on earth they had been talking of, it usually transpired that they had found an infinite amount to say about nothing. It was a little worrying to hear Colonel Chichele and Major Harbottle describe their wives as "pals," but the fact could not be denied, and after all we were in the Punjab. They were pals too, but the terms were different.

People discussed it according to their lights, and girls said in pretty wonderment that Mrs. Harbottle and Mrs. Chichele were like men, they never kissed each other. I think Judy prescribed these conditions. Anna was far more a person who did as the world told her. But it was a poor negation to describe all that they never did; there was no common little convention of attachment that did not seem to be tacitly omitted between them. I hope one did not too cynically observe that they offered these to their husbands instead; the redeeming observation was their husbands'

---

1 brevet: a document conferring a privilege from a sovereign or government, especially a rank in the army, without the appropriate pay. OED
2 the Maidan: an open space, esplanade or parade-ground. OED

complete satisfaction. This they maintained to the end. In the natural order of things Robert Harbottle should have paid heavily for interfering as he did in Paris between a woman and what she was entitled to live for. As a matter of fact he never paid anything at all; I doubt whether he ever knew himself a debtor. Judy kept her temperament under like a current and swam with the tides of the surface, taking refreshing dips only now and then which one traced in her eyes and her hair when she and Robert came back from leave. That sort of thing is lost in the sands of India, but it makes an oasis as it travels, and it sometimes seemed to me a curious pity that she and Anna should sit in the shade of it together, while Robert and Peter Chichele, their titular companions, blundered on in the desert. But after all, if you are born blind — and the men were both immensely liked, and the shooting was good.

Ten years later Somers joined. The Twelfth were at Peshawur.[1] Robert Harbottle was Lieutenant-Colonel by that time and had the regiment. Distinction had incrusted, in the Indian way, upon Peter Chichele, its former colonel; he was General Commanding the District and K.C.B.[2] So we were all still together in Peshawur. It was great luck for the Chicheles, Sir Peter's having the district, though his father's old regiment would have made it pleasant enough for the boy in any case. He came to us, I mean, of course, to two or three of us, with the interest that hangs about a victim of circumstances; we understood that he wasn't a "born soldier." Anna had told me on the contrary that he was a sacrifice to family tradition made inevitable by the General's unfortunate investments. Bellona's bridegroom[3] was not a rôle he fancied, though he would make a kind of compromise as best man; he would agree, she said, to be a war correspondent and write picturesque specials for the London halfpenny press. There was the humor of the poor boy's despair in it, but she conveyed it, I remember, in exactly the same tone with which she had said to me years before that he wanted to drive a milk-cart. She carried quite her half of the family tradition, though she could talk of sacrifice and make her eyes wistful, contemplating for Somers the limitations of the drill-book

---

1 Peshawur: a city in what is now Pakistan. EN
2 K.C.B.: Knight Commander of the Bath. OED
3 Bellona's bridegroom: Bellona was the Roman goddess of war; a spirited woman of commanding presence. OED. In other words, Robert does not wish to make a career of being a military man.

and the camp of exercise, proclaiming and insisting upon what she would have done if she could only have chosen for him. Anna Chichele saw things that way. With more than a passable sense of all that was involved, if she could have made her son an artist in life or a commander-in-chief, if she could have given him the seeing eye or the Order of the Star of India,[1] she would not have hesitated for an instant. Judy, with her single mind, cried out, almost at sight of him, upon them both, I mean both Anna and Sir Peter. Not that the boy carried his condemnation badly, or even obviously; I venture that no one noticed it in the mess; but it was naturally plain to those of us who were under the same. He had put in his two years with a British regiment at Meerut[2] — they nurse subalterns[3] that way for the Indian army — and his eyes no longer played with the tinsel vision of India; they looked instead into the arid stretch beyond. This preoccupation conveyed to the Surgeon-Major's wife the suggestion that Mr. Chichele was the victim of a hopeless attachment. Mrs. Harbottle made no such mistake; she saw simply, I imagine, the beginnings of her own hunger and thirst in him, looking back as she told us across a decade of dusty sunsets to remember then. The decade was there, close to the memory of all of us; we put, from Judy herself downward, an absurd amount of confidence in it.

She looked so well the night she met him. It was English mail day; she depended a great deal upon her letters, and I suppose somebody had written her a word that brought her that happy, still excitement that is the inner mystery of words. He went straight to her with some speech about his mother having given him leave, and for twenty minutes she patronized him on a sofa as his mother would not have dreamed of doing.

Anna Chichele, from the other side of the room, smiled on the pair.

"I depend on you and Judy to be good to him while we are away," she said. She and Sir Peter were going on leave at the end of the week to Scotland, as usual, for the shooting.

Following her glance I felt incapable of the proportion she assigned me. "I will see after his socks with pleasure," I said. "I think, don't you, we may leave the rest to Judy?"

---

1 Order of the Star of India: a knighthood. OED
2 Meerut: a town northeast of Delhi.
3 subalterns: of inferior rank; below the rank of Captain. OED

Her eyes remained upon the boy, and I saw the passion rise in them, at which I turned mine elsewhere. Who can look unperturbed upon such a privacy of nature as that? "Poor old Judy!" she went on. "She never would be bothered with him in all his dear hobble-dehoy time; she resented his claims, the unreasonable creature, used to limit me to three anecdotes a week; and now she has him on her hands, if you like. See the pretty air of deference in the way he listens to her! He has nice manners, the villain, if he is a Chichele!"

"Oh, you have improved Sir Peter's," I said kindly.

"I do hope Judy will think him worth while. I can't quite expect that he will be up to her, bless him, she is so much cleverer, isn't she, than any of us? But if she will just be herself with him it will make such a difference."

The other two crossed the room to us at that, and Judy gaily made Somers over to his mother, trailing off to find Robert in the billiard-room.

"Well, what has Mrs. Harbottle been telling you?" Anna asked him.

The young man's eye followed Judy, his hand went musingly to his mustache.

"She was telling me," he said, "that people in India were sepulchers of themselves, but that now and then one came who could roll away another's stone."

"It sounds promising," said Lady Chichele to me.

"It sound cryptic," I laughed to Somers, but I saw that he had the key.

I can not say that I attended diligently to Mr. Chichele's socks, but the part corresponding was freely assigned me. After his people went I saw him often. He pretended to find qualities in my tea, implied that he found them in my talk. As a matter of fact it was my inquiring attitude that he loved, the knowledge that there was no detail that he could give me about himself, his impressions and experiences, that was unlikely to interest me. I would not for the world imply that he was egotistical or complacent, absolutely the reverse, but he possessed an articulate soul which found its happiness in expression, and I like to listen. I feel that these are complicated words to explain a very simple relation, and I pause to wonder what is left to me if I wished to describe his commerce with Mrs. Harbottle. Luckily there is an alternative; one needn't do it. I wish I had somewhere on paper Judy's own account of it at this period, however. It is a thing she would have enjoyed writing and more enjoyed communicating, at this period.

There was a grave reticence in his talk about her which amused me in the beginning. Mrs. Harbottle had been for ten years important enough to us all, but her serious significance, the light and the beauty in her, had plainly been reserved for the discovery of this sensitive and intelligent person not very long from Sandhurst[1] and exactly twenty-six. I was barely allowed a familiar reference, and anything approaching a flippancy was met with penetrating silence. I was almost rebuked for lightly suggesting that she must occasionally find herself bored in Peshawur.

"I think not anywhere," said Mr. Chichele; "Mrs. Harbottle is one of the few people who sound the privilege of living."

This to me, who had counted Mrs. Harbottle's yawns on so many occasions! It became presently necessary to be careful, tactful, in one's implications about Mrs. Harbottle, and to recognize a certain distinction in the fact that one was the only person with whom Mr. Chichele discussed her at all.

The day came when we talked of Robert; it was bound to come in the progress of any understanding and affectionate colloquy which had his wife for inspiration. I was familiar, of course, with Somers's opinion that the Colonel was an awfully good sort; that had been among the preliminaries and become understood as the base of all references. And I liked Robert Harbottle very well myself. When his adjutant called him a born leader of men, however, I felt compelled to look at the statement consideringly.

"In a tight place," I said — dear me, what expressions had the freedom of our little frontier drawing-rooms! — "I would as soon depend on him as on anybody. But as for leadership —— "

"He is such a good fellow that nobody here does justice to his soldierly qualities," said Mr. Chichele, "except Mrs. Harbottle."

"Has she been telling you about them?" I inquired.

"Well," he hesitated, "she told me about the Mulla Nulla affair. She is rather proud of that. Any woman would be."

"Poor dear Judy!" I mused.

Somers said nothing, but looked at me, removing his cigarette, as if my words would be the better of explanation.

---

1 Sandhurst: home of the Royal Military College, England.

"She has taken refuge in them — in Bob Harbottle's soldierly qualities — ever since she married him," I continued.

"Taken refuge," he repeated, coldly, but at my uncompromising glance his eyes fell.

"Well?" I said.

"You mean —— "

"Oh, I mean what I say," I laughed. "Your cigarette has gone out — have another."

"I think her devotion to him splendid."

"Quite splendid. Have you seen the things he brought her from the Simla[1] Art Exhibition? He said they were nice bits of color, and she has hung them in the drawing-room, where she will have to look at them every day. Let us admire her — dear Judy."

"Oh," he said, with a fine air of detachment, "do you think they are so necessary, those agreements?"

"Well," I replied, "we see that they are not indispensable. More sugar? I have only given you one lump. And we know, at all events," I added, unguardedly, "that she could never have had an illusion about him."

The young man looked up quickly. "Is that story true?" he asked.

"There was a story, but most of us have forgotten it. Who told you?"

"The doctor."

"The Surgeon-Major," I said, "has an accurate memory and a sense of proportion. As I suppose you were bound to get it from somebody, I am glad you got it from him."

I was not prepared to go on, and saw with some relief that Somers was not either. His silence, as he smoked, seemed to me deliberate; and I had oddly enough at this moment for the first time the impression that he was a man and not a boy. Then the Harbottles themselves joined us, very cheery after a gallop from the Wazir-Bagh. We talked of old times, old friendships, good swords that were broken, names that had carried far, and Somers effaced himself in the perfect manner of the British subaltern. It was a long, pleasant gossip, and I thought Judy seemed rather glad to let her husband dictate its level, which, of course, he did. I noticed when the three rode away together that the Colonel

---

1 Simla: In Himachal Pradesh, 7,000 feet up in the Himalayas. Simla was the summer capital of British India during the hot months. TH

was beginning to sit down rather solidly on his big New Zealander; and I watched the dusk come over from the foot-hills for a long time thinking more kindly that I had spoken of Robert Harbottle.

I have often wondered how far happiness is contributed to a temperament like Judy Harbottle's, and how far it creates its own; but I doubt whether, on either count, she found as much in any other winter of her life except perhaps the remote ones by the Seine. Those ardent hours of hers, when everything she said was touched with the flame of her individuality, came oftener; she suddenly cleaned up her palette and began to translate in one study after another the language of the frontier country, that spoke only in stones and in shadows under the stones and in sunlight over them. There is nothing in the Academy[1] of this year, at all events, that I would exchange for the one she gave me. She lived her physical life at a pace which carried us all along with her; she hunted and drove and danced and dined with such sincere intention as convinced us all that in hunting and driving and dancing and dining there were satisfactions that had been somehow overlooked. The Surgeon-Major's wife said it was delightful to meet Mrs. Harbottle, she seemed to enjoy everything so thoroughly; the Surgeon-Major looked at her critically and asked her if she were quite sure she hadn't a night temperature. He was a Scotchman. One night Colonel Harbottle, hearing her give away the last extra, charged her with renewing her youth.

"No, Bob," she said, "only imitating it."

Ah, that question of her youth. It was so near her — still, she told me once, she heard the beat of its flying, and the pulse in her veins answered the false signal. That was afterward, when she told the truth. She was not so happy when she indulged herself otherwise. As when she asked one to remember that she was a middle-aged woman, with middle-aged thoughts and satisfactions.

"I am now really happiest," she declared, "when the Commissioner takes me in to dinner, when the General Commanding leads me to the dance."

She did her best to make it an honest conviction. I offered her a recent success not crowned by the Academy, and she put it down

---

1 the Academy: perhaps the Royal Academy of Painting, Sculpture, and Architecture in England — or the annual exhibition of the Society.

on the table. "By and by," she said. "At present I am reading Pascal and Bossuet."[1] Well, she was reading Pascal and Bossuet. She grieved aloud that most of our activities in India were so indomitably youthful, owing to the accident that most of us were always so young. "There is no dignified distraction in this country," she complained, "for respectable ladies nearing forty." She seemed to make these declarations in the presence of Somers Chichele, who would look at her with a little queer smile — a bad translation, I imagine, of what he felt.

She gave herself so generously to her seniors that somebody said Mrs. Harbottle's girdle was hung with brass hats.[2] It seems flippant to add that her complexion was as honest as the day, but the fact is that the year before Judy had felt compelled, like the rest of us, to repair just a little the ravages of the climate. If she had never done it one would not have looked twice at the absurdity when she said of the powder-puff in the dressing-room, "I have raised that thing to the level of an immorality," and sailed in to dance with an uncompromising expression and a face uncompromised. I have not spoken of her beauty; for one thing it was not always there, and there were people who would deny it altogether, or whose considered comment was, "I wouldn't call her plain." They, of course, were people in whom she declined to be interested, but even for those of us who could evoke some demonstration of her vivid self her face would not always light in correspondence. When it did there was none that I like better to look at; and I envied Somers Chichele his way to make it the pale, shining thing that would hold him lifted, in return, for hours together, with I know not what mystic power of a moon upon the tide. And he? Oh, he was dark and delicate, by nature simple, sincere, delightfully intelligent. His common title to charm was the rather sweet seriousness that rested on his upper lip, and a certain winning gratification in his attention; but he had a subtler one in his eyes, which must be always seeking and smiling over what they found; those eyes of perpetual inquiry for the exquisite which ask so little help to create it. A personality to button up in a uniform, good heavens!

---

1 Pascal and Bossuet: Blaise Pascal (1623-62), a French scholar and scientist. Jacques Bénigne Bossuet (1627-1704), a French prelate and a famous orator.

2 brass hats: slang, derogatory term for an officer of high rank in the British army (or other Services). OED

As I begin to think of them together I remember how the maternal note appeared in her talk about him.

"His youth is pathetic," she told me, "but there is nothing that he does not understand."

"Don't apologize, Judy," I said. We were so brusque on the frontier. Besides, the matter still suffered a jocular presentment. Mrs. Harbottle and Mr. Chichele were still "great friends"; we could still put them next each other at our dinner-parties without the feeling that it would be "marked." There was still nothing unusual in the fact that when Mrs. Harbottle was there Mr. Chichele might be taken for granted. We were so broad-minded also, on the frontier.

It grew more obvious, the maternal note. I began positively to dread it, almost as much, I imagine, as Somers did. She took her privileges all in Anna's name, she exercised her authority quite as Lady Chichele's proxy. She went to the very limit. "Anna Chichele," she said actually in his presence, "is a fortunate woman. She has all kinds of cleverness, and she has her tall son. I have only one little talent, and I have no tall son." Now it was not in nature that she could have had a son as tall as Somers, nor was that desire in her eyes. All civilization implies a good deal of farce, but this was a poor refuge, a cheap device; I was glad when it fell away from her sincerity, when the day came on which she looked into my fire and said simply, "An attachment like ours has no terms."

"I wonder," I said.

"For what come and goes," she went on dreamily, "how could there be a formula?"

"Look here, Judy," I said, "you know me very well. What if the flesh leaps with the spirit?"

She looked at me, very white. "Oh no," she said, "no."

I waited, but there seemed nothing more that she could say; and in the silence the futile negative seemed to wander round the room repeating itself like an echo, "Oh no, no." I poked the fire presently to drown the sound of it. Judy sat still, with her feet crossed and her hands thrust into the pockets of her coat, staring into the coals.

"Can you live independently, satisfied with your interests and occupations?" she demanded at last. "Yes, I know you can. I can't. I must exist more than half in other people. It is what they think and feel that matters to me, just as much as what I think and feel. The best of life is in that communication."

"It has always been a passion with you, Judy," I replied. "I can imagine how much you must miss —— "

"Whom?"

"Anne Chichele," I said softly.

She got up and walked about the room, fixing here and there an intent regard upon things which she did not see. "Oh, I do," she said at one point, with the effect of pulling herself together. She took another turn or two, and then finding herself near the door she went out. I felt as profoundly humiliated for her as if she had staggered.

The next night was one of those that stand out so vividly, for no reason that one can identify, in one's memory. We were dining with the Harbottles, a small party, for a tourist they had with them. Judy and I and Somers and the traveler had drifted out into the veranda, where the scent of Japanese lilies came and went on the spring wind to trouble the souls of any taken unawares. There was a brightness beyond the foot-hills where the moon was coming, and I remember how one tall clump swayed out against it, and seemed in passionate perfume to lay a burden on the breast. Judy moved away from it and sat clasping her knees on the edge of the veranda. Somers, when his eyes were not upon her, looked always at the lily.

Even the spirit of the globe-trotter was stirred, and he said, "I think you Anglo-Indians live in a kind of little paradise."

There was an instant's silence, and then Judy turned her face into the lamplight from the drawing-room. "With everything but the essentials," she said.

We stayed late; Mr. Chichele and ourselves were the last to go. Judy walked with us along the moonlit drive to the gate, which is so unnecessary a luxury in India that the servants always leave it open. She swung the stiff halves together.

"Now," she said, "it is shut."

"And I," said Somers Chichele, softly and quickly, "am on the other side."

Even over that depth she could flash him a smile. "It is the business of my life," she gave him in return, "to keep this gate shut." I felt as if they had forgotten us. Somers mounted and rode off without a word; we were walking in a different direction. Looking back, I saw Judy leaning immovable on the gate, while Somers turned in his saddle, apparently to repeat the form of lifting his hat. And all about them stretched the stones of Kabul valley, vague and formless in the tide of the moonlight ...

Next day a note from Mrs. Harbottle informed me that she had gone to Bombay for a fortnight. In a postscript she wrote, "I shall wait for the Chicheles there, and come back with them." I remember reflecting that if she could not induce herself to take a passage to England in the ship that brought them, it seemed the right thing to do.

She did come back with them. I met the party at the station. I knew Somers would meet them, and it seemed to me, so imminent did disaster loom, that some one else should be there, some one to offer a covering movement of a flank support wherever it might be most needed. And among all our smiling faces disaster did come, or the cold premonition of it. We were all perfect, but Somers's lip trembled. Deprived for a fortnight he was eager for the draft, and he was only twenty-six. His lip trembled, and there, under the flickering station-lamps, suddenly stood that of which there never could be again any denial, for those of us who saw.

Did we make, I wonder, even a pretense of disguising the consternation that sprang up among us, like an armed thing, ready to kill any further suggestion of the truth? I don't know. Anna Chichele's unfinished sentence dropped as if someone had given her a blow upon the mouth. Coolies[1] were piling the luggage into a hired carriage at the edge of the platform. She walked mechanically after them, and would have stepped in with it but for the sight of her own gleaming landau drawn up within a yard or two, and the General waiting. We all got home somehow, taking it with us, and I gave Lady Chichele twenty-four hours to come to me with her face all one question and her heart all one fear. She came in twelve.

"Have you seen it — long?" Prepared as I was her directness was demoralizing.

"It isn't a mortal disease."

"Oh, for Heaven's sake ——— "

"Well, not with certainty, for more than a month."

She made a little spasmodic movement with her hands, then dropped them pitifully. "Couldn't you do *anything?*"

I looked at her, and she said at once, "No, of course you couldn't."

For a moment or two I took my share of the heavy sense of it, my trivial share, which yet was an experience sufficiently exciting. "I am afraid it will have to be faced," I said.

"What will happen?" Anna cried. "Oh, what will happen?"

---

1 Coolies: a term used to refer to unskilled Native labourers in Eastern countries. OED

"Why not the usual thing?" Lady Chichele looked up quickly as if at a reminder. "The ambiguous attachment of the country," I went on, limping but courageous, "half declared, half admitted, that leads vaguely nowhere, and finally perishes as the man's life enriches itself — the thing we have seen so often."

"Whatever Judy is capable of it won't be the usual thing. You know that."

I had to confess in silence that I did.

"It flashed at me — the difference in her — in Bombay." She pressed her lips together and then went on unsteadily. "In her eyes, her voice. She was mannered, extravagant, elaborate. With me! All the way up I wondered and worried. But I never thought — " She stopped; her voice simply shook itself into silence. I called a servant.

"I am going to give you a good stiff peg,"[1] I said. I apologize for the "peg," but not for the whisky and soda. It is a beverage on the frontier, of which the vulgarity is lost in the value. While it was coming I tried to talk of other things, but she would only nod absently in the pauses.

"Last night we dined with him, it was guest night at the mess, and she was there. I watched her, and she knew it. I don't know whether she tried, but anyway, she failed. The covenant between them was written on her forehead whenever she looked at him, though that was seldom. She dared not look at him. And the little conversation that they had — you would have laughed — it was a comedy of stutters. The facile Mrs. Harbottle!"

"You do well to be angry, naturally," I said; "but it would be fatal to let yourself go, Anna."

"Angry? Oh, I am *sick*. The misery of it! The terror of it! If it were anybody but Judy! Can't you imagine the passion of a temperament like that in a woman who has all these years been feeding on herself? I tell you she will take him from my very arms. And he will go — to I dare not imagine what catastrophe! Who can prevent it? Who can prevent it?"

"There is you," I said.

Lady Chichele laughed hysterically. "I think you ought to say, 'There are you.' I — what can I do? Do you realize that it's *Judy*? My friend — my other self? Do you think we can drag all that out of it? Do you think a tie like that can be broken by an accident — by a misfortune? With it all I *adore* Judy Harbottle. I love her, as I

---

1 peg: a measure of spirits or wine. OED

have always loved her, and — it's damnable, but I don't know whether, whatever happened, I wouldn't go on loving her."

"Finish your peg," I said. She was sobbing.

"Where I blame myself most," she went on, "is for not seeing in him all that makes him mature to her — that makes her forget the absurd difference between them, and take him simply and sincerely as I know she does, as the contemporary of her soul if not of her body. I saw none of that. Could I, as his mother? Would he show it to me? I thought him just a charming boy, clever, too, of course, with nice instincts and well plucked; we were always proud of that, with his delicate physique. Just a boy! I haven't yet stopped thinking how different he looks without his curls. And I thought she would be just kind and gracious and delightful to him because he was my son."

"There, of course," I said, "is the only chance."

"Where — what?"

"He is your son."

"Would you have me appeal to her? Do you know I don't think I could?"

"Dear me, no. Your case must present itself. It must spring upon her and grow before her out of your silence, and if you can manage it, your confidence. There is a great deal, after all, remember, to hold her in that. I can't somehow imagine her failing you. Otherwise —— "

Lady Chichele and I exchanged a glance of candid admission.

"Otherwise she would be capable of sacrificing everything — everything. Of gathering her life into an hour. I know. And do you know if the thing were less impossible, less grotesque, I should not be so much afraid? I mean that the *absolute* indefensibility of it might bring her a recklessness and a momentum which might —— "

"Send her over the verge," I said. "Well, go home and ask her to dinner."

There was a good deal more to say, of course, than I have thought proper to put down here, but before Anna went I saw that she was keyed up to the heroic part. This was none the less to her credit because it was the only part, the dictation of a sense of expediency that despaired while it dictated. The noble thing was her capacity to take it, and, amid all that warred in her, to carry it out on the brave high lines of her inspiration. It seemed a literal inspiration, so perfectly calculated that it was hard not to think sometimes, when one saw them together, that Anna had been lulled into a simple resumption of the old relation. Then from the least thing possible — the lift of an eyelid — it flashed upon one that between these two every moment was dramatic, and one took up the word with a curious sense of detachment and futility, but with one's heart beating like a trip-hammer with the mad excitement of it. The acute thing was the splendid sincerity of Judy Harbottle's response. For days she was profoundly on her guard, then suddenly she seemed to become practically, vividly aware of what I must go on calling the great chance, and passionately to fling herself upon it. It was the strangest cooperation without a word or a sign to show it conscious — a playing together for stakes that could not be admitted, a thing to hand upon breathless. It was there between them — the tenable ground of what they were to each other: they occupied it with almost an equal eye upon the tide that threatened, while I from my mainland tower also made an anguished calculation of the chances. I think, in spite of the menace, they found real beatitudes; so keenly did they set about the business that it brought them moments finer than any they could count in the years that were behind them, the flat and colorless years that were gone. Once or twice the wild idea even visited me that it was, after all, the projection of his mother in Somers that had so seized Judy Harbottle, and that the original was all that was needed to help the happy process of detachment. Somers himself at the time was a good deal away on escort duty: they had a clear field.

I can not tell exactly when — between Mrs. Harbottle and myself — it became a matter for reference more or less overt, I mean her defined problem, the thing that went about between her and the sun. It will be imagined that it did not come up like the weather; indeed, it was hardly ever to be envisaged and never to be held; but it was always there, and out of our joint consciousness it would sometimes leap and pass, without shape or face. It might slip between two sentences, or it might remain, a dogging shadow, for an hour. Or a week would go by while, with a strong hand, she held it out of sight altogether and talked of Anna — always of Anna. Her eyes shone with the things she told me then: she seemed to keep herself under the influence of them as if they had the power of narcotics. At the end of a time like this she turned to me in the door as she was going and stood silent, as if she could neither go nor stay. I had been able to make nothing of her that afternoon: she had seemed preoccupied with the pattern of the carpet which she traced continually with her riding crop, and finally I, too, had relapsed. She sat haggard, with the fight forever in her eyes, and the day seemed too somber about her in her corner. When she turned in the door, I looked up with sudden prescience of a crisis.

"Don't jump," she said, "it was only to tell you that I have persuaded Robert to apply for furlough. Eighteen months. From the first of April. Don't touch me." I suppose I made a movement toward her. Certainly I wanted to throw my arms about her; with the instinct, I suppose, to steady her in her great resolution.

"At the end of that time, as you know, he will be retired. I had some trouble, he is so keen on the regiment, but I think — I have succeeded. You might mention it to Anna."

"Haven't you?" sprang past my lips.

"I can't. It would be like taking an oath to tell her, and — I can't take an oath to go. But I mean to."

"There is nothing to be said," I brought out, feeling indeed that there was not. "But I congratulate you, Judy."

"No there is nothing to be said. And you congratulate me, no doubt!"

She stood for a moment quivering in the isolation she made for herself; and I felt a primitive angry revolt against the delicate trafficking of souls that could end in such ravage and disaster. The price was too heavy; I would have denuded her, at the moment, of all that had led her into this, and turned her out a clod with fine shoulders like fifty other women in Peshawur. Then, perhaps, because I held myself silent and remote and she had no emotion of fear from me, she did not immediately go.

"It will beat itself away, I suppose, like the rest of the unreasonable pain of the world," she said at last; and that, of course, brought me to her side. "Things will go back to their proportions. This," she touched an open rose, "will claim its beauty again. And life will become — perhaps — what it was before." Still I found nothing to say, I could only put my arm in hers and walk with her to the edge of the veranda where the syce[1] was holding her horse. She stroked the animal's neck. "Everything in me answered him," she informed me, with the grave intelligence of a patient who relates a symptom past. As she took the reins she turned to me again. "His spirit came to mine like a homing bird," she said, and in her smile even the pale reflection of happiness was sweet and stirring. It left me hanging in

---

1 syce: a groom. OED

imagination over the source and the stream, a little blessed in the mere understanding.

Too much blessed for confidence, or any safe feeling that the source was bound. Rather I saw it leaping over every obstacle, flashing to its destiny. As I drove to the Club next day I decided that I would not tell Anna Chichele of Colonel Harbottle's projected furlough. If to Judy telling her would be like taking an oath that they would go, to me it would at least be like assuming sponsorship for their intention. That would be heavy indeed. From the 1st of April — we were then in March. Anna would hear it soon enough from the General, would see it soon enough, almost, in the *Gazette*,[1] when it would have passed into irrecoverable fact. So I went by her with locked lips, kept out of the way of those eyes of the mother that asked and asked, and would have seen clear to any depth, any hiding-place of knowledge like that. As I pulled up at the Club I saw Colonel Harbottle talking concernedly to the wife of our Second-in-Command, and was reminded that I had not heard for some days how Major Watkins was going on. So I, too, approached Mrs. Watkins in her victoria[2] to ask. Robert Harbottle kindly forestalled her reply. "Hard luck, isn't it? Watkins has been ordered home at once. Just settled into their new house, too — last of the kit came up from Calcutta[3] yesterday, didn't it, Mrs. Watkins? But it's sound to go — Peshawur is the worst hole in Asia to shake off dysentery in."

We agreed upon this and discussed the sale-list of her new furniture that Mrs. Watkins would have to send round the station, and considered the chances of a trooper[4] — to the Watkinses with two children and not a penny but his pay it did make it easier not to have to go by a liner — and Colonel Harbottle and I were half-way to the reading-room before the significance of Major Watkin's sick-leave flashed upon me.

"But this," I cried, "will make a difference to your plans. You won't —— "

"Be able to ask for that furlough Judy wants. Rather not. I'm afraid she's disappointed — she was tremendously set on going — but it doesn't matter tuppence to me."

---

1 the *Gazette*: newspaper containing lists of government appointments and promotions, names of bankrupts, and other public notices. OED
2 victoria: a low light four-wheeled vehicle with a collapsible top. OED
3 Calcutta: the capital of British India from 1833 to 1912. EN
4 trooper: a ship used to transport soldiers or troops. OED

I sought out Mrs. Harbottle, at the end of the room. She looked radiant; she sat on the edge of the table and swung a light-hearted heel. She was talking to people who in themselves were a witness to high spirits, Captain the Hon. Freddy Gisborne, Mrs. Flamboys.

At the sight of me her face clouded, fell suddenly into the old weary lines. It made me feel somehow a little sick; I went back to my cart and drove home.

For more than a week I did not see her except when I met her riding with Somers Chichele along the peach-bordered road that leads to the Wazir-Bagh. The trees were all in blossom and made a picture that might well catch dreaming hearts into a beatitude that would correspond. The air was full of spring and the scent of violets, those wonderful Peshawur violets that grow in great clumps, tall and double. Gracious clouds came and trailed across the frontier barrier; blue as an idyll it rose about us; the city smiled in her gardens.

She had it all in her face, poor Judy, all the spring softness and more, the morning she came, intensely controlled, to announce her defeat. I was in the drawing-room doing the flowers; I put them down to look at her. The wonderful telegram from Simla arrived — that was the wonderful part — at the same time; I remember how the red, white, and blue turban of the telegraph peon[1] bobbed up behind her shoulder in the veranda. I signed and laid it on the table; I suppose it seemed hardly likely that anything could be important enough to interfere at the moment with my impression of what love, unbound and victorious, could do with a face I thought I knew. Love sat there careless of the issue, full of delight. Love proclaimed that between him and Judith Harbottle it was all over — she had met him, alas, in too narrow a place — and I marveled at the paradox with which he softened every curve and underlined every vivid note of personality in token that it had just begun. He sat there in great serenity, and though I knew that somewhere behind lurked a vanquished woman, I saw her through such a radiance that I could not be sure of seeing her at all ...

She went back to the very first of it; she seemed herself intensely interested in the facts; and there is no use in pretending that, while she talked, the moral consideration was at all present with

---

1 peon: a messenger. OED

me either; it wasn't. Her extremity was the thing that absorbed us; she even, in tender thoughtfulness, diagnosed it from its definite beautiful beginning.

"It was there, in my heart, when I woke one morning, exquisite and strange, the assurance of a gift. How had it come there, while I slept? I assure you when I closed my eyes it did not exist for me .... Yes, of course, I had seen him, but only somewhere at dinner ... As the day went on it changed — it turned into a clear pool, into a flower. And I — think of my not understanding! I was pleased with it! For a long time, for days, I never dreamed that it could be anything but a little secret joy. Then, suddenly — oh, I had not been perceiving enough! — it was in all my veins, a tide, an efflorescence,[1] a thing of my very life.

"Then — it was a little late — I understood, and since —— "

"I began by hating it — being furious, furious — and afraid, too. Sometimes it was like a low cloud, hovering and traveling always with me, sometimes like a beast of prey that went a little way off and sat looking at me ...

"I have — done my best. But there is nothing to do, to kill, to abolish. How can I say, 'I will not let you in,' when it is already there? How can I assume indifference when this thing is imposed upon every moment of my day? And it has grown so sweet — the longing — that — isn't it strange? — I could more willingly give him up than the desire of him. That seems as impossible to part with as life itself."

She sat reflective for a moment, and I saw her eyes slowly fill.

"Don't — don't *cry*, Judy," I faltered, wanting to horribly, myself. She smiled them dry.

"Not now. But I am giving myself, I suppose, to many tears."

"God help you," I said. What else was there to say?

"There is no such person," she replied, gaily. "There is only a blessed devil."

"Then you go all the way — to the logical conclusion?"

She hardly hesitated. "To the logical conclusion. What poor words!"

"May I ask — when?"

"I should like to tell you that quite definitely, and I think I can. The English mail leaves to-night."

"And you have arranged to take it?"

---

1 efflorescence: flowering.

"We have arranged nothing. Do you know" — she smiled as if at the fresh colors of an idyll — "we have not even come to the admission? There has been between us no word, no vision. Ah, we have gone in bonds, and dumb! Hours we have had, exquisite hours of the spirit, but never a moment of the heart, a moment confessed. It was mine to give — that moment, and he has waited — I know — wondering whether perhaps it would ever come. And to-day — we are going for a ride to-day, and I do not think we shall come back."

"O Judy," I cried, catching at her sleeve, "he is only a boy!"

"There were times when I thought that conclusive. Now the misery of it has gone to sleep; don't waken it. It pleases me to believe that the years are a convention. I never had any dignity, you know, and I seem to have missed the moral deliverance. I only want — oh, you know what I want. Why don't you open your telegram?"

I had been folding and fingering the brown envelope as if it had been a scrap of waste-paper.

"It is probably from Mrs. Watkins about the victoria," I said, feeling its profound irrelevance. "I wired an offer to her in Bombay. However" — and I read the telegram, the little solving telegram from Army Headquarters. I turned my back on her to read it again, and then I replaced it very carefully and put it in my pocket. It was a moment to take hold of with both hands, crying on all one's gods for steadiness.

"How white you look!" said Mrs. Harbottle with concern. "Not bad news?"

"On the contrary, excellent news. Judy, will you stay to lunch?"

She looked at me, hesitating. "Won't it seem rather a compromise on your part? When you ought to be rousing the city —— "

"I don't intend to rouse the city," I said.

"I have given you the chance."

"Thank you," I said, grimly, "but the only real favor you can do me is to stay and lunch." It was then just on one.

"I'll stay," she said, "if you will promise not to make any sort of effort. I shouldn't mind, but it would distress you."

"I promise absolutely," I said, and ironical joy rose up in me, and the telegram burned in my pocket.

She would talk of it, though I found it hard to let her go on, knowing and knowing and knowing as I did that for that day at least it could not be. There was very little about herself that she wanted to tell me; she was there confessed a woman whom joy had overcome; it was understood that we both accepted that situation.

But in the details which she asked me take charge of it was plain that she also kept a watchful eye upon fate — matters of business. We were in the drawing-room. The little round clock in its Amritsar[1] case marked half-past three. Judy put down her coffee-cup and rose to go. As she glanced at the clock the light deepened in her eyes, and I, with her hand in mine, felt like an agent of the Destroyer — for it was half-past three — consumed myself with fear lest the blow had miscarried. Then as we stood, suddenly, the sound of hoofs at a gallop on the drive, and my husband threw himself off at the door and tore through the hall to his room; and in the certainty that overwhelmed me even Judy, for an instant, stood dim and remote.

"Major Jim seems to be in a hurry," said Mrs. Harbottle, light-ly. "I have always liked your husband. I wonder whether he will say to-morrow that he always liked me."

"Dear Judy, I don't think he will be occupied with you to-morrow."

"Oh, surely, just a little, if I go to-night."

"You won't go to-night."

She looked at me helplessly. I felt as if I were insisting upon her abasement instead of her salvation. "I wish —— "

"You're not going — you're not! You can't! Look!"

I pulled it out of my pocket and thrust it at her — the telegram. It came, against every regulation, from my good friend the Deputy Adjutant-General, in Simla, and it read, "*Row Khurram 12th proba-bly ordered front three hours' time.*"

Her face changed — how my heart leaped to see it change! — and that took command there which will command trampling, even in the women of the camp, at news like this.

"What luck that Bob couldn't take his furlough!" she exclaimed, single-thoughted. "But you have known this for hours" — there was even something of the Colonel's wife, authority, inci-siveness. "Why didn't you tell me? Ah — I see."

I stood before her abashed, and that was ridiculous, while she measured me as if I presented in myself the woman I took her to be. "It wasn't like that," she said. I had to defend myself. "Judy," I said, "if you weren't in honor bound to Anna, how could I know that you would be in honor bound to the regiment? There was a train at three."

---

1 Amritsar: a city in northern India, in the state of Punjab. EN

"I beg to assure you that you have overcalculated," said Mrs. Harbottle. Her eyes were hard and proud. "And I am not sure" — a deep red swept over her face, a man's blush — "in the light of this I am not sure that I am not in honor bound to Anna."

We had reached the veranda, and at her signal her coachman drove quickly up. "You have kept me here three hours when there was the whole of Bob's kit to see to," she said, as she flung herself in; "you might have thought of that."

It was a more than usually tedious campaign, and Colonel Robert Harbottle was ambushed and shot in a place where one must believe pure boredom induced him to take his men. The incident was relieved, the newspapers said — and they are seldom so clever in finding relief for such incidents — by the dash and courage shown by Lieutenant Chichele, who, in one of those feats which it has lately been the fashion to criticize, carried the mortally wounded body of his Colonel out of range at conspicuous risk of depriving the Queen of another officer. I helped Judy with her silent packing; she had forgiven me long before that; and she settled almost at once into the flat in Chelsea which has since been credited with so delightful an atmosphere, went back straight into her own world. I have always kept her first letters about it, always shall. For months after, while the expedition still raged after snipers and rifle-thieves, I discussed with Lady Chichele the probable outcome of it all. I have sometimes felt ashamed of leaping as straight as I did with Anna to what we thought the inevitable. I based no calculation on all Mrs. Harbottle had gone back to, just as I had based no calculation on her ten years' companionship in arms when I kept her from the three o'clock train. This last was a retrospection in which Anna naturally could not join me; she never knew, poor dear, how fortunate as to its moment was the campaign she deplored, and nothing to this day can have disturbed her conviction that the bond she was at such magnificent pains to strengthen, held against the strain, as long, happily, as the supreme need existed. "How right you were!" she often said. "She did, after all, love me best, dear, wonderful Judy!" Her distress about poor Robert Harbottle was genuine enough, but one could not be surprised at a certain ambiguity; one tear for Robert, so to speak, and two for her boy. It could hardly be, for him, a marriage after his mother's heart. And she laid down with some emphasis that Somers was brilliantly entitled to all he was likely to get — which was natural, too …

I had been from the beginning so much "in it" that Anna showed me, a year later, though I don't believe she liked doing it, the letter in part of which Mrs. Harbottle shall finally excuse herself. "Somers will give you this," I read, "and with it take back your son. You will not find, I know, anything grotesque in the charming enthusiasm with which he has offered his life to me; you understand too well, you are too kind. And if you wonder that I can so render up a dear thing which I might keep and would once have taken, think how sweet in the desert is the pool, and how barren was the prospect from Balclutha."

It was like her to abandon in pride a happiness that asked so much less humiliation: I don't know why, but it was like her. And of course, when one thought of it, she had consulted all sorts of high expediencies. But I sat silent with remembrance, quieting a pang in my heart, trying not to calculate how much it had cost Judy Harbottle to take her second chance.

Part II

A Mother in India

CHAPTER I

THERE were times when we had to go without puddings to pay John's uniform bills, and always I did the facings myself with a cloth-ball[1] to save getting new ones. I would have polished his sword, too, if I had been allowed; I adored his sword. And once, I remember, we painted and varnished our own dog-cart,[2] and very smart it looked, to save fifty rupees. We had nothing but our pay — John had his company when we were married, but what is that? — and life was made up of small knowing economies, much more amusing in recollection than in practise. We were sodden poor, and that is a fact, poor and conscientious, which was worse. A big fat spider of a money-lender came one day into the veranda and tempted us — we lived in a hut, but it had a veranda — and John threatened to report him to the police. Poor when everybody else had enough to live in the open-handed Indian fashion, that was what made it so hard; we were alone in our sordid little ways. When the expectation of Cecily came to us we made out to be delighted, knowing that the whole station pitied us, and when Cecily came herself, with a swamping burst of expense, we kept up the pretense splendidly. She was peevish, poor little thing, and she threatened convulsions from the beginning, but we both knew that it was abnormal not to love her a great deal, more than life, immediately and increasingly; and we applied ourselves honestly to do it, with the thermometer at a hundred and two, and the nurse leaving at the end of a fortnight because she discovered that I had only six of everything for the table. To find out a husband's virtues, you must marry a poor man. The regiment was under-officered as usual, and John had to take parade at daylight quite three times a week; but he walked up and down the veranda with Cecily constantly till two in the morning, when a little coolness came. I usually lay awake the rest of the night in fear that a scorpion would drop from the ceiling on her. Nevertheless, we were of excellent mind toward Cecily; we were in such terror, not so much of failing in our duty toward her as toward the ideal standard of mankind. We were very anxious

---

1 cloth-ball: cleaning material (?).
2 dog-cart: a two-wheeled driving cart with cross seats back to back. OED

indeed not to come short. To be found too small for one's place in nature would have been odious. We would talk about her for an hour at a time, even when John's charger was threatening glanders[1] and I could see his mind perpetually wandering to the stable. I would say to John that she had brought a new element into our lives — she had indeed! — and John would reply, "I know what you mean," and go on to prophesy that she would "bind us together." We didn't need binding together; we were more to each other, there in the desolation of that arid frontier outpost, than most husbands and wives; but it seemed a proper and hopeful thing to believe, so we believed it. Of course, the real experience would have come, we weren't monsters; but fate curtailed the opportunity. She was just five weeks old when the doctor told us that we must either pack her home immediately or lose her, and the very next day John went down with enteric.[2] So Cecily was sent to England with a sergeant's wife who had lost her twins, and I settled down under the direction of a native doctor, to fight for my husband's life, without ice or proper food, or sick-room comforts of any sort. Ah! Fort Samila, with the sun glaring up from the sand! — however, it is a long time ago now. I trusted the baby willingly to Mrs. Berry and to Providence, and did not fret; my capacity for worry, I suppose, was completely absorbed. Mrs. Berry's letter, describing the child's improvement on the voyage and safe arrival came, I remember, the day on which John was allowed his first solid mouthful; it had been a long siege. "Poor little wretch!" he said when I read it aloud; and after that Cecily became an episode.

She had gone to my husband's people; it was the best arrangement. We were lucky that it was possible; so many children had to be sent to strangers and hirelings. Since an unfortunate infant must be brought into the world and set adrift, the haven of its grandmother and its Aunt Emma and its Aunt Alice certainly seemed providential. I had absolutely no cause for anxiety, as I often told people, wondering that I did not feel a little all the same. Nothing, I knew, could exceed the conscientious devotion of all three Farnham ladies to the child. She would appear upon their somewhat barren horizon as a new and interesting duty, and the small additional income she also represented would be almost nominal compensation for the care she would receive. They were excellent

---

1 glanders: horse disease.
2 enteric: typhoid.

persons of the kind that talk about matins and vespers, and attend both. They helped little charities and gave little teas, and wrote little notes, and made deprecating allowance for the eccentricities of their titled or moneyed acquaintances. They were the subdued, smiling, unimaginatively dressed women on a small definite income that you meet at every rectory garden-party in the country, a little snobbish, a little priggish, wholly conventional, but apart from these weaknesses, sound and simple and dignified, managing their two small servants with a display of the most exact traditions, and keeping a somewhat vague and belated but constant eye upon the doings of their country as chronicled in a biweekly paper. They were all immensely interested in royalty, and would read paragraphs aloud to each other about how the Princess Beatrice or the Princess Maud[1] had opened a fancy bazaar, looking remarkably well in plain gray poplin trimmed with Irish lace — an industry which, as is well known, the Royal Family has set its heart on rehabilitating. Upon which Mrs. Farnham's comment invariably would be, "How thoughtful of them, dear!" and Alice would usually say, "Well, if I were a princess, I should like something nicer than plain gray poplin." Alice, being the youngest, was not always expected to think before she spoke. Alice painted in water-colors, but Emma was supposed to have the most common sense.

They took turns in writing to us with the greatest regularity about Cecily; only once, I think, did they miss the weekly mail, and that was when she threatened diphtheria and they thought we had better be kept in ignorance. The kind and affectionate terms of these letters never altered except with the facts they described — teething, creeping, measles, cheeks growing round and rosy, all were conveyed in the same smooth, pat, and proper phrases, so absolutely empty of any glimpse of the child's personality that after the first few months it was like reading about a somewhat uninteresting infant in a book. I was sure Cecily was not uninteresting, but her chroniclers were. We used to wade through the long, thin sheets and saw how much more satisfactory it would be when Cecily could write to us herself. Meanwhile we noted her weekly progress with much the feeling one would have about a far-

---

1 Princess Beatrice or the Princess Maud: Princess Beatrice (d. 1944) was the youngest daughter of Queen Victoria; Princess Maud (d. 1938) was the youngest daughter of Victoria's son, who became Edward VII. EN

away little bit of property that was giving no trouble and coming on exceedingly well. We would take possession of Cecily at our convenience; till then, it was gratifying to hear of our unearned increment in dear little dimples and sweet little curls.

She was nearly four when I saw her again. We were home on three months' leave; John had just got his first brevet for doing something which he does not allow me to talk about in the Black Mountain country; and we were fearfully pleased with ourselves. I remember that excitement lasted well up to Port Said.[1] As far as the Canal,[2] Cecily was only one of the pleasures and interests we were going home to: John's majority[3] was the thing that really gave savor to life. But the first faint line of Europe brought my child to my horizon; and all the rest of the way she kept her place, holding out her little arms to me, beckoning me on. Her four motherless years brought compunction to my heart and tears to my eyes; she should have all the compensation that could be. I suddenly realized how ready I was — how ready! — to have her back. I rebelled fiercely against John's decision that we must not take her with us on our return to the frontier; privately, I resolved to dispute it, and, if necessary, I saw myself abducting the child — my own child. My days and nights as the ship crept on were full of a long ache to possess her; the defrauded tenderness of the last four years rose up in me and sometimes caught at my throat. I could think and talk and dream of nothing else. John indulged me as much as was reasonable, and only once betrayed by a yawn that the subject was not for him endlessly absorbing. Then I cried and he apologized. "You know," he said, "it isn't exactly the same thing. I'm not her mother." At which I dried my tears and expanded, proud and pacified. I was her mother!

Then the rainy little station and Alice, all-embracing in a damp waterproof, and the drive in the fly, and John's mother at the gate and a necessary pause while I kissed John's mother. Dear thing, she wanted to hold our hands and look into our faces and tell us how little we had changed for all our hardships; and on the way

---

1 Port Said: a city port in Egypt, on the Mediterranean Sea, at the entrance to the Suez Canal.
2 the Canal: the Suez canal, opened 1869.
3 majority: the rank of Major. OED

to the house she actually stopped to point out some alterations in the flower-borders. At last the drawing-room door and the smiling housemaid turning the handle and the unforgettable picture of a little girl, a little girl unlike anything we had imagined, starting bravely to trot across the room with the little speech that had been taught her. Half-way she came; I suppose our regards were too fixed, too absorbed, for there she stopped with a wail of terror at the strange faces, and ran straight back to the outstretched arms of her Aunt Emma. The most natural thing in the world, no doubt. I walked over to a chair opposite with my handbag and umbrella and sat down — a spectator, aloof and silent. Aunt Emma fondled and quieted the child, apologizing for her to me, coaxing her to look up, but the little figure still shook with sobs, hiding its face in the bosom that it knew. I smiled politely, like any other stranger, at Emma's deprecations, and sat impassive, looking at my alleged baby breaking her heart at the sight of her mother. It is not amusing even now to remember the anger that I felt. I did not touch her or speak to her; I simply sat observing my alien possession, in the frock I had not made and the sash I had not chosen, being coaxed and kissed and protected and petted by its Aunt Emma. Presently I asked to be taken to my room, and there I locked myself in for two atrocious hours. Just once my heart beat high, when a tiny knock came and a timid, docile little voice said that tea was ready. But I heard the rustle of a skirt, and guessed the directing angel in Aunt Emma, and responded, "Thank you, dear, run away and say that I am coming," with a pleasant visitor's inflection which I was able to sustain for the rest of the afternoon.

"She goes to bed at seven," said Emma.

"Oh, does she?" said I. "A very good hour, I should think."

"She sleeps in my room," said Mrs. Farnham.

"We give her mutton broth very often, but seldom stock soup," said Aunt Emma. "Mamma thinks it is too stimulating."

"Indeed?" said I, to all of it.

They took me up to see her in her crib, and pointed out, as she lay asleep, that though she had "a general look" of me, her features were distinctively Farnham.

"Won't you kiss her?" asked Alice. "You haven't kissed her yet, and she is used to so much affection."

"I don't think I could take such an advantage of her," I said.

They looked at each other, and Mrs. Farnham said that I was plainly worn out. I mustn't sit up to prayers.

If I had been given anything like reasonable time I might have made a fight for it, but four weeks — it took a month each way in those days — was too absurdly little; I could do nothing. But I would not stay at mamma's. It was more than I would ask of myself, that daily disappointment under the mask of gratified discovery, for long.

I spent an approving, unnatural week, in my farcical character, bridling my resentment and hiding my mortification with pretty phrases; and then I went up to town and drowned my sorrows in the summer sales. I took John with me. I may have been Cecily's mother in theory, but I was John's wife in fact.

We went back to the frontier, and the regiment saw a lot of service. That meant medals and fun for my husband, but economy and anxiety for me, though I managed to be allowed as close to the firing line as any woman.

Once the Colonel's wife and I, sitting in Fort Samila, actually heard the rifles of a punitive expedition cracking on the other side of the river — that was a bad moment. My man came in after fifteen hours' fighting, and went sound asleep, sitting before his food with his knife and fork in his hands. But service makes heavy demands besides those on your wife's nerves. We had saved two thousand rupees, I remember, against another run home, and it all went like powder, in the Mirzai expedition; and the run home diminished to a month in a boarding-house in the hills.

Meanwhile, however, we had begun to correspond with our daughter, in large round words of one syllable, behind which, of course, was plain the patient guiding hand of Aunt Emma. One could hear Aunt Emma suggesting what would be nice to say, trying to instil a little pale affection for the far-off papa and mamma. There was so little Cecily and so much Emma — of course, it could not be otherwise — that I used to take, I fear, but a perfunctory joy in these letters. When we went home again I stipulated absolutely that she was to write to us without any sort of supervision — the child was ten.

"But the spelling!" cried Aunt Emma, with lifted eyebrows.

"Her letters aren't exercises," I was obliged to retort; "she will do the best she can."

We found her a docile little girl, with nice manners, a thoroughly unobjectionable child. I saw quite clearly that I could not have brought her up so well; indeed, there were moments when I fancied that Cecily, contrasting me with her aunts, wondered a little what my bringing up could have been like. With this reserve of criticism on Cecily's part, however, we got on very tolerably, largely because I found it impossible to assume any responsibility toward her, and in moments of doubt or discipline referred her to her aunts. We spent a pleasant summer with a little girl in the house whose interest in us was amusing, and whose outings it was gratifying to arrange; but when we went back, I had no desire to take her with us. I thought her very much better where she was.

Then came the period which is filled, in a subordinate degree, with Cecily's letters. I do not wish to claim more than I ought; they were not my only or even my principal interest in life. It was a long period; it lasted till she was twenty-one. John had had promotion in the meantime, and there was rather more money, but he had earned his second brevet with a bullet through one lung, and the doctors ordered our leave to be spent in South Africa. We had photographs, we knew she had grown tall and athletic and comely, and the letters were always very creditable. I had the unusual and qualified privilege of watching my daughter's development from ten to twenty-one, at a distance of four thousand miles, by means of the written word. I wrote myself as provocatively as possible; I sought for every string, but the vibration that came back across the seas to me was always other than the one I looked for, and sometimes there was none. Nevertheless, Mrs. Farnham wrote me that Cecily very much valued my communications. Once when I had described an unusual excursion in a native state, I learned that she had read my letter aloud to the sewing circle. After that I abandoned description, and confined myself to such intimate personal details as no sewing circle could find amusing. The child's own letters were simply a mirror of the ideas of the Farnham ladies; that must have been so, it was not altogether my jaundiced eye. Alice and Emma and grandmamma paraded the pages in turn. I very early gave up hope of discoveries in my daughter, though as much of the original as I could detect was satisfactorily simple and sturdy. I found little things to criticize, of course, tendencies to correct; and by return post I criticized and corrected, but the distance and the deliberation seemed to touch my maxims with a kind of arid frivolity, and sometimes I tore them up. One quick, warm-blooded scolding would have been worth a sheaf of them. My studied little phrases could only inoculate her with a dislike for me without protecting her from anything under the sun.

However, I found she didn't dislike me, when John and I went home at last to bring her out. She received me with just a hint of kindness, perhaps, but on the whole very well.

CHAPTER II

JOHN was recalled, of course, before the end of our furlough, which knocked various things on the head; but that is the sort of thing one learned to take with philosophy in any lengthened term of Her Majesty's service. Beside, there is usually sugar for the pill; and in this case it was a Staff command bigger than anything we expected for at least five years to come. The excitement of it when it was explained to her gave Cecily a charming color. She took a good deal of interest in the General, her papa; I think she had an idea that his distinction would alleviate the situation in India, however it might present itself. She accepted that prospective situation calmly; it had been placed before her all her life. There would always be a time when she should go and live with papa and mamma in India, and so long as she was of an age to receive the idea with rebel tears she was assured that papa and mamma would give her a pony. The pony was no longer added to the prospect; it was absorbed no doubt in the general list of attractions calculated to reconcile a young lady to a parental roof with which she had no practical acquaintance. At all events, when I feared the embarrassment and dismay of a pathetic parting with darling grandmamma and the aunties, and the sweet cat and the dear vicar and all the other objects of affection, I found an agreeable unexpected philosophy.

I may add that while I anticipated such broken-hearted farewells I was quite prepared to take them easily. Time, I imagined, had brought philosophy to me also, equally agreeable and equally unexpected.

It was a Bombay ship, full of returning Anglo-Indians. I looked up and down the long saloon tables with a sense of relief and of solace; I was again among my own people. They belonged to Bengal[1] and to Burma,[2] to Madras[3] and to the Punjab, but they were all my people. I could pick out a score that I knew in fact, and there was none that in imagination I didn't know. The look of wider seas and skies,

---

1 Bengal: formerly a province of North-East British India.
2 Burma: now Myanmar, a country in Southeast Asia.
3 Madras: a city in southeastern India, on the Bay of Bengal.

the casual experienced glance, the touch of irony and of tolerance, how well I knew it and how well I liked it! Dear old England, sitting in our wake, seemed to hold by comparison a great many soft, unsophisticated people, immensely occupied about very particular trifles. How difficult it had been, all the summer, to be interested! These of my long acquaintance belonged to my country's Executive, acute, alert, with the marks of travail on them. Gladly I went in and out of the women's cabins and listened to the argot[1] of the men; my own ruling, administering, soldiering little lot.

Cecily looked at them askance. To her the atmosphere was alien, and I perceived that gently and privately she registered objections. She cast a disapproving eye upon the wife of a Conservator of Forests,[2] who scanned with interest a distant funnel and laid a small wager that it belonged to the Messageries Maritimes.[3] She looked with a straightened lip at the crisply stepping women who walked the deck in short and rather shabby skirts with their hands in their jacket-pockets talking transfers and promotions; and having got up at six to make a water-color sketch of the sunrise, she came to me in profound indignation to say that she had met a man in his pajamas; no doubt, poor wretch, on his way to be shaved. I was unable to convince her that he was not expected to visit the barber in all his clothes.

At the end of the third day she told me that she wished these people wouldn't talk to her; she didn't like them. I had turned in the hour we left the Channel and had not left my berth since, so possibly I was not in the most amiable mood to receive a douche of cold water. "I must try to remember, dear," I said, "that you have been brought up altogether in the society of pussies and vicars and elderly ladies, and of course you miss them. But you must have a little patience. I shall be up to-morrow, if this beastly sea continues to go down; and then we will try to find somebody suitable to introduce to you."

"Thank you, mamma," said my daughter, without a ray of suspicion. Then she added consideringly, "Aunt Emma and Aunt Alice do seem quite elderly ladies beside you, and yet you are older than either of them, aren't you? I wonder how that is."

---

1 argot: the jargon of a group or class. OED
2 Conservator of Forests: one who preserves and protects the forests. OED
3 Messageries Maritimes: the name of a shipping-line. OED

It was so innocent, so admirable, that I laughed at my own expense; while Cecily, doing her hair, considered me gravely. "I wish you would tell me why you laugh, mamma," quoth she; "you laugh so often."

We had not to wait after all for my good offices of the next morning. Cecily came down at ten o'clock that night quite happy and excited; she had been talking to a bishop, such a dear bishop. The bishop had been showing her his collection of photographs, and she had promised to play the harmonium for him at the eleven-o'clock service in the morning. "Bless me!" said I, "is it Sunday?" It seemed she had got on very well indeed with the bishop, who knew the married sister, at Tunbridge,[1] of her very greatest friend. Cecily herself did not know the married sister, but that didn't matter — it was a link. The bishop was charming. "Well, my love," said I — I was teaching myself to use these forms of address for fear she would feel an unkind lack of them, but it was difficult — "I am glad that somebody from my part of the world has impressed you favorably at last. I wish we had more bishops."

"Oh, but my bishop doesn't belong to your part of the world," responded my daughter sleepily. "He is traveling for his health."

It was the most unexpected and delightful thing to be packed into one's chair next morning by Dacres Tottenham. As I emerged from the music saloon after breakfast — Cecily had stayed below to look over her hymns and consider with her bishop the possibility of an anthem — Dacres's face was the first I saw; it simply illuminated, for me, that portion of the deck. I noticed with pleasure the quick toss of the cigar overboard as he recognized and bore down upon me. We were immense friends; John liked him too. He was one of those people who make a tremendous difference; in all our three hundred passengers there could be no one like him, certainly no one whom I could be more glad to see. We plunged at once into immediate personal affairs, we would get at the heart of them later. He gave his vivid word to everything he had seen and done; we laughed and exclaimed and were silent in a concert of admirable understanding. We were still unraveling, still demanding and explaining when the ship's bell began to ring for church, and almost simultaneously Cecily advanced toward us. She had a proper Sunday hat on, with flowers under the brim, and

---

1 Tunbridge: Tunbridge Wells in southeastern England; until the late nineteenth century, it was a fashionable spa frequented by royalty. EN

a church-going frock; she wore gloves and clasped a prayer-book. Most of the women who filed past to the summons of the bell were going down as they were, in cotton blouses and serge skirts, in tweed caps or anything, as to a kind of family prayers. I knew exactly how they would lean against the pillars of the saloon during the psalms. This young lady would be little less than a rebuke to them. I surveyed her approach; she positively walked as if it were Sunday.

"My dear," I said, "how *endimanchée*[1] you look! The bishop will be very pleased with you. This gentleman is Mr. Tottenham, who administers Her Majesty's pleasure in parts of India about Allahabad.[2] My daughter, Dacres." She was certainly looking very fresh, and her calm gray eyes had the repose in them that has never known itself to be disturbed about anything. I wondered whether she bowed so distantly also because it was Sunday, and then I remembered that Dacres was a young man, and that the Farnham ladies had probably taught her that it was right to be very distant with young men.

"It is almost eleven, mamma."

"Yes, dear. I see you are going to church."

"Are you not coming, mamma?"

I was well wrapped up in an extremely comfortable corner. I had *La Duchesse Bleue* uncut in my lap, and an agreeable person to talk to. I fear that in any case I should not have been inclined to attend the service, but there was something in my daughter's intonation that made me distinctly hostile to the idea. I am putting things down as there were, extenuating nothing.

"I think not, dear."

"I've turned up two such nice seats."

"Stay, Miss Farnham, and keep us in countenance," said Dacres, with his charming smile. The smile displaced a look of discreet and amused observation. Dacres had an eye always for a situation, and this one was even newer to him than to me.

"No, no. She must run away and not bully her mamma," I said. "When she comes back we will see how much she remembers of the sermon;" and as the flat tinkle from the companion began to

---

1 *endimanchée*: in one's Sunday best. OF

2 Allahabad: a holy city in northern India, in Uttar Pradesh state, at the confluence of the Yamuna and Ganges rivers, named by Akbar in 1575. EN

show signs of diminishing, Cecily, with one grieved glance, hastened down.

"You amazing lady!" said Dacres. "A daughter — and such a tall daughter! I somehow never —— "

"You knew we had one?"

"There was theory of that kind, I remember, about ten years ago. Since then — excuse me — I don't think you've mentioned her."

"You talk as if she were a skeleton in the closet!"

"You *didn't* talk — as if she were."

"I think she was, in a way, poor child. But the resurrection day hasn't confounded me as I deserved. She's a very good girl."

"If you had asked me to pick out your daughter —— "

"She would have been the last you would indicate! Quite so," I said. "She is like her father's people. I can't help that."

"I shouldn't think you would if you could," Dacres remarked absently; but the sea air, perhaps, enabled me to digest his thoughtlessness with a smile.

"No," I said, "I am just as well pleased. I think a resemblance to me would confuse me, often."

There was a trace of scrutiny in Dacres's glance. "Don't you find yourself in sympathy with her?" he asked.

"My dear boy, I have seen her just twice in twenty-one years! You see, I've always stuck to John."

"But between mother and daughter — I may be old-fashioned, but I had an idea that there was an instinct that might be depended on."

"I am depending on it," I said, and let my eyes follow the little blue waves that chased past the handrail. "We are making very good speed, aren't we? Thirty-five knots since last night at ten. Are you in the sweep?"

"I never bet on the way out — can't afford it. Am I old-fashioned?" he insisted.

"Probably. Men are very slow in changing their philosophy about women. I fancy their idea of the maternal relation is firmest fixed of all."

"We see it a beatitude!" he cried.

"I know," I said wearily, "and you never modify the view."

Dacres contemplated the portion of the deck that lay between us. His eyes were discreetly lowered, but I saw embarrassment and speculation and a hint of criticism in them.

"Tell me more about it," said he.

"Oh, for heaven's sake don't be sympathetic!" I exclaimed. "Lend me a little philosophy instead. There is nothing to tell. There she is and there I am, in the most intimate relation in the world, constituted when she is twenty-one and I am forty." Dacres started slightly at the ominous word; so little do men realize that the women they like can ever pass out of the constated years of attraction. "I find the young lady very tolerable, very creditable, very nice. I find the relation atrocious. There you have it. I would like to break the relation into pieces," I went on recklessly, "and throw it into the sea. Such things should be tempered to one. I should feel it much less if she occupied another cabin, and would consent to call me Elizabeth or Jane. It is not as if I had been her mother always. One grows fastidious at forty — new intimacies are only possible then on a basis of temperament —— "

I paused; it seemed to me that I was making excuses, and I had not the least desire in the world to do that.

"How awfully rough on the girl!" said Dacres Tottenham.

"That consideration has also occurred to me," I said candidly, "though I have perhaps been even more struck by its converse."

"You had no earthly business to be her mother," said my friend, with irritation.

I shrugged my shoulders — what would you have done? — and opened *La Duchesse Bleue.*

CHAPTER III

MRS. MORGAN, wife of a judge of the High Court of Bombay, and I sat amidships on the cool side in the Suez Canal. She was outlining "Soiled Linen" in chain-stitch on a green canvas bag; I was admiring the Egyptian sands. "How charming," said I, "is this solitary desert in the endless oasis we are compelled to cross!"

"Oasis in the desert, you mean," said Mrs. Morgan; "I haven't noticed any, but I happened to look up this morning as I was putting on my stockings, and I saw through my port-hole the most lovely mirage."

I had been at school with Mrs. Morgan more than twenty years agone, but she had come to the special enjoyment of the dignities of life while I still liked doing things. Mrs. Morgan was the kind of person to make one realize how distressing a medium is middle age. Contemplating her precipitous lap, to which conventional attitudes were certainly more becoming, I crossed my own knees with energy, and once more resolved to be young until I was old.

"How perfectly delightful for you to be taking Cecily out!" said Mrs. Morgan placidly.

"Isn't it?" I responded, watching the gliding sands.

"But she was born in sixty-nine — that makes her twenty-one. Quite time, I should say."

"Oh, we couldn't put it off any longer. I mean — her father has such a horror of early débuts. He simply would not hear of her coming before."

"Doesn't want her to marry in India, I dare say — the only one," purred Mrs. Morgan.

"Oh, I don't know. It isn't such a bad place. I was brought out there to marry, and I married. I've found it very satisfactory."

"You always did say exactly what you thought, Helena," said Mrs. Morgan excusingly.

"I haven't much patience with people who bring their daughters out to give them the chance they never would have in England, and then go about devoutly hoping they won't marry in India," I said. "I shall be very pleased if Cecily does as well as your girls have done."

"Mary in the Indian Civil[1] and Jessie in the Imperial Service Troops," sighed Mrs. Morgan complacently. "And both, my dear, within a year. It *was* a blow."

"Oh, it must have been!" I said civilly.

There was no use in bandying words with Emily Morgan.

"There is nothing in the world like the satisfaction and pleasure one takes in one's daughters," Mrs. Morgan went on limpidly. "And one can be in such *close* sympathy with one's girls. I have never regretted having no sons."

"Dear me, yes. To watch oneself growing up again — call back the lovely April of one's prime, etcetera — to read every thought and anticipate every wish — there is no more golden privilege in life, dear Emily. Such a direct and natural avenue for affection, such a wide field for interest!"

I paused, lost in the volume of my admirable sentiments.

"How beautifully you talk, Helena! I wish I had the gift."

"It doesn't mean very much," I said truthfully.

"Oh, I think it's everything! And how companionable a girl is! I quite envy you, this season, having Cecily constantly with you and taking her about everywhere. Something quite new for you, isn't it?"

"Absolutely," said I; "I am looking forward to it immensely. But it is likely she will make her own friends, don't you think?" I added anxiously.

"Hardly the first season. My girls didn't. I was practically their only intimate for months. Don't be afraid; you won't be obliged to go shares in Cecily with anybody for a good long while," added Mrs. Morgan kindly. "I know just how you feel about *that*."

The muddy water of the Ditch chafed up from under us against its banks with a smell that enabled me to hide the emotions Mrs. Morgan evoked behind my handkerchief. The pale desert was pictorial with the drifting, deepening purple shadows of clouds, and in the midst a blue glimmer of the Bitter Lakes,[2] with a white sail on them. A little frantic Arab boy ran alongside keeping pace with the ship. Except for the smell, it was like a dream, we moved so quietly; on, gently on and on between the

---

1 Indian Civil: Indian Civil Service. Formed in 1861, it consisted of British administrators, to ensure the pervasiveness of British rule in India. TH

2 the Bitter Lakes: near the Suez Canal (the "Ditch").

ridgy clay banks and the rows of piles. Peace was on the ship; you could hear what the Fourth[1] in his white ducks[2] said to the quartermaster[3] in his blue denims; you could count the strokes of the electric bell in the wheel-house; peace was on the ship as she pushed on, an ever-venturing, double-funneled impertinence, through the sands of the ages. My eyes wandered along a plank-line in the deck till they were arrested by a petticoat I knew, when they returned of their own accord. I seemed to be always seeing that petticoat.

"I think," resumed Mrs. Morgan, whose glance had wandered in the same direction, "that Cecily is a very fine type of our English girls. With those dark gray eyes, a *little* prominent possibly, and that good color — it's rather high now perhaps, but she will lose quite enough of it in India — and those regular features, she would make a splendid Britannia.[4] Do you know, I fancy she must have a great deal of character. Has she?"

"Any amount. And all of it good," I responded, with private dejection.

"No faults at all?" chaffed Mrs. Morgan.

I shook my head. "Nothing," I said sadly, "that I can put my finger on. But I hope to discover a few later. The sun may bring them out."

"Like freckles. Well, you are a lucky woman. Mine had plenty, I assure you. Untidiness was no name for Jessie, and Mary — I'm *sorry* to say that Mary sometimes fibbed."

"How lovable of her! Cecily's neatness is a painful example to me, and I don't believe she would tell a fib to save my life."

"Tell me," said Mrs. Morgan, as the lunch-bell rang and she gathered her occupation into her work-basket, "who is that talking to her?"

"Oh, an old friend," I replied easily; "Dacres Tottenham, a dear fellow, and most benevolent. He is trying on my behalf to reconcile her to the life she'll have to lead in India."

"She won't need much reconciling, if she's like most girls," observed Mrs. Morgan, "but he seems to be trying very hard."

---

1 the Fourth: Fourth Officer.
2 white ducks: white trousers.
3 quartermaster: on ship, a petty officer who attends to the steering of the ship and other duties. OED
4 Britannia: personification of Britain.

That was quite the way I took it — on my behalf — for several days. When people have understood you very adequately for ten years you do not expect them to boggle at any problem you may present at the end of the decade. I thought Dacres was moved by a fine sense of compassion. I thought that with his admirable perception he had put a finger on the little comedy of fruitfulness in my life that laughed so bitterly at the tragedy of the barren woman, and was attempting, by delicate manipulation, to make it easier. I really thought so. Then I observed that myself had preposterously deceived me, that it wasn't like that at all. When Mr. Tottenham joined us, Cecily and me, I saw that he listened more than he talked, with an ear specially cocked to register any small irony which might appear in my remarks to my daughter. Naturally he registered more than there were, to make up perhaps for dear Cecily's obviously not registering any. I could see, too, that he was suspicious of any flavor of kindness; finally, to avoid the strictures of his upper lip, which really, dear fellow, began to bore me, I talked exclusively about the distant sails and the Red Sea littoral.[1] When he no longer joined us as we sat or walked together, I perceived that his hostility was fixed and his *parti pris*.[2] He was brimful of compassion, but it was all for Cecily, none for the situation or for me. (She would have marveled, placidly, why he pitied her. I am glad I can say that.) The primitive man in him rose up as Pope of nature and excommunicated me as a creature recusant to her functions. Then deliberately Dacres undertook an office of consolation; and I fell to wondering, while Mrs. Morgan spoke her convictions plainly out, how far an impulse of reparation for a misfortune with which he had nothing to do might carry a man.

I began to watch the affair with an interest which even to me seemed queer. It was not detached, but it was semi-detached, and, of course, on the side for which I seem, in this history, to be perpetually apologizing. With certain limitations it didn't matter an atom whom Cecily married. So that he was sound and decent, with reasonable prospects, her simple requirements and ours for her would be quite met. There was the ghost of a consolation in that; one needn't be anxious or exacting.

I could predict with a certain amount of confidence that in her first season she would probably receive three or four proposals, any

---

1 littoral: shore.
2 *parti pris*: position taken, mind made up.

one of which she might accept with as much propriety and satisfaction as any other one. For Cecily it was so simple; prearranged
by nature like her digestion, one could not see any logical basis for
difficulties. A nice upstanding sapper,[1] a dashing Bengal Lancer[2]—
oh, I could think of half a dozen types that would answer excel-
lently. She was the kind of young person, and that was the sum-
ming up of it, to marry a type and be typically happy. I hoped and
expected that she would. But Dacres!

Dacres should exercise the greatest possible discretion. He was
not a person who could throw the dice indifferently with fate. He
could respond to so much, and he would inevitably, sooner or later,
demand so much response! He was governed by a preposterously
exacting temperament, and he wore his nerves outside. And what
vision he had! How he explored the world he lived in and drew
out of it all there was, all there was! I could see him in the years to
come ranging alone the fields that were sweet and the horizons
that lifted for him, and ever returning to pace the common dusty
mortal road by the side of a purblind[3] wife. On general principles,
as a case to point at, it would be a conspicuous pity. Nor would it
lack the aspect of a particular, a personal misfortune. Dacres was
occupied in quite the natural normal degree with his charming
self; he would pass his misery on, and who would deserve to escape
it less than his mother-in-law?

I listened to Emily Morgan, who gleaned in the ship more
information about Dacres Tottenham's people, pay, and prospects
than I had ever acquired, and I kept an eye upon the pair which
was, I flattered myself, quite maternal. I watched them without
acute anxiety, deploring the threatening destiny, but hardly nearer
to it than one is in the stalls to the stage. My moments of real concern for Dacres were mingled more with anger than with sorrow
— it seemed inexcusable that he, with his infallible divining-rod
for temperament, should be on the point of making such an ass of
himself. Though I talk of the stage there was nothing at all dramatic
to reward my attention, mine and Emily Morgan's. To my imagination, excited by its idea of what Dacres Tottenham's courtship
ought to be, the attentions he paid to Cecily were most humdrum.

---

1 sapper: a soldier of the Royal Engineers, especially one who undermines
   enemy fortifications.
2 Bengal Lancer: cavalry regiments of the British army.
3 purblind: dim-witted. OED

He threw rings into buckets with her — she was good at that — and quoits[1] upon the "bull" board; he found her chair after the decks were swabbed in the morning and established her in it; he paced the deck with her at convenient times and seasons. They were humdrum, but they were constant and cumulative. Cecily took them with an even breath that perfectly matched. There was hardly anything, on her part, to note — a little discreet observation of his comings and goings, eyes scarcely lifted from her book, and later just a hint of proprietorship, as the evening she came up to me on deck, our first night in the Indian Ocean. I was lying in my long chair looking at the thick, low stars and thinking it was a long time since I had seen John.

"Dearest mamma, out here and nothing over your shoulders! You *are* imprudent. Where is your wrap? Mr. Tottenham, will you please fetch mamma's wrap for her?"

"If mamma so instructs me," he said audaciously.

"Do as Cecily tells you," I laughed, and he went and did it, while I, by the light of a quartermaster's lantern, distinctly saw my daughter blush.

Another time, when Cecily came down to undress, she bent over me as I lay in the lower berth with unusual solicitude. I had been dozing, and I jumped.

"What is it, child?" I said. "Is the ship on fire?"

"No mamma, the ship is not on fire. There is nothing wrong. I'm so sorry I startled you. But Mr. Tottenham has been telling me all about what you did for the soldiers the time plague broke out in the lines at Mian-Mir. I think it was splendid, mamma, and so does he."

"Oh, *Lord*!" I groaned. "Good night."

---

1 quoits: iron rings thrown at iron pegs. OED

CHAPTER IV

IT remained in my mind, that little thing that Dacres had taken the trouble to tell my daughter; I thought about it a good deal. It seemed to me the most serious and convincing circumstance that had yet offered itself to my consideration. Dacres was no longer content to bring solace and support to the more appealing figure of the situation; he must set to work, bless him! to improve the situation itself. He must try to induce Miss Farnham, by telling her everything he could remember to my credit, to think as well of her mother as possible, in spite of the strange and secret blows which that mother might be supposed to sit up at night to deliver to her. Cecily thought very well of me already; indeed, with private reservations as to my manners and — no, *not* my morals, I believe I exceeded her expectations of what a perfectly new and untrained mother would be likely to prove. It was my theory that she found me all she could understand me to be. The maternal virtues of the outside were certainly mine; I put them on with care every morning and wore them with patience all day. Dacres, I assured myself, must have allowed his preconception to lead him absurdly by the nose not to see that the girl was satisfied, that my impatience, my impotence, did not at all make her miserable. Evidently, however, he had created our relations differently; evidently he had set himself to their amelioration. There was portent in it; things seemed to be closing in. I bit off a quarter of an inch of wooden pen-handle in considering whether or not I should mention it in my letter to John, and decided that it would be better just perhaps to drop a hint. Though I could not expect John to receive it with any sort of perturbation. Men are different; he would probably think Tottenham well enough able to look after himself.

I had embarked on my letter, there at the end of a corner-table of the saloon, when I saw Dacres saunter through. He wore a very conscious and elaborately purposeless air; and it jumped with my mood that he had nothing less than the crisis of his life in his pocket, and was looking for me. As he advanced toward me between the long tables doubt left me and alarm assailed me. "I'm glad to find you in a quiet corner," said he, seating himself, and confirmed my worst anticipations.

"I'm writing to John," I said, and again applied myself to my pen-handle. It is a trick Cecily has since done her best in vain to cure me of.

"I am going to interrupt you," he said. "I have not had an opportunity of talking to you for some time."

"I like that!" I exclaimed derisively.

"And I want to tell you that I am very much charmed with Cecily."

"Well," I said, "I am not going to gratify you by saying anything against her."

"You don't deserve her, you know."

"I won't dispute that. But, if you don't mind — I'm not sure that I'll stand being abused, dear boy."

"I quite see it isn't any use. Though one spoke with the tongues of men and of angels ―― "[1]

"And had not charity," I continued for him. "Precisely. I won't go on, but your quotation is very apt."

"I so bow down before her simplicity. It makes a wide and beautiful margin for the rest of her character. She is a girl Ruskin[2] would have loved."

"I wonder," said I. "He did seem fond of the simple type, didn't he?"

"Her mind is so clear, so transparent. The motive spring of everything she says and does is so direct. Don't you find you can most completely depend upon her?"

"Oh yes," I said; "certainly. I nearly always know what she is going to say before she says it, and under given circumstances I can tell precisely what she will do."

"I fancy her sense of duty is very beautifully developed."

"It is," I said. "There is hardly a day when I do not come in contact with it."

"Well, that is surely a good thing. And I find that calm poise of hers very restful."

"I would not have believed that so many virtues could reside in one young lady," I said, taking refuge in flippancy, "and to think that she should be my daughter!"

"As I believe you know, that seems to me rather a cruel stroke of destiny, Mrs. Farnham."

---

1 Corinthians 13.1.
2 John Ruskin (1819-1900), English art critic.

"Oh yes, I know! You have a constructive imagination, Dacres. You don't seem to see that the girl is protected by her limitations, like a tortoise. She lives within them quite secure and happy and content. How determined you are to be sorry for her!"

Mr. Tottenham looked at the end of this lively exchange as though he sought for a polite way of conveying to me that I rather was the limited person. He looked as if he wished he could say things. The first of them would be, I saw, that he had quite a different conception of Cecily, that it was illuminated by many trifles, nuances of feeling and expression, which he had noticed in his talks with her whenever they had skirted the subject of her adoption by her mother. He knew her, he was longing to say, better than I did; when it would have been natural to reply that one could not hope to compete in such a direction with an intelligent young man, and we should at once have been upon delicate and difficult ground. So it was as well perhaps that he kept silence until he said, as he had come prepared to say, "Well, I want to put that beyond a doubt — her happiness — if I'm good enough. I want her, please, and I only hope that she will be half as willing to come as you are likely to be to let her go."

It was a shock when it came, plump, like that; and I was horrified to feel how completely every other consideration was lost for the instant in the immense relief that it prefigured. To be my whole complete self again, without the feeling that a fraction of me was masquerading about in Cecily! To be freed at once, or almost, from an exacting condition and an impossible ideal! "Oh!" I exclaimed, and my eyes positively filled. "You *are* good, Dacres, but I couldn't let you do that."

His undisguised stare brought me back to a sense of the proportion of things. I saw that in the combination of influences that had brought Mr. Tottenham to the point of proposing to marry my daughter consideration for me, if it had a place, would be fantastic. Inwardly I laughed at the egotism of raw nerves that had conjured it up, even for an instant, as a reason for gratitude. The situation was not so peculiar, not so interesting, as that. But I answered his stare with a smile; what I had said might very well stand.

"Do you imagine," he said, seeing that I did not mean to amplify it, "that I want to marry her out of any sort of *good*ness?"

"Benevolence is your weakness, Dacres."

"I see. You think one's motive is to withdraw her from a relation which ought to be the most natural in the world, but which is, in her particular and painful case, the most equivocal."

"Well, come," I remonstrated. "You have dropped one or two things, you know, in the heat of your indignation, not badly calculated to give one that idea. The eloquent statement you have just made, for instance — it carries all the patness of old conviction. How often have you rehearsed it?"

I am a fairly long-suffering person, but I began to feel a little annoyed with my would-be son-in-law. If the relation were achieved it would give him no prescriptive right to bully me; and we were still in very early anticipation of that.

"Ah!" he said disarmingly. "Don't let us quarrel. I'm sorry you think that; because it isn't likely to bring your favor to my project, and I want you friendly and helpful. Oh, confound it!" he exclaimed, with sudden temper. "You ought to be. I don't understand this aloofness. I half suspect it's pose. You undervalue Cecily — well, you have no business to undervalue me. You know me better than anybody in the world. Now are you going to help me to marry your daughter?"

"I don't think so," I said slowly, after a moment's silence, which he sat through like a mutinous schoolboy. "I might tell you that I don't care a button whom you marry, but that would not be true. I do care more or less. As you say, I know you pretty well. I'd a little rather you didn't make a mess of it; and if you must I should distinctly prefer not to have the spectacle under my nose for the rest of my life. I can't hinder you, but I won't help you."

"And what possesses you to imagine that in marrying Cecily I should make a mess of it? Shouldn't your first consideration be whether *she* would?"

"Perhaps it should, but, you see, it isn't. Cecily would be happy with anybody who made her comfortable. You would ask a good deal more than that, you know."

Dacres, at this, took me up promptly. Life, he said, the heart of life, had particularly little to say to temperament. By the heart of life I suppose he meant married love. He explained that its roots asked other sustenance, and that it throve best of all on simple elemental goodness. So long as a man sought in women mere casual companionship, perhaps the most exquisite thing to be experienced was the stimulus of some spiritual feminine counterpart; but when he desired of one woman that she should be always and intimately with him, the background of his life, the mother of children, he was better advised to avoid nerves and sensibilities, and try for the repose of the common — the uncommon — domestic virtues. Ah, he said, they were sweet, like lavender. (Already, I told him, he smelled the housekeeper's linen-chest.) But I did not interrupt him much, I couldn't, he was too absorbed. To temperamental pairing, he declared, the century owed its breed of decadents. I asked him if he had ever really recognized one; and he retorted that if he hadn't he didn't wish to make a beginning in his own family. In a quarter of an hour he repudiated the theories of a lifetime, a gratifying triumph for simple elemental goodness. Having denied the value of the subtler pretensions to charm in woman as you marry her, he went artlessly on to endow Cecily with as many of them as could possibly be desirable. He actually persuaded himself to say that it was lovely to see the reflections of life in her tranquil spirit; and when I looked at him incredulously he grew angry, and hinted that Cecily's sensitiveness to reflections and other things might be a trifle beyond her mother's ken. "She responds instantly, intimately, to the beautiful everywhere," he declared.

"Aren't the opportunities of life on board ship rather limited to demonstrate that?" I inquired. "I know — you mean sunsets. Cecily is very fond of sunsets. She is always asking me to come and look at them."

"I was thinking of last night's sunset," he confessed. "We looked at it together."

"What did she say?" I asked idly.

"Nothing very much. That's just the point. Another girl would have raved and gushed."

"Oh, well, Cecily never does that," I responded. "Nevertheless she is a very ordinary human instrument. I hope I shall have no temptation ten years hence to remind you that I warned you of her quality."

"I wish, not in the least for my own profit, for I am well convinced already, but simply to win your cordiality and your approval — never did an unexceptional wooer receive such niggard encouragement! — I wish there were some sort of test for her quality. I would be proud to stand by it, and you would be convinced. I can't find words to describe my objection to your state of mind."

The thing seemed to me to be a foregone conclusion. I saw it accomplished, with all its possibilities of disastrous commonplace. I saw all that I have here taken the trouble to foreshadow. So far as I was concerned, Dacres's burden would add itself to my philosophies, *voilà tout.*[1] I should always be a little uncomfortable about it,

---

1 *voilà tout*: that's all.

because it had been taken from my back; but it would not be a matter for the wringing of hands. And yet — the hatefulness of the mistake! Dacres's bold talk of a test made no suggestion. Should my invention be more fertile? I thought of something.

"You have said nothing to her yet?" I asked.

"Nothing. I don't think she suspects for a moment. She treats me as if no such fell design were possible. I'm none too confident, you know," he added, with a longer face.

"We go straight to Agra.[1] Could you come to Agra?"

"Ideal!" he cried. "The memory of Mumtaz! The garden of the Taj! I've always wanted to love under the same moon as Shah Jehan.[2] How thoughtful of you!"

"You must spend a few days with us in Agra," I continued. "And as you say, it is the very place to shrine your happiness, if it comes to pass there."

"Well, I am glad to have extracted a word of kindness from you at last," said Dacres, as the stewards came to lay the table. "But I wish," he added regretfully, "you could have thought of a test."

---

1 Agra: city in northern India.
2 Mumtaz; the Taj; Shah Jehan: Shah Jehan governed India for thirty years during the Mughal Empire. He built a number of majestic buildings, including the Taj Mahal, which was a tribute to his beloved queen, Arjumand Banu Bagam, known as Mumtaz Mahal: *Elect of the Palace*. Building of the Taj Mahal began in 1632 and was finished about 1643. EN

CHAPTER V

FOUR days later we were in Agra. A time there was when the name would have been the key of dreams to me; now it stood for John's headquarters. I was rejoiced to think I would look again upon the Taj; and the prospect of living with it was a real enchantment; but I pondered most the kind of house that would be provided for the General Commanding the District, how many the dining-room would seat, and whether it would have a roof of thatch or of corrugated iron — I prayed against corrugated iron. I confess these my preoccupations. I was forty, and at forty the practical considerations of life hold their own even against domes of marble, world-renowned, and set about with gardens where the bulbul[1] sings to the rose. I smiled across the years at the raptures of my first vision of the place at twenty-one, just Cecily's age. Would I now sit under Arjamand's cypresses[2] till two o'clock in the morning to see the wonder of her tomb at a particular angle of the moon? Would I climb one of her tall white ministering minarets[3] to see anything whatever? I very greatly feared that I would not. Alas for the aging of sentiment, of interest! Keep your touch with life and your seat in the saddle as long as you will, the world is no new toy at forty. But Cecily was twenty-one, Cecily who sat stolidly finishing her lunch while Dacres Tottenham talked about Akbar[4] and his philosophy. "The sort of man," he said, "that Carlyle[5] might have smoked a pipe with."

"But surely," said Cecily reflectively, "tobacco was not discovered in England then. Akbar came to the throne in 1526."

"Nor Carlyle either for that mater," I hastened to observe. "Nevertheless, I think Mr. Tottenham's proposition must stand."

"Thanks, Mrs. Farnham," said Dacres. "But imagine Miss Farnham's remembering Akbar's date! I'm sure you didn't!"

"Let us hope she doesn't know too much about him," I cried gaily, "or there will be nothing to tell!"

---

1 bulbul: type of thrush.
2 cypresses: trees symbolic of mourning.
3 minarets: tall slender turrets from which hours of prayer are called. OED
4 Akbar: one of the leaders during the Mughal Empire. EN
5 Carlyle: Thomas Carlyle (1795-1881), Scottish historian and social critic.

"Oh, really and truly very little!" said Cecily, "but as soon as we heard papa would be stationed here Aunt Emma made me read up about those old Moguls and people. I think I remember the dynasty. Baber, wasn't he the first? and then Humayon, and after him Akbar, and then Jehangir, and then Shah Jehan.[1] But I've forgotten every date but Akbar's."

She smiled her smile of brilliant health and even spirits as she made the damaging admission, and she was so good to look at, sitting there simple and wholesome and fresh, peeling her banana with her well-shaped fingers, that we swallowed the dynasty as it were whole, and smiled back upon her. John, I may say, was extremely pleased with Cecily; he said she was a very satisfactory human accomplishment. One would have thought, positively, the way he plumed himself over his handsome daughter, that he alone was responsible for her. But John, having received his family, straightway set off with his Staff on a tour of inspection, and thereby takes himself out of this history. I sometimes think that if he had stayed — but there has never been the lightest recrimination between us about it, and I am not going to hint one now.

"Did you read," asked Dacres, "what he and the Court poet wrote over the entrance gate to the big mosque at Fettehpur-Sikri?[2] It's rather nice. 'The world is a looking-glass, wherein the image has come and is gone — take as thine own nothing more than what thou lookest upon.'"

My daughter's thoughtful gaze was, of course, fixed upon the speaker, and in his own glance I saw a sudden ray of consciousness; but Cecily transferred her eyes to the opposite wall, deeply considering, and while Dacres and I smiled across the table, I saw that she had perceived no reason for blushing. It was a singularly narrow escape.

---

1 Baber etc.: Cecily is listing the leaders of the Mughal Empire (the date Duncan has Cecily give for Akbar's coming to the throne is incorrect):

Baber	1483-1530
Humayan r.	1508-56
Akbar	1542-1605
Jehangir r.	1605-27
Shah Jehan r.	1628-57. TH

2 the mosque at Fattehpur-Sikri: Akbar built a city that was abandoned after only fourteen years. The buildings stand preserved. The entrance gate is the largest of its kind in the world. TH

"No," she said, "I didn't; what a curious proverb for an emperor to make! He couldn't possibly have been able to see all his possessions at once."

"If you have finished," Dacres addressed her, "do let me show you what your plain and immediate duty is to the garden. The garden waits for you — all the roses expectant —— "

"Why, there isn't one!" cried Cecily, pinning on her hat. It was pleasing, and just a trifle pathetic, the way he hurried her out of the scope of any little dart; he would not have her even within range of amused observation. Would he continue, I wondered vaguely, as, with my elbows on the table, I tore into strips the lemon-leaf that floated in my finger-bowl — would he continue, through life, to shelter her from his other clever friends as now he attempted to shelter her from her mother? In that case he would have to domicile her, poor dear, behind the curtain, like the native ladies — a good price to pay for a protection of which, bless her heart! she would be all unaware. I had quite stopped bemoaning the affair; perhaps the comments of my husband, who treated it with broad approval and satisfaction, did something to soothe my sensibilities. At all events, I had gradually come to occupy a high fatalistic ground toward the pair. If it was written upon their foreheads that they should marry, the inscription was none of mine; and, of course, it was true, as John had indignantly stated, that Dacres might do very much worse. One's interest in Dacres Tottenham's problematical future had in no way diminished; but the young man was so positive, so full of intention, so disinclined to discussion — he had not reopened the subject since that morning in the saloon of the Caledonia — that one's feeling about it rather took the attenuated form of a shrug. I am afraid, too, that the pleasurable excitement of such an impending event had a little supervened; even at forty there is no disallowing the natural interests of one's sex. As I sat there pulling my lemon-leaf to pieces, I should not have been surprised or in the least put about if the two had returned radiant from the lawn to demand my blessing. As to the test of quality that I had obligingly invented for Dacres on the spur of the moment without his knowledge or connivance, it had some time ago faded into what he apprehended it to be — a mere idyllic opportunity, a charming background, a frame for his project, of prettier sentiment than the funnels and the handrails of a ship.

Mr. Tottenham had ten days to spend with us. He knew the place well; it belonged to the province to whose service he was dedicated, and he claimed with impressive authority the privilege of showing it to Cecily by degrees — the Hall of Audience[1] to-day, the Jessamine Tower[2] to-morrow, the tomb of Akbar[3] another, and the Deserted City[4] yet another day. We arranged the expeditions in conference, Dacres insisting only upon the order of them, which I saw was to be cumulative, with the Taj at the very end, on the night precisely of the full of the moon, with a better chance of roses. I had no special views, but Cecily contributed some; that we should do the Hall of Audience in the morning, so as not to interfere with the club tennis in the afternoon, that we should bicycle to Akbar's tomb and take a cold luncheon — if we were sure there would be no snakes — to the Deserted City, to all of which Dacres gave loyal assent. I indorsed everything; I was the encouraging chorus, only stipulating that my number should be swelled from day to day by the addition of such persons as I should approve. Cecily, for instance, wanted to invite the Bakewells because we had come out in the same ship with them, but I could not endure the Bakewells, and it seemed to me that our having made the voyage with them was the best possible reason for declining to lay eyes on them for the rest of our natural lives. "Mamma has such strong prejudices," Cecily remarked, as she reluctantly gave up the idea; and I waited to see whether the graceless Tottenham would unmurmuringly take down the Bakewells. How strong must be the sentiment that turns a man into a boa-constrictor without a pang of transmigration![5] But no, this time he was faithful to the principles of his pre-Cecilian existence. "They are rather Boojums,"[6] he declared. "You would think so, too, if you knew them better. It is that kind of excellent person that makes the real burden of India." I could have patted him on the back.

Thanks to the rest of the chorus, which proved abundantly available, I was no immediate witness to Cecily's introduction to

---

1 Hall of Audience: the Diwanni-Khas, site of Akbar's imperial throne. TH
2 Jessamine Tower: the Jasmine Tower (?).
3 tomb of Akbar: Akbar is buried in a beautiful mausoleum in Sikandra, a few miles from Agra. TH
4 Deserted City: presumably another reference to Fattehpur-Sikri.
5 transmigration: pass into a different body. OED
6 Boojums: a tree native to the Puerto Litertad area and the Baja California Peninsula of northwestern Mexico — resembles a giant upside-down turnip. EN

the glorious fragments which sustain in Agra the memory of the Moguls. I may as well say that I arranged with care that if anybody must be standing by when Dacres disclosed them, it should not be I. If Cecily had squinted, I should have been sorry, but I would have found in it no personal humiliation. There were other imperfections of vision, however, for which I felt responsible and ashamed; and with Dacres, though the situation, Heaven knows, was none of my seeking, I had a little the feeling of a dealer who offers a defective *bibelot*[1] to a connoisseur. My charming daughter — I was fifty times congratulated upon her appearance and her manners — had many excellent qualities and capacities which she never inherited from me; but she could see no more than the bulk, no further than the perspective; she could register exactly as much as a camera.

This was a curious thing, perhaps, to displease my maternal vanity, but it did; I had really rather she squinted; and when there was anything to look at I kept out of the way. I can not tell precisely, therefore, what the incidents were that contributed to make Mr. Tottenham, on our return from these expeditions, so thoughtful, with a thoughtfulness which increased, toward the end of them, to a positive gravity. This would disappear during dinner under the influence of food and drink. He would talk nightly with new enthusiasm and fresh hope — or did I imagine it? — of the loveliness he had arranged to reveal on the following day. If again my imagination did not lead me astray, I fancied this occurred later and later in the course of the meal as the week went on; as if his state required more stimulus as time progressed. One evening, when I expected it to flag altogether, I had a whim to order champagne and observe the effect; but I am glad to say that I reproved myself, and refrained.

Cecily, meanwhile, was conducting herself in a manner which left nothing to be desired. If, as I sometimes thought, she took Dacres very much for granted, she took him calmly for granted; she seemed a prey to none of those fluttering uncertainties, those suspended judgments and elaborate indifferences which translate themselves so plainly in a young lady receiving addresses. She turned herself out very freshly and very well; she was always ready for everything, and I am sure that no glance of Dacres Tottenham's found aught but direct and decorous response. His society on these

---

1 *bibelot*: a small curio or artistic trinket. OED

occasions gave her solid pleasure; so did the drive and the lunch; the satisfactions were apparently upon the same plane. She was aware of the plum, if I may be permitted a brusque but irresistible simile; and with her mouth open, her eyes modestly closed, and her head in a convenient position, she waited, placidly, until it should fall in. The Farnham ladies would have been delighted with the result of their labors in the sweet reason and eminent propriety of this attitude. Thinking of my idiotic sufferings when John began to fix himself upon my horizon, I pondered profoundly the power of nature in differentiation.

One evening, the last, I think, but one, I had occasion to go to my daughter's room, and found her writing in her commonplace-book. She had a commonplace-book,[1] as well as a Where Is It?[2] an engagement-book, an account-book, a diary, a Daily Sunshine,[3] and others with purposes too various to remember. "Dearest mamma," she said, as I was departing, "there is only one 'p' in 'opulence,' isn't there?"

"Yes," I replied, with my hand on the door-handle, and added curiously, for it was an odd word in Cecily's mouth, "Why?"

She hardly hesitated. "Oh," she said, "I am just writing down one or two things Mr. Tottenham said about Agra before I forget them. They seemed so true."

"He has a descriptive touch," I remarked.

"I think he describes beautifully. Would you like to hear what he said to-day?"

"I would," I replied sincerely.

"'Agra,'" read this astonishing young lady, "'is India's one pure idyl. Elsewhere she offers other things, foolish opulence, tawdry pageant, treachery of eunuchs and jealousies of harems, thefts of kings' jewels and barbaric retributions; but they are all actual, visualized, or part of a past that shows to the backward glance hardly more relief and vitality than a Persian painting' — I should like to see a Persian painting — 'but here the immortal tombs and pleasure-houses rise out of color delicate and subtle; the vision holds across three hundred years; the print of the court is still in the dust of the city.'"

---

1 a commonplace-book: a book in which one records favourite sayings, notable passages. OED.
2 a Where Is It?: an address book (?).
3 a Daily Sunshine: a book with uplifting maxims (?).

"Did you really let him go on like that?" I exclaimed. "It has the license of a lecture!"

"I encouraged him to. Of course he didn't say it straight off. He said it naturally; he stopped now and then to cough. I didn't understand it all; but I think I have remembered every word."

"You have a remarkable memory. I'm glad he stopped to cough. Is there any more?"

"One little bit. 'Here the Moguls wrought their passions into marble, and held them up with great refrains from their religion, and set them about with gardens; and here they stand in the twilight of the glory of those kings and the noonday splendor of their own.'"

"How clever of you!" I exclaimed. "How wonderfully clever of you to remember!"

"I had to ask him to repeat one or two sentences. He didn't like that. But this is nothing. I used to learn pages letter-perfect for Aunt Emma. She was very particular. I think it is worth preserving, don't you?"

"Dear Cecily," I responded, "you have a frugal mind."

There was nothing else to respond. I could not tell her just how practical I thought her, or how pathetic her little book.

CHAPTER VI

WE drove together, after dinner, to the Taj. The moonlight lay in an empty splendor over the broad sandy road, with the acacias pricking up on each side of it and the gardens of the station bungalows stretching back into clusters of crisp shadows. It was an exquisite February night, very still. Nothing seemed abroad but two or three pariah dogs, upon vague and errant business, and the Executive Engineer going swiftly home from the club on his bicycle. Even the little shops of the bazaar were dark and empty; only here and there a light showed barred behind the carved balconies of the upper rooms, and there was hardly any tom-tomming. The last long slope of the road showed us the river curving to the left, through a silent white waste that stretched indefinitely into the moonlight on one side, and was crowned by Akbar's fort on the other. His long high line of turrets and battlements still guarded a hint of their evening rose, and dim and exquisite above them hovered the three dome-bubbles of the Pearl Mosque. It was a night of perfect illusion, and the illusion was mysterious, delicate, and faint. I sat silent as we rolled long, twenty years nearer to the original joy of things when John and I drove through the same old dream.

Dacres, too, seemed preoccupied; only Cecily was, as they say, herself. Cecily was really more than herself, she exhibited an unusual flow of spirits. She talked continually, she pointed out this and that, she asked who lived here and who lived there. At regular intervals of about four minutes she demanded if it wasn't simply too lovely. She sat straight up with her vigorous profile and her smart hat; and the silhouette of her personality sharply refused to mingle with the dust of any dynasty. She was a contrast, a protest; positively she was an indignity. "Do lean back, dear child," I exclaimed at last. "You interfere with the landscape."

She leaned back, but she went on interfering with it in terms of sincerest enthusiasm.

When we stopped at the great archway of entrance I begged to be left in the carriage. What else could one do, when the golden moment had come, but sit in the carriage and measure it? They climbed the broad stone steps together and passed under the lofty gravures into the garden, and I waited. I waited and remembered. I am not, as perhaps by this time is evident, a person of overwhelming sentiment, but I think the smile upon my lips was gentle, so plainly I could see, beyond the massive archway and across a score of years, all that they saw at that moment — Arjamand's garden, and the long straight tank of marble cleaving it full of sleeping water and the shadows of the marshaling cypresses; her wide dark garden of roses and of pomegranates, and at the end the Vision, marvelous, aerial, the soul of something — is it beauty? is it sorrow? — that great white pride of love in mourning such as only here in all the round of our little world lifts itself to the stars, the unpaintable, indescribable Taj Mahal. A gentle breath stole out with a scent of jessamine and such a memory! I closed my eyes and felt the warm luxury of a tear.

Thinking of the two in the garden, my mood was very kind, very conniving. How foolish after all were my cherry-stone theories of taste and temperament before that uncalculating thing which sways a world and builds a Taj Mahal! Was it probable that Arjamand and her Emperor had loved fastidiously, and yet how they had loved! I wandered away into consideration of the blind forces which move the world, in which comely young persons like my daughter Cecily had such a place; I speculated vaguely upon the value of the subtler gifts of sympathy and insight which seemed indeed, at that enveloping moment, to be mere flowers strewn upon the tide of deeper emotions. The garden sent me a fragrance of roses; the moon sailed higher and picked out the little kiosks set along the wall. It was a charming, charming thing to wait, there at the portal of the silvered, scented garden, for an idyl to come forth.

When they reappeared, Dacres and my daughter, they came with casual steps and cheerful voices. They might have been a couple of tourists. The moonlight fell full upon them on the platform under the arch. It showed Dacres measuring with his stick the length of the Sanscrit letters[1] which declared the stately texts, and Cecily's expression of polite, perfunctory interest. They looked up at the height above them; they looked back at the vision behind. Then they sauntered toward the carriage, he offering a formal hand to help her down the uncertain steps, she gracefully accepting it.

---

1   Sanscrit letters: the ancient and sacred language of the Hindus in India.
    OED

"You — you have not been long," said I. "I hope you didn't hurry on my account."

"Miss Farnham found the marble a little cold under foot," replied Dacres, putting Miss Farnham in.

"You see," explained Cecily, "I stupidly forgot to change into thicker soles. I have only my slippers. But, mamma, how lovely it is! Do let us come again in the daytime. I am dying to make a sketch of it."

Mr. Tottenham was to leave us on the following day. In the morning, after "little breakfast," as we say in India, he sought me in the room I had set aside to be particularly my own.

Again I was writing to John, but this time I waited for precisely his interruption. I had got no further than "My dearest husband," and my pen-handle was a fringe.

"Another fine day," I said, as if the old, old Indian joke could give him ease, poor man!

"Yes," said he, "we are having lovely weather."

He had forgotten that it was a joke. Then he lapsed into silence while I renewed my attentions to my pen.

"I say," he said at last, with so strained a look about his mouth that it was almost a contortion, "I haven't done it, you know."

"No," I responded, cheerfully, "and you're not going to. Is that it? Well!"

"Frankly —— " said he.

"Dear me, yes! Anything else between you and me would be grotesque," I interrupted, "after all these years."

"I don't think it would be a success," he said, looking at me resolutely with his clear blue eyes, in which still lay, alas! the possibility of many delusions.

"No," I said, "I never did, you know. But the prospect had begun to impose upon me."

"To say how right you were would seem, under the circumstances, the most hateful form of flattery."

"Yes," I said, "I think I can dispense with your verbal indorsement." I felt a little bitter. It was, of course, better that the connoisseur should have discovered the flaw before concluding the transaction; but although I had pointed it out myself I was not entirely pleased to have the article returned.

"I am infinitely ashamed that it should have taken me all these days — day after day and each contributory — to discover what you saw so easily and so completely."

"You forget that I am her mother," I could not resist the temptation of saying.

"Oh, for God's sake don't jeer! Please be absolutely direct, and tell me if you have reason to believe that to the extent of a thought, of a breath — to any extent at all — she cares."

He was, I could see, very deeply moved; he had not arrived at this point without trouble and disorder not lightly to be put on or off. Yet I did not hurry to his relief, I was still possessed by a vague feeling of offense. I reflected that any mother would be, and I quite plumed myself upon my annoyance. It was so satisfactory, when one had a daughter, to know the sensations of even any mother. Nor was it soothing to remember that the young man's whole attitude toward Cecily had been based upon criticism of me, even though he sat before me whipped with his own lash. His temerity had been stupid and obstinate; I could not regret his punishment.

I kept him waiting long enough to think all this, and then I replied, "I have not the least means of knowing."

I can not say what he expected, but he squared his shoulders as if he had received a blow and might receive another. Then he looked at me with a flash of the old indignation. "You are not near enough to her for that!" he exclaimed.

"I am not near enough to her for that."

Silence fell between us. A crow perched upon an opened venetian and cawed lustily. For years afterward I never heard a crow caw without a sense of vain, distressing experiment. Dacres got up and began to walk about the room. I very soon put a stop to that. "I can't talk to a pendulum," I said, but I could not persuade him to sit down again.

"Candidly," he said at length, "do you think she would have me?"

"I regret to say that I think she would. But you would not dream of asking her."

"Why not? She is a dear girl," he responded, inconsequently.

"You could not possibly stand it."

Then Mr. Tottenham delivered himself of this remarkable phrase: "I could stand it," he said, "as well as you can."

There was far from being any joy in the irony with which I regarded him and under which I saw him gather up his resolution to go; nevertheless I did nothing to make it easy for him. I refrained from imparting my private conviction that Cecily would accept the first presentable substitute that appeared, although it was strong.

I made no reference to my daughter's large fund of philosophy and small balance of sentiment. I did not even — though this was reprehensible — confess the test, the test of quality in these ten days with the marble archives of the Moguls, which I had almost wantonly suggested, which he had so unconsciously accepted, so disastrously applied. I gave him quite fifteen minutes of his bad quarter of an hour, and when it was over I wrote truthfully but furiously to John ....

That was ten years ago. We have since attained the shades of retirement, and our daughter is still with us when she is not with Aunt Emma and Aunt Alice — grandmamma has passed away. Mr. Tottenham's dumb departure that day in February — it was the year John got his C.B.[1] — was followed, I am thankful to say, by none of the symptoms of unrequited affection on Cecily's part. Not for ten minutes, so far as I was aware, was she the maid forlorn. I think her self-respect was of too robust a character, thanks to the Misses Farnham. Still less, of course, had she any reproaches to serve upon her mother, although for a long time I thought I detected — or was it my guilty conscience? — a spark of shrewdness in the glance she bent upon me when the talk was of Mr. Tottenham and the probabilities of his return to Agra. So well did she sustain her experience, or so little did she feel it, that I believe the impression went abroad that Dacres had been sent disconsolate away. One astonishing conversation I had with her some six months later, which turned upon the point of a particularly desirable offer. She told me something then, without any sort of embarrassment, but quite lucidly and directly, that edified me much to hear. She said that while she was quite sure that Mr. Tottenham thought of her only as a friend — she had never had the least reason for any other impression — he had done her a service for which she could not thank him enough — in showing her what a husband might be. He had given her a standard; it might be high, but it was unalterable. She didn't know whether she could describe it, but Mr. Tottenham was different from the kind of man you seemed to meet in India. He had his own ways of looking at things, and he talked so well. He had given her an ideal, and she intended to profit by it. To know that men like

---

1 C.B.: Companion of the Bath. OED

Mr. Tottenham existed, and to marry any other kind would be an act of folly which she did not intend to commit. No, Major the Hon. Hugh Taverel did not come near it — very far short, indeed! He had talked to her during the whole of dinner the night before about jackal-hunting with a bobbery pack[1] — not at all an elevated mind. Yes, he might be a very good fellow, but as a companion for life she was sure he would not be at all suitable. She would wait.

And she has waited. I never thought she would, but she has. From time to time men have wished to take her from us, but the standard has been inexorable, and none of them has reached it. When Dacres married the charming American whom he caught like a butterfly upon her Eastern tour, Cecily sent them as a wedding present an alabaster model of the Taj, and I let her do it — the gift was so exquisitely appropriate. I suppose he never looks at it without being reminded that he didn't marry Miss Farnham, and I hope that he remembers that he owes it to Miss Farnham's mother. So much I think I might claim; it is really very little considering what it stands for. Cecily is permanently with us — I believe she considers herself an intimate. I am very reasonable about lending her to her aunts, but she takes no sort of advantage of my liberality; she says she knows her duty is at home. She is growing into a firm and solid English maiden lady, with a good color and great decision of character. That she always had.

I point out to John, when she takes our crumpets away from us, that she gets it from him. I could never take away anybody's crumpets, merely because they were indigestible, least of all my own parents'. She has acquired a distinct affection for us, by some means best known to herself; but I should have no objection to that if she would not rearrange my bonnet-strings. That is a fond liberty to which I take exception; but it is one thing to take exception and another to express it.

Our daughter is with us, permanently with us. She declares that she intends to be the prop of our declining years; she makes the statement often, and always as if it were humorous. Nevertheless I sometimes notice a spirit of inquiry, a note of investigation in her encounters with the opposite sex that suggests an expectation not yet extinct that another and perhaps a more appreciative Dacres

---

1   a bobbery pack: a pack of hounds of various breeds or of no breed. OED

Tottenham may flash across her field of vision — alas, how improbable! Myself I can not imagine why she should wish it; I have grown in my old age into a perfect horror of cultivated young men; but if such a person should by a miracle at any time appear, I think it is extremely improbable that I will interfere on his behalf.

Part III

An Impossible Ideal

CHAPTER I

TO understand how we prized him, Dora Harris and I, it is necessary to know Simla. I suppose people think of that place, if they ever do think of it, as an agreeable retreat in the wilds of the Himalayas where deodars[1] and scandals grow, and where the Viceroy[2] if he likes may take off his decorations and go about in flannels. I know how useless it would be to try to give a more faithful impression, and I will hold back from the attempt as far as I can. Besides, my little story is itself an explanation of Simla. Ingersoll Armour might have appeared almost anywhere else without making social history. He came and bloomed among us in the wilderness, and such and such things happened. It sounds too rude a generalization to say that Simla is a wilderness; I hasten to add that it is a waste as highly cultivated as you like, producing many things more admirable than Ingersoll Armour. Still he bloomed there conspicuously alone. Perhaps there would have been nothing to tell if we had not tried to gather him. That was wrong; Nature in Simla expects you to be content with cocked hats.[3]

There are artists almost everywhere and people who paint even in the Himalayas, though Miss Harris and I in our superior way went yearly to the Simla Fine Arts Exhibition chiefly to amuse ourselves by scoffing. It was easy to say clever things about the poor little exhibits; and one was grateful to the show on this account, for nothing is more depressing east of Suez than the absence of provocation to say clever things. There one afternoon in May as we marched about enjoying ourselves, we came upon Ingersoll Armour, not in the flesh, but in half a dozen studies hanging in the least conspicuous corner and quite the worst light in the room.

"Eh, what?" said I, and Dora exclaimed:

"I *say!*"

"Sent out from home," I said, ever the oracle.

"Not at all," replied Dora. "Look, they are Indian subjects. *Simla* subjects," she went on, with excitement.

---

1 deodars: the Himalayan cedar; the tallest of the cedar family, with drooping branches bearing large barrel-shaped cones. OED
2 Viceroy: a ruler exercising authority on behalf of a sovereign in a colony, province, etc. OED
3 cocked hats: senior bureaucrats.

I turned up the catalogue. "Ninety-seven, 'Ksumti Bazar'; ninety-eight, 'Clouds on the Chor'; ninety-nine, 'The House of a Friend' — Lord, what apricot blossoms! Yes, they're all Simla."

"For goodness' sake," said Dora, "who painted them? You've got the catalogue!"

"'I. Armour,'" I read.

"'I. Armour,'" she repeated, and we looked at each other, saying in plain silence that to the small world of Simla I. Armour was unknown.

"Not on Government House list,[1] I venture to believe," said Dora. That in itself may show to what depths we sink. Yet it was a trenchant and a reasonable speculation.

"It may be a newcomer," I suggested, but she shook her head. "All newcomers call upon us," she said. "There in the middle of the Mall we escape none of them. He isn't a calling person."

"Why do you say 'he'? You are very confident with your pronouns. There's a delicacy of feeling —— "

"Which exactly does not suggest a woman. We are undermined by delicacy of feeling; we're not strong enough to express it with brushes. A man can make it a quality, a decorative characteristic, and so we see it. With a woman it's everything — all over the place — and of no effect. Oh, I assure you, I. Armour is a man."

"Who shall stand against you! Let him be a man. He has taste."

"Taste!" exclaimed Miss Harris, violently, and from the corners of her mouth I gathered that I had said one of those things which she would store up and produce to prove that I was not, for all my pretensions, a person of the truest feeling. "He sees things."

"There's an intensity," I ventured.

"That's better. Yes, an intensity. A perfect passion of color. Look at that." She indicated a patch of hillsides perhaps six inches by four, in which the light seemed to come and go as it does in a sapphire.

We stood and gazed. It was a tremendous thing; only half a dozen studies with feeling and knowledge in them, but there in that remote fastness thrice barred against the arts a tremendous thing, a banquet for our famished eyes. What they would have said to us in London is a different matter, and how good they really were I do not find the courage to pronounce, but they had merit

---

1 Government House list: the list of people whose status entitled them to be invited to official government functions.

enough to prick our sense of beauty delightfully where we found them — oh, they were good!

"Heaven send it isn't a Tommy,"[1] said Dora, with a falling countenance. "There is something absolutely inaccessible about a Tommy."

"How could it be?" I asked.

"Oh, there are some inspired ones. But it isn't — that's a French technique. It's an Englishman or an American who has worked in Paris. What in the name of fortune is he doing here?"

"Oh," I said, "we have had them, you know. Val Prinsep[2] came out at the time of the Prince of Wales's visit."

"Do you remember *that*?"

"It's a matter of history," I said, evasively, "and Edwin Weeks traveled through India not so many years ago. I saw his studio in Paris afterward. Between his own canvases and Ahmedabad balconies and Delhi embroideries and Burmese Buddhas and other things he seemed to have carried off the whole place."

"But they don't come up here ever. They come in the cold weather, and as they can get plenty of snow and ice at home, they stay down in the plains with the palm-trees."

"Precisely; they do," I said.

"And besides," Dora went on, with increasing excitement, "this isn't a master. You see, he doesn't send a single picture — only these tiny things. And there's a certain tentativeness" — Miss Harris, her parasol handle pressed against her lips, looked at me with an eagerness that was a pleasure to look at in itself.

"A certain weakness, almost a lack of confidence, in the drawing," I said.

"What does that signify?"

"Why, immaturity, of course — not enough discipline. He's a student. Not that it amounts to a defect, you know" — she was as jealous already as if she possessed the things — "only a sign to read by. I should be grateful for more signs. Why should a student come to Simla?"

"To teach, perhaps," I suggested. Naturally one sought only among reasons of utility.

"It's the Kensington person who teaches. When they have worked in the ateliers and learned as much as this they never do. They paint fans and menu cards, and starve, but they don't teach."

---

1 a Tommy: a British private soldier. OED
2 Val Prinsep: an artist (1838–1904).

Sir William Lamb, Member of Council for the Department of Finance, was borne by the stream to our sides. The simile will hardly stand conscientious examination, for the stream was a thin one and did no more than trickle past, while Sir William weighed fifteen stone, and was so eminent that it could never inconvenience him at its deepest. Dora detached her gaze from the pictures and turned her back upon them; I saw the measure of precaution. It was unavailing, however. "What have we here?" said Sir William. Dora removed her person from his line of vision, and he saw what we had there.

"The work of a friend of yours?" Sir William was spoken of as a "cautious" man. He had risen to his present distinction on stepping-stones of mistakes he conspicuously had not made.

"No," said Dora, "we were wondering who the artist could be."

Sir William looked at the studies, and had a happy thought. "If you ask me, I should say a child of ten," he said. He was also known as a man of humor.

"Miss Harris had just remarked a certain immaturity," I ventured.

"Oh well," said Sir William, "this isn't the Royal Academy, is it? I always say it's very good of people to send their things here at all. And some of them are not half bad — I should call this year's average very high indeed."

"Are you pleased with the picture that has taken your prize, Sir William?" asked Dora.

"I have bought it." Sir William's chest underwent before our eyes an expansion of conscious virtue. Living is so expensive in Simla; the purchase of a merely decorative object takes almost the proportion of an act of religion, even by a Member of Council drawing four hundred pounds a month.

"First-rate it is, first-rate. Have you seen it? 'Our Camp in Tirah.' Natives cooking in the foreground, fellows standing about smoking, and a whole pile of tinned stores dumped down in one corner, exactly as they would be, don't you know! Oh, I think the Committee made a very good choice indeed, a very good choice."

Sir William moved on, and Dora was free to send me an expressive glance. "Isn't that just *like* this place?" she demanded. "Let me see, the Viceroy's medal, the Society's silver medal, five prizes from Members of Council. Highly Commended's as thick as blackberries, and these perfectly fresh, original, admirable things completely ignored. What an absurd, impossible corner of the earth it is!"

"You look very cross, you two," said Mrs. Sinclair, trailing past. "Come and see the crazy china exhibit, all made of little bits, you know. They say the photograph frames are simply lovely."

Mrs. Sinclair's invitation was not sincere. Miss Harris was able to answer it with a laugh and a wave. We remained beside the serious fact of exhibits 97–103.

"Who are the judges this year?" I asked, not that I did not know precisely who they were likely to be. There is a custom in these matters, and I had been part of Simla for eleven years.

Dora took the catalogue from my hand and turned its pages over.

"Mr. Cathcart, of course; the Private Secretary to the Viceroy would be on the Committee almost *ex officio*, wouldn't he? Impossible to conceive a Private Secretary to the Viceroy whose opinion would not be valuable upon any head. The member for Public Works — I suppose he can build bridges, or could once, therefore he can draw, or could once; besides, look at his precedence and his pay! General Haycock — isn't he head of the Ordnance Department? I can't think of any other reason for putting him on. Oh yes — he's a K.C.B., and he is inventing a way of taking colored photographs. Mr. Tilley, the old gentleman that teaches elementary drawing to the little girls in the diocesan school, that's all right. And Mr. Jay, of course, because Mr. Jay's water-colors are the mainstay of the exhibition, and he must be given a chance of expressing his opinion of them." She handed me back the catalogue. "I have never been really angry with them before," she said.

"Are you really angry now?" I asked.

"Furious," Dora replied, and indeed her face expressed indignation. Its lines were quite tense, and a spark shone oddly in the middle of the eyes. One could not credit her with beauty, but as her lady friends were fond of saying, there was something "more" in her face. I saw a good deal more at this moment, and it gave me pleasure, as all her feelings did when they came out like that. I hasten to add that she was not unpleasing; her features had a symmetry and a mobility, and her eyes could take any transient charm they chose to endow themselves with; though there were moments when she compared very badly with the other young ladies of Simla with their high spirits and their pretty complexions, very badly indeed. Those were occasions when the gay monotony of the place pressed, I imagine, a little heavily upon her, and the dulness she felt translated itself in her expression. But she was by no means unpleasing.

"I must go and see Lady Pilkey's picture," I said.

"What is the use?" said Dora. "It's a landscape in oils — a view of the Himalayas, near Narkanda. There are the snows in the background, very thin and visionary through a gap in the trees, and two hills, one hill on each side. Dark green trees, pine-trees, with a dead one in the left foreground covered with a brilliant red creeper. Right foreground occupied by a mountain path and a solitary native figure with its back turned. Society's silver medal."

"When did you see it?" I asked.

"I haven't seen it — this year. But I saw the one she sent last, and the one the year before that. You can trust my memory, really."

"No," I said, "I can't. I'm dining there to-night. I must have an original impression."

"Congratulate her on the warm blaze of color in the foreground. It's perfectly safe," urged Miss Harris, but I felt compelled to go myself to see Lady Pilkey's landscape. When I returned I found her still sitting in grave absorption before the studies that had taken us so by surprise. Her face was full of a soft new light; I had never before seen the spring touched in her that could flood it like that.

"You were very nearly right," I announced; "but the blaze of color was in the middle distance, and there was a torrent in the foreground that quite put it out. And the picture does take the Society's silver medal."

"I can not decide," she replied without looking at me, "between the Kattiawar[1] fair thing and those hills in the rain. I can only have one — father won't hear of more than one."

"You can have two," I said bluntly, so deeply interested I was in the effect the things had on her. "And I will have a third for myself. I can't withstand those apricot-trees."

I thought there was moisture in the eyes she turned upon me, an unusual thing — a most unusual thing — in Dora Harris; but she winked it back, if it was there, too quickly for any certainty.

"You are a dear," she said. Once or twice before she had called me a dear. It reminded me, as nothing else ever did, that I was a contemporary of her father's. It is a feeble confession, but I have known myself refrain from doing occasional agreeable things apprehending that she might call me a dear.

---

1   Kattiawar (Kathiawar): a peninsula of western India in the state of Gujarat. EN

CHAPTER II

DORA had been out three seasons when these things happened. I remember sharing Edward Harris's anxiety in no slight degree as to how the situation would resolve itself when she came, the situation consisting so considerably in his eyes of the second Mrs. Harris, who had complicated it further with three little red-cheeked boys, all of the age to be led about the station on very small ponies, and not under any circumstances to be allowed in the drawing-room when one went to tea with their mother. No one, except perhaps poor Ted himself, was more interested than I to observe how the situation did resolve itself, in the decision of Mrs. Harris that the boys, the two eldest at least, must positively begin the race for the competitive examinations of the future without further delay, and that she must as positively be domiciled in England "to be near" them, at all events until they had well made the start. I should have been glad to see them ride their ponies up and down the Mall a bit longer, poor little chaps; they were still very cherubic to be invited to take a view of competitive examinations, however distant; but Mrs. Harris's conviction was not to be overcome. So they went home to begin, and she went with them, leaving Dora in possession of her father, her father's house, his pay, his precedence, and all that was his. Not that I would suggest any friction; I am convinced that there was nothing like that — at least, nothing that met the eye, or the ear. Dora adored the three little boys and was extremely kind to their mother. She regarded this lady, I have reason to believe, with the greatest indulgence, and behaved toward her with the greatest consideration; I mean she had unerring intuitions as to just when, on afternoons when Mrs. Harris was at home from dusk till dinner, she should be dying for a walk. One could imagine her looking with her gray eyes at dear mamma's horizon and deciding that papa was certainly not enough to fill it by himself, deciding at the same time that he was never likely to be ousted there, only accompanied, in a less important and entirely innocent degree. It may be surprising that any one should fly from so broad-minded a step-daughter; but the happy family party lasted a bare three months. I think Mrs. Harris had a perception — she was the kind of woman who arrived obscurely at the very correct conclusions — that she was contributing to her step-daughter's amusement in a manner which her most benevolent intentions had not contemplated, and she was not by any means the little person to go on doing that indefinitely, perhaps increasingly. Besides, it was in the natural order of things that Dora should marry, and Mrs. Harris doubtless foresaw a comfortable return for herself in the course of a year or two, when the usual promising junior in "the Department" should gild his own prospects and promote the general well-being by acquiring its head for a father-in-law. Things always worked out if you gave them time. How much time you ought to give them was doubtless by now a pretty constant query with the little lady in her foggy exile; for two years had already passed and Dora had found no connection with any young man of the Department more permanent than those prescribed at dinners and at dances. It is doubtful, indeed, if she had had the opportunity. There was no absolute means of knowing; but if offers were made they never transpired, and Mrs. Harris, far away in England, nourished a certainty that they never were made. Speaking with her intimate knowledge of the sex she declared that Dora frightened the men, that her cleverness was of a kind to paralyze any sentiment of the sort that might be expected. It depended upon Mrs. Harris's humor whether this was Dora's misfortune or her crime. She, Dora, never frightened me, and by the time her cleverness dawned upon me, my sentiment about her had become too robust to be paralyzed. On the contrary, the agreeable stimulus it gave me was one of the things I counted most valuable in my life out there. It hardly mattered, however, that I should confess this; I was not a young man in Harris's department. I had a department of my own; and Dora, though she frisked with me gloriously and bullied me continually, must ever have been aware of the formidable fact that I joined the Service two years before Edward Harris did. The daughter of three generations of bureaucrats was not likely to forget that at one time her father had been junior to me in the same office, though in the course of time and the march of opportunity he had his own show now, and we nodded to each other on the Mall with an equal sense of the divine right of secretaries. It may seem irrelevant, but I feel compelled to explain here that I had remained a bachelor while Harris had married twice, and that I had kept up my cricket, while Harris had let his figure take all the soft curves of middle age. Nevertheless the fact remained. Sometimes I fancied it gave a certain piquancy to my relations with his daughter, but I could never believe that the laugh was on my side.

If we met at dinner-parties, it would be sometimes Edward Harris and sometimes myself who would take the dullest and stoutest woman down. If she fell to him the next in precedence was bestowed upon me, and there might not be a pin to choose between them for phlegm and inflation. It is a preposterous mistake to suppose that the married ladies of Simla are in the majority brilliant and fascinating creatures, who say things in French for greater convenience, and lead a man on. After fifteen years I am ready to swear that I have been led on to nothing more compromising than a subscription to the Young Women's Christian Association, though no one could have been more docile or more intelligent. During one viceroyalty of happy memory half a dozen clever and amusing men and women came together in Simla — it was a mere fortuitous occurrence, aided by a joyous ruler who hated being bored as none before or since have hated it — and the place has lived socially upon the reputation of that meteoric term ever since. Whereas the domestic virtues are no more deeply rooted anywhere than under the deodars; nor could any one, I hasten to add, chronicle the fact with more profound satisfaction than myself. A dinner-party, however, is not a favorable setting for the domestic virtues; it does them so little justice that one could sometimes almost wish them left at home, and I was talking of Simla dinner-parties, where I have encountered so many. How often have I been consulted as to the best school for boys in England, or instructed as to how much I should let my man charge me for shoe-blacking, or advised as to the most effectual way of preventing the butler from stealing my cheroots, while Dora Harris, remote as a star, talked to a cavalry subaltern about wind-galls and splints! At these moments I felt my seniority bitterly; to give Dora to a cavalry subaltern was such plain waste.

It was an infinite pleasure to know any one as well as I seemed to know Dora Harris. She, I believe, held no one else upon the same terms of intimacy, though she found women, of course, with whom she fluttered and embraced; and while there were, naturally, men with whom I exchanged the time o' day in terms more or less cordial, I am certain that I kept all my closest thoughts for her. It is necessary again to know Simla to understand how our friendship was gilded by the consideration that it was on both sides perfectly spontaneous. Social life in the poor little place is almost a pure farce with the number of its dictated, prompted intimacies, not controlled by general laws of expediency as at home, but each on its own basis of hope and expectancy, broadly and ludicrously obvious as a case by itself. There is a conspiracy of stupidity about it, for we are all in the same hat, every one of us; there is none so exalted that he does not urgently want a post that somebody else can give him. So we continue to exchange our depreciated smiles, and only privately admit that the person who most desires to be agreeable to us is the person whom we regard with the greatest suspicion. As between Dora Harris and myself there could be, naturally, no ax to grind. We amused ourselves by looking on penetratingly but tolerantly at the grinding of other people's.

That was a very principal bond between us, that uncompromising clearness with which we looked at the place we lived in, and on the testimony of which we were so certain that we didn't like it. The women were nearly all so much in heaven in Simla, the men so well satisfied to be there too, at the top of the tree, that our dissatisfaction gave us to one another the merit of originality, almost proved in one another a superior mind. It was not that either of us would have preferred to grill out our days in the plains; we always had a saving clause for the climate, the altitude, the scenery; it was Simla intrinsic, Simla as its other conditions made it, with which we found such liberal fault. Again I should have to explain Simla, at the length of an essay at least, to justify our condemnation. This difficulty confronts me everywhere. I must ask you instead to imagine a small colony of superior — very superior — officials, of British origin and traditions, set on the top of a hill, years and miles away from literature, music, pictures, politics, existing like a harem on the gossip of the Viceroy's intentions, and depending for amusement on tennis and bumble-puppy,[1] and then consider, you yourself, whether you are the sort of person to be unquestionably happy there. If you see no reason to the contrary, pray do not go on. There were times when Dora declared that she couldn't breathe for want of an atmosphere, and times when I looked round and groaned at the cheerful congratulatory aridity in every man's eye — men who had done things at Oxford in my own year, and come out like me to be mummified into a last state like this. Thank Heaven, there was never any cheerful congratulation in my eye; one could always put there, when the thought inspired it, a saving spark of rank ingratitude instead.

It was as if we had the most desirable things — roses, cool airs, far snowy ranges — to build what we like with, and we built Simla

---

1 bumble-puppy: a game.

— altitude, 7,000, population 2,500, headquarters of the Government of India during the summer months. An ark it was, of course; an ark of refuge from the horrible heat that surged below, and I wondered as I climbed the steeps of Summer Hill in search of I. Armour's inaccessible address, whether he was to be the dove bearing beautiful testimony of a world coming nearer. I rejected the simile, however, as over-sanguine; we had been too long abandoned on our Ararat.[1]

---

1 Ararat: The final landing-place of Noah's Ark.

CHAPTER III

A DOG of no sort of caste stood in the veranda and barked at me offensively. I picked up a stone, and he vanished like the dog of a dream into the house. It was such a small house that it wasn't on the municipal map at all: it looked as if some one had built it for amusement with anything that was lying about. Nevertheless, it had a name, it was called Amy Villa, freshly painted in white letters on a shiny black board, and nailed against the nearest tree in the orthodox Simla fashion. It looked as if the owner of the place had named it as a duty toward his tenant, the board was so new, and in that case the reflection presented itself that the tenant might have cooperated to call it something else. It was disconcerting somehow to find that our dove had perched, even temporarily, in Amy Villa. Nor was it soothing to discover that the small white object stuck in the corner of the board was Mr. Ingersoll Armour's card.

In Simla we do not stick our cards about in that way at the mercy of the wind and the weather; we paint our names nearly under the names of our houses with "I.C.S." for Indian Civil Service, or "P.W.D." for Public Works Department, or whatever designation we are entitled to immediately after, so that there can be no mistake. This strikes newcomers sometimes as a little professional, especially when a hand accompanies, pointing; but it is the only possible way where there are no streets and no numbers, but where houses are dropped about a hilltop as if they had fallen from a pepper-pot. In sticking his card out like that Mr. Armour seemed to imagine himself *au quatrième* or *au cinquième* somewhere on the south side of the Seine; it betrayed rather a ridiculous lack of conformity. He was high enough up, however, to give any illusion; I had to stop to find the wind to announce myself. There was nobody else to do it if I except the dog.

I walked into the veranda and shouted. Then I saw that one end of it was partly glazed off, and inside sat a young man in his shirt-sleeves with his back to the door.

In reply he called out, "That you, Rosario?" and I stood silent, taken somewhat aback.

There was only one Rosario in Simla, and he was a subordinate in my own office. Again the hateful need to explain. Between subordinate clerks and officials in Simla there is a greater gulf fixed than was ever imagined in parable. Besides, Rosario had a plain strain of what we call "the country" in him, a plain strain, that is, of the color of the country. It was certainly the first time in my official career that I had been mistaken for Rosario.

Armour turned round and saw me — that I was a stranger.

He got up at once. "Oh," he said, "I thought it was Rosario."

"It isn't," I replied, "my name is Philips. May I ask whether you were expecting Mr. Rosario? I can come again, you know."

"Oh, it doesn't matter. Sit down. He may drop in or he may not — I rather thought he would to-day. It's a pull up,[1] isn't it, from the Mall?[2] Have a whisky-and-soda."

I stood on the threshold spellbound. It was just the smell that bound me, the good old smell of oil paints and turpentine and mediums and varnish and new canvas that you never by any chance put your nose into in any part of Asia. It carried me back twenty years to old haunts, old friends, old joys, ideals, theories. Ah, to be young and have a temperament! For I had one then — that instant in Armour's veranda proved it to me forever.

"No, thanks," I said. "If you don't mind I'll just have the smell."

The young fellow knew at once that I liked the smell. "Well, have a chair, anyhow," he said, and took one himself and sat down opposite me, letting his lean brown hands fall between his knees.

"Do you mind," I said, "if for a minute I sit still and look round?"

He understood again.

"I haven't brought much," he said, "I left pretty near everything in Paris."

"You have brought a world." Then after a moment, "Did you do that?" I asked, nodding toward a canvas tacked against the wall. It was the head of a half-veiled Arab woman turned away.

The picture was in the turning away, and the shadow the head-covering made over the cheek and lips.

"Lord, no! That's Dagnan Bouveret.[3] I used to take my things to him, and one day he gave me that. You have an eye," he added, but without patronage. "It's the best thing I've got."

I felt the warmth of an old thrill.

"Once upon a time," I said, "I was allowed to have an eye." The wine, untasted all those years, went to my head. "That's a vigorous bit above," I continued.

---

1 pull up: steep ascent.
2 the Mall: the main street in Simla.
3 Dagnan Bouveret: French painter (1859–1929).

"Oh, well! It isn't really up to much, you know. It's Rosario's. He photographs mostly, but he has a notion of color."

"Really?" said I, thinking with regard to my eye that the sun of that atrocious country had put it out. "I expect I've lost it," I said aloud.

"Your eye? Oh, you'll easily get a fresh one. Do you go home for the exhibitions?"

"I did once," I confessed. "My first leave. A kind of paralysis overtakes one here. Last time I went for the grouse."

He glanced at me with his light clear eyes as if for the first time he encountered a difficulty.

"It's a magnificent country for painting," he said.

"But not for pictures," I rejoined. He paid no attention, staring at the ground and twisting one end of his mustache.

"The sun on those old marble tombs — broad sun and sand ―― "

"You mean somewhere about Delhi."

"I couldn't get anywhere near it." He was not at that moment anywhere near me. "But I have thought out a trick or two — I mean to have another go when it cools off again down there." He returned with a smile, and I saw how delicate his face was. The smile turned down with a little gentle mockery in its lines. I had seen that particular smile only on the faces of one or two beautiful women. It had a borrowed air upon a man, like a tiara or an earring.

"There's plenty to paint," he said, looking at me with an air of friendly speculation.

"Indeed, yes. And it has never been done. We are sure it has never been done."

" 'We' — you mean people generally?"

"Not at all. I mean Miss Harris, Miss Harris and myself."

"Your daughter?"

"My name is Philips," I reminded him pleasantly, remembering that the intelligence of clever people is often limited to a single art. "Miss Harris is the daughter of Mr. Edward Harris, Secretary to the Government of India in the Legislative Department. She is fond of pictures. We have a good many tastes in common. We have always suspected that India had never been painted, and when we saw your things at the Town Hall we knew it."

His queer eyes dilated, and he blushed.

"Oh," he said, "it's only one interpretation. It all depends on what a fellow sees. No fellow can see everything."

"Till you came," I insisted, "nobody had seen anything."

He shook his head, but I could read in his face that this was not news to him.

"That is mainly what I came up to tell you," I continued, "to beg that you will go on and on. To hope that you will stay a long time and do a great deal. It is such an extraordinary chance that any one should turn up who can say what the country really means."

He stuck his hands in his pockets with a restive movement. "Oh, don't make me feel responsible," he said, "I hate that"; and then suddenly he remembered his manners. "But it's certainly nice of you to think so," he added.

There was something a little unusual in his inflection which led me to ask at this point whether he was an American, and to discover that he came from somewhere in Wisconsin, not directly, but by way of a few years in London and Paris. This accounted in a way for the effect of freedom in any fortune about him for which I already liked him, and perhaps partly for the look of unembarrassed inquiry and experiment which sat so lightly in his unlined face. He came, one realized, out of the fermentation of new conditions; he never could have been the product of our limits and systems and classes in England. His surroundings, his "things," as he called them, were as old as the sense of beauty, but he seemed simply to have put them where he could see them, there was no pose in their arrangement. They were all good, and his delight in them was plain; but he was evidently in no sense a connoisseur beyond that of natural instinct. Some of those he had picked up in India I could tell him about, but I had no impression that he would remember what I said. There was one Bokhara tapestry[1] I examined with a good deal of interest.

"Yes," he said, "they told me I shouldn't get anything as good as that out here, so I brought it," but I had to explain to him why it was anomalous that this should be so.

"It came a good many miles over desert from somewhere," he remarked, as I made a note of inquiry as to the present direction of trade in woven goods from Persia, "I had to pound it for a week to get the dust out."

---

1 Bokhara tapestry (or Bukhara): a city in western Uzbekistan, known for its manufacturing of textiles. EN

We spent an hour looking over work he had done down in the plains, and then I took my leave. It did not occur to me at the moment to ask Armour to come to the club or to offer to do anything for him; all the hospitality, all that was worth offering seemed so much more at his disposition than at mine. I only asked if I might come again, mentioning somewhat shyly that I must have the opportunity of adding, at my leisure, to those of his pictures that were already mine by transaction with the secretary of the Art Exhibition. I left him so astonished that this had happened, so plainly pleased, that I was certain he had never sold anything before in his life. This impression gave me the uplifted joy of a discoverer to add to the satisfactions I had already drawn from the afternoon; and I almost bounded down the hill to the Mall. I left the pi dog[1] barking in the veranda, and I met Mr. Rosario coming up, but in my unusual elation I hardly paused to consider either of them further.

The mare and her groom were waiting on the Mall, and it was only when I got on her back that the consciousness visited me of something forgotten. It was my mission — to propose to take Armour, if he were "possible," to call upon the Harrises. Oh, well, he was possible enough; I supposed he possessed a coat, though he hadn't been wearing it; and I could arrange it by letter. Meanwhile, as was only fair, I turned the mare in the direction of the drawing-room where I had reason to believe that Miss Dora Harris was quenching her impatience in tea.

---

1   pi dog: Mongrel dog (from piebald). OED

CHAPTER IV

THE very next morning I met Armour on my way to office. He was ambling along on the leanest and most ill-groomed of bazaar ponies, and he wore a bowler. In Simla sun hats are admissible, straw hats are presentable, and soft felt hats are superior, but you must not wear a bowler. I might almost say that if one's glance falls upon a bowler, one hardly looks further; the expectation of finding an acquaintance under it is so vain. In this instance, I did look further, fortunately, though in doing so I was compelled to notice that the bowler was not lifted in answer to my salutation. Of no importance in itself, of course, but betraying in Armour a certain lack of observation. I felt the Departmental Head crumble in me, however, as I recognized him, and I pulled the mare up in a manner which she plainly resented. It was my opportunity to do cautiously and delicately what I had omitted the afternoon before; but my recollection is that I was very clumsy.

I said something about the dust, and he said something about the glare, and then I could think of nothing better than to ask him if he wouldn't like to meet a few Simla people.

"Oh, I know lots of people, thanks," he said. "It's kind of you to think of it, all the same, but I've got any amount of friends here."

I thought of Mr. Rosario, and stood, or sat, confounded.

The mare fidgeted; I knocked a beast of a fly off her, and so gained time.

"This is my second season up here, you know."

"Your second season!" I exclaimed. "Where on earth have you been hiding?"

"Well, I didn't exhibit last year, you see. I'd heard it was a kind of a toy show, so I thought I wouldn't. I think now that was foolish. But I got to know quite a number of families."

"But I am sure there are numbers that you haven't met," I urged, "or I should have heard of it."

He glanced at me with a slight flush. "If you mean society people," he said, "I don't care about that kind of thing, Mr. Philips. I'm not adapted to it, and I don't want to be. If any one offered to introduce me to the Viceroy, I would ask to be excused."

"Oh, the Viceroy," I responded, disrespectfully, "is neither here nor there. But there are some people, friends of my own, who would like very much to meet you."

"By the name of Harris?" he asked. I was too amazed to do anything but nod. By the name of Harris! The Secretary of the Government of India in the Legislative Department! The expression, not used as an invocation, was inexcusable.

"I remember you mentioned them yesterday."

"Yes," I said, "there's a father and daughter. Miss Harris is very artistic."

His face clouded, as well it might, at the word. "Does she paint?" he asked, so apprehensively that I could not forbear a smile at Dora's expense. I could assure him that she did not paint, that she had not painted, at all events, for years, and presently I found myself in the ridiculous position of using argument to bring a young man to the Harrises. In the end I prevailed, I know, out of sheer good nature on Armour's part; he was as innocent as a baby of any sense of opportunity.

We arranged it for the following Friday, but as luck would have it, His Excellency sent for me at the very hour; we met the messenger. I felt myself unlucky, but there was nothing for it but that Armour should go alone, which he did, with neither diffidence nor alacrity, but as if it were all in the day's work, and he had no reason to be disobliging.

The files were very heavy during the succeeding fortnight, and the Viceroy quite importunate in his demand for my valuable suggestions. I was worked off my legs, and two or three times was obliged to deny myself in replying to notes from Dora suggesting Sunday breakfast or afternoon tea. Finally, I shook myself free; it was the day she wrote:

"You must come — I can't keep it to myself any longer."

I half thought Armour would be there, but he wasn't; that is, he was absent corporeally, but the spirit and expression of him littered every convenient part. Some few things lay about that I had seen in the studio, to call it so, but most of the little wooden panels looked fresh, almost wet, and the air held strongly the fragrance of Armour's north veranda. In one corner there used to be a Madonna on a carved easel; the Madonna stood on the floor, and the easel with working pegs in it held an unfinished canvas. Dora sat in the midst with a distinct flush — she was inclined to be sallow — and made me welcome in terms touched with extravagance. She did not rush, however, upon the matter that was dyeing her cheeks, and I showed myself as little impetuous. She poured out the tea, and we sat there inhaling, as it were, the aroma of the thing, while keeping it consciously in the background.

I imagine there was no moment in the time I describe when we enjoyed Ingersoll Armour so much as at this one, when he lay in his nimbus half known and wholly suppressed, between us. There were later instances, perhaps, of deeper satisfaction, but they were more or less perplexed, and not unobscured by anxiety. That afternoon it was all to know and to be experienced, with just a delicious foretaste.

I said something presently about Lady Pilkey's picnic on the morrow, to which we had both been bidden.

"Shall I call for you?" I asked. "You will ride, of course."

"Thanks, but I've cried off — I'm going sketching." Her eyes plainly added, "with Ingersoll Armour," but she as obviously shrank from the roughness of pitching him in that unconsidered way before us. For some reason I refrained from taking the cue. I would not lug him in either.

"That is a new accomplishment," was as much as I felt I could say with dignity, and she responded:

"Yes, isn't it?"

I felt some slight indignation on Lady Pilkey's account. "Do you really think you ought to do things like that at the eleventh hour?" I asked, but Dora smiled at a glance, the hypocrisy out of my face.

"What does anything matter?" she demanded.

I knew perfectly well the standard by which nothing mattered, and there was no use, of course, in going on pretending that I did not.

"I assured him that you didn't paint," I said, accusingly.

"Oh, I had to — otherwise what was there to go upon? He would have been found only to be lost again. You did not contemplate that?" Miss Harris inquired sweetly.

"I should have thought it was the surest way of losing him."

"I can't think why you should be so rude. He observes progress already."

"With a view to claiming and holding him, would it be of any use," I asked, "for me to start in oils?"

Miss Harris eyed me calmly.

"I don't know," she said, "but it doesn't seem the same thing somehow. I think you had better leave it to me."

"Indeed, I won't," I said; "there is too much in it," and we smiled across the gulf of our friendly understanding.

I crossed to the mantelpiece and picked up one of the little wet panels. There was that in it which explained my friend's exultation much more plainly than words.

"That is what I am to show him to-morrow," she explained; "I think I have done as he told me. I think it's pretty right."

Whether it was pretty right or pretty wrong, she had taken in an extraordinary way an essence out of him. It wasn't of course good, but his feeling was reflected in it, at once so brilliantly and so profoundly that it was startling to see.

"Do you think he'll be pleased?" she asked, anxiously.

"I think he'll be astounded," I said, reserving the rest, and she cried in her pleasure, "Oh, you dear man!"

"I see you have taken possession of him," I went on.

"Ah, body and soul," Dora rejoined, and it must have been something like that. I could imagine how she did it; with what wiles of simplicity and candid good-fellowship she had drawn him to forgetfulness and response, and how presently his enthusiasm leaped up to answer hers and they had been caught altogether out of the plane of common relations, and he had gone away on that disgraceful bazaar pony with a ratified arrangement to return next day which had been almost taken for granted from the beginning.

I confess, though I had helped to bring it about, the situation didn't altogether please me. I did not dream of foolish dangers, but it seemed to take a little too much for granted; I found myself inwardly demanding whether, after all, a vivid capacity to make color conscious was a sufficient basis on which to bring to Edward Harris's house a young man about whom we knew nothing whatever else. An instant's regard showed the scruple fraudulent, it fled before the rush of pleasure with which I gazed at the tokens he had left behind him. I fell back on my wonder, which was great, that Dora should have possessed the technique necessary to take him at a point where he could give her so much that was valuable.

"Oh, well," she said when I uttered it, "you know I made the experiment! I found out in South Kensington[1] — you can learn that much there — that I never would be able to paint well enough to make it worth while. So I dropped it and took a more general line toward life. But I find it very easy to imagine myself dedicated to that particular one again."

"You never told me," I said. Why had I been shut out of that experience?

"I tell you now," Dora replied, absently, "when I am able to offer you the fact with illustrations." She laughed and dropped a still illu-

---

1 South Kensington: an area of London, England, associated with the arts.

minated face in the palm of her hand. "He has wonderfully revived me," she declared. "I could throw, honestly, the whole of Simla overboard for this."

"Don't," I urged, feeling, suddenly an integral part of Simla.

"Oh, no — what end would be served? But I don't care who knows," she went on with a rush, "that in all life this is what I like best, and people like Mr. Armour are the people I value most. Heavens, how few of them there are! And wherever they go how the air clears up round them! It makes me quite ill to think of the life we lead here — the poverty of it, the preposterous dulness of it .... "

"For goodness' sake," I said, obscurely irritated, "don't quote the bishop. The life holds whatever we put into it."

"For other people it does, and for us it holds what other people put into it," she retorted. "I don't know whether you think it's adequately filled with gold lace and truffles."

"Why should I defend it?" I asked, not knowing indeed why. "But it has perhaps a dignity, you know. Ah, you are too fresh from your baptism," I continued, as she shook her head and went to the piano. The quality, whatever it was, that the last fortnight had generated in her, leaped from her fingers; she played with triumph, elation, intention. The notes seemed an outlet for the sense of beauty and for power to make it. I had never heard her play like that before.

It occurred to me to ask when she had done, how far, after a fortnight, she could throw light on Armour's aims and history, where he had come from, and the great query with which we first received him, what he could be doing in Simla. I gathered that she had learned practically nothing, and had hardly concerned herself to learn anything. What difference did it make? she asked me. Why should we inquire? Why tack a theory of origin to a phenomenon of joy? Let us say the wind brought him, and build him a temple. She was very whimsical up to the furthest stretch of what could possibly be considered tea-time. When I went away I saw her go again and sit down at the piano. In the veranda I remembered something, stopped, and went back. I had to go back. "You did not tell me," I said, "when he was coming again."

"Oh, to-morrow — to-morrow, of course." Dora paused to reply.

I resented, as I made my way to the Club, the weight of official duties that made it so impossible for me to keep at all closely in touch with this young man.

CHAPTER V

THE art of the photographer usually arouses in me all that is splenetic, and I had not submitted myself to him for years before Dora made such a preposterous point of it — years in which, as I sadly explained to her, I might have submitted to the ordeal with much more "pleasing" results. She had often insisted before, but I could never see that she made out a particularly good case for the operation until one afternoon when she showed me the bold counterfeit presentment of an Assistant Adjutant-General or some such person, much flattered as to features but singularly faithful in its reproduction of the straps and buttons attached. To my post also there belongs a uniform and a cocked hat sufficiently dramatic, but persons who serve the State primarily with the intelligence are supposed to have a mind above buttons; and when I decided that my photograph should compete with the Assistant Adjutant-General's, I gave him every sartorial advantage. I gathered that the offer, cabinet size, of this gentleman had been a spontaneous one; that certainly could not be said of mine. Most unwillingly I turned one morning into Kauffer's; and I can not now imagine why I did it, for emulation of the Assistant Adjutant-General was really not motive enough, unless it was with an instinct prepared to stumble upon matter germane in an absurd degree to this little history.

I had the honor to be subjected to the searching analysis of Mr. Kauffer himself. It was he who placed the chair and arranged the screw, he who fixed the angle of my chin and gently disposed my fingers on my knee. He gave me, I remember, a recent portrait of the Viceroy to fix my eye upon, doubtless with the purpose of inspiring my countenance with the devotion which would sit suitably upon one of His Excellency's slaves, and when it was all over he conducted me into another apartment in order that I might see the very latest viceregal group — a domestic one, including the Staff. The walls of the room contained what is usually there, the enlarged photograph, the colored photograph, the amateur theatrical group, the group of His Excellency's Executive Council, the native dignitary with a diamond-tipped aigrette in the front of his turban. The copy in oils of some old Italian landscape, very black and yellow, also held its invariable place, and above it, very near the ceiling, a line of canvases which, had I not been led past them to inspect our ruler and his family, who sat transfixed on an easel in a resplendent frame, would probably have escaped my attention. I did proper homage to the easel, and then turned to these pictures. It was plain enough who had painted them. Armour's broad brush stood out all over them. They were mostly Indian sporting subjects, the incident a trifle elliptical, the drawing unequal, but the verve and feeling unmistakable, and color to send a quiver of glorious acquiescence through you like a pang. What astonished me was the number of them; there must have been at least a dozen, all the same size and shape, all hanging in a line of dazzling repetition. Here then was the explanation of Armour's seeming curious lack of output, and plain denial of the supposition that he spent the whole of his time in doing the little wooden "pochade"[1] things whose sweetness and delicacy had so feasted our eyes elsewhere. It was part, no doubt, of his absolutely uncommercial nature — we had experienced together passages of the keenest embarrassment over my purchase of some of his studies — that he had not mentioned these more serious things exposed at Kauffer's; one had the feeling of coming unexpectedly on treasure left upon the wayside and forgotten.

"Hullo!" I said, at a standstill, "I see you've got some of Mr. Armour's work there."

Mr. Kauffer, with his hands behind him, made the sound which has its counterpart in a shrug. "Yass," he said, "I haf some of Mr. Armour's work there. This one, that one, all those remaining pictures — they are all the work of Mr. Armour."

"I didn't know that any of his things were to be seen outside his studio," I observed.

"So? They are to be seen here. There is no objection."

"Why should there be any objection?" I demanded, slightly nettled. "People must see them before they buy them."

"Buy them!" Kauffer's tone was distinctly exasperated. "Who will buy those pictures? No-body. They are all, every one of them to *refuse*."

"If you know Mr. Armour well enough," I said, "you should advise him to exhibit some of his local studies and sketches here. They might sell better."

My words seemed unfortunately chosen. Mr. Kauffer turned an honest angry red.

---

1 pochade: a rough sketch. OED

"Do I not know Mr. Armour well enough — und better!" he exclaimed. "What this man wass doing when I in Paris find him oudt? Shtarving, mein Gott! I see his work. I see he paint a very goot horse, very goot animal subject. I bring him oudt on contract, five hundred rupees the monnth to paint for me, for my firm. Sir, it is now nine monnth. I am yoost four tousand five hundred rupees out of my pocket by this gentleman!"

To enable me to cope with this astonishing tale I asked Mr. Kauffer for a chair, which he obligingly gave me, and begged that he also would be seated. The files at my office were my business, and this was not, but no matter of Imperial concern seemed at the moment half so urgently to require probing. "Surely," I said, "that is an unusual piece of enterprise for a photographic firm to employ an artist to paint on a salary. I don't know even a regular dealer who does it."

Mr. Kauffer at once and frankly explained. It was unusual and entirely out of the regular line of business. It was, in fact, one of the exceptional forms of enterprise inspired in this country by the native prince. We who had to treat with the native prince solely on lofty political lines were hardly likely to remember how largely he bulked in the humbler relations of trade; but there was more than one Calcutta establishment, Mr. Kauffer declared, that would be obliged to put up its shutters without this inconstant and difficult, but liberal customer. I waited with impatience. I could not for the life of me see Armour's connection with the native prince, who is seldom a patron of the arts for their own sakes.

"Surely," I said, "you could not depend upon the Indian nobility to buy landscapes. They never do. I know of only one distinguished exception, and he lives a thousand miles from here, in Bengal."

"No, not landscape," returned Mr. Kauffer; "but that Indian nobleman will buy his portrait. We send our own man — photographic artist — to his State, and he photograph the Chief and his arab,[1] the Chief and his Prime Minister, the Chief in his durbar,[2] palace, gardens, stables — everything. Presently the Chief goes on a big shoot. He says he will not have a plain photograph — besides, it is difficult. He will have a painting, and he will pay."

"Ah," I said, "I begin to see."

"You see? Then I send this Armour. Look!" Mr. Kauffer continued with rising excitement, baited apparently by the unfortunate

---

1 arab: horse.
2 durbar: the court of an Indian ruler. OED

canvas to which he pointed, "When Armour go to make that I say you go paint ze Maharajah of Gridigurh spearing ze wild pig. You see what he make?"

"Well," I said, "it is a wonderfully spirited, dashing thing, and the treatment of all that canebrake[1] and jungle grass is superb."

"Ze treatment — pardon me, sir, I overboil — do you know which is ze Maharajah?"

"I can't say I do."

"Neider does he. Ze Maharajah refuse zat picture; he is a good fellow, too. He says it is a portrait of ze pig."

"But it is so good," I protested, "of the pig."

"But that does not interest the Maharajah, you onderstand, no. You see this one? Nawab[2] of Kandore on his State elephant."

"No doubt about it," I said. "I know the Nawab well, the young scoundrel. How dignified he looks!"

There was a note of real sorrow in Kauffer's voice. "Dignified? Oh, yes; dignified, but, you observe, also black. The Nawab will not be painted black. At once it is on my hands."

"But he is black," I remonstrated. "He's the darkest native I've ever seen among the nobility."

"No matter for that. He will not be black. When I photograph that Nawab — any nawab — I do not him black make. But zis ass of Armour — ach!"

It was a fascinating subject, and I could have pursued it all along the line of poor Armour's rejected canvases, but the need to get away from Kauffer with his equal claim upon my sympathy was too great. To have cracked my solemn mask by a single smile would have been to break down irrepressibly, and never since I set foot in India had I felt a parallel desire to laugh and to weep. There was a pang in it which I recognize as impossible to convey, arising from the point of contact, almost unimaginable yet so clear before me, of the uncompromising ideals of the atelier[3] and the naive demands of the Oriental, with an unhappy photographer caught between and wriggling. The situation was really monstrous, the fatuous rejection of all that fine scheming and exquisite manipulation, and it did not grow less so as Mr. Kauffer continued to unfold it. Armour had not, apparently, proceeded to the scene of his labors

---

1 canebrake: a tract of land overgrown with canes. OED
2 Nawab: governor. OED
3 atelier: workshop or studio.

without instructions. In the pig-sticking delineation he had been specially told that the Maharajah and the pig were to be in the middle, with the rest nowhere and nothing between. Other injunctions were as clear, and as clearly disregarded. Armour, like the Maharajahs, had simply "*refuse*" to abandon his premeditated conceptions of how the thing should be done. And here was the result, for the laughter of the gods and anybody else that might see. I asked Kauffer unguardedly if no sort of pressure could be brought to bear upon these chaps to make them pay up. His face beaming with hope and intelligence, he suggested that I should approach the Foreign Office in his behalf; but this I could not quite see my way to. The coercion of native rulers, I explained, was a difficult and a dangerous art, and to insist, for example, that one of them should recognize his own complexion might be to run up a disproportionate little bill of our own. I did, however, compound something with Kauffer; I hope it wasn't a felony. "Look here," I said to Kauffer, "this isn't official, you know, in any way, but how would it do to write that scamp Kandore a formal letter regretting that the portrait does not suit him, and asking his permission to dispose of it to me? Of course it is yours to do as you like with already, but that is not reason why you shouldn't ask. I should like it, but the Porcha tiger[1] beat will do as well."

Kauffer nearly fell upon my neck.

"That Kandore will buy it to put in one bonfire first," he assured me, and I sincerely hoped for his sake that it would be the case.

"Of course it's understood," I bethought me to say, "that I get it, if I do get it, at Mr. Armour's price. I'm not a Maharajah, you know, and it isn't a portrait of me."

"Of course!" said Kauffer, "but I sink I sell you that Porcha; it is ze best of ze two."

---

1 Porcha tiger: possibly a reference to an artistic rendering of a tiger shaped out of *gutta-percha*, a substitute for rubber made from the thickened juice of various trees found in the Malayan archipelago — used extensively in the arts. OED

CHAPTER VI

I VENTURED for a few days to keep the light which chance had shed for me upon Armour's affairs to myself. The whole thing considered in connection with his rare and delicate talent, seemed too derogatory and disastrous to impart without the sense of doing him some kind of injury in the mere statement. But there came a point when I could no longer listen to Dora Harris's theories to account for him, wild idealizations as most of them were of any man's circumstances and intentions. "Why don't you ask him point-blank?" I said, and she replied, frowning slightly, "Oh, I couldn't do that. It would destroy something — I don't know what, but something valuable — between us." This struck me as an exaggeration, considering how far, by that time, they must have progressed toward intimacy, and my mouth was opened. She heard me without the exclamations I expected, her head bent over the pencil she was sharpening, and her silence continued after I had finished. The touch of comedy I gave the whole thing — surely I was justified in that! — fell flat, and I extracted from her muteness a sense of rebuke; one would think I had been taking advantage of the poor devil.

At last, having broken the lead of her pencil three times, she turned a calm, considering eye upon me.

"You have known this for a fortnight?" she asked. "That doesn't seem somehow quite fair."

"To whom?" I asked, and her answer startled me.

"To either of us," she said.

How she advised herself to that effect is more than I can imagine, but the print of her words is indelible, that is what she said.

"Oh, confound it!" I exclaimed. "I couldn't help finding out, you know."

"But you could help keeping it to yourself in that — in that base way," she replied, and almost — the evening light was beginning to glimmer uncertainly through the deodars — I could swear I saw the flash of a tear on her eyelid.

"I beg your pardon," she went on a moment later, "but I do hate having to pity him. It's intolerable — that."

I picked up a dainty edition of Aucassin and Nicolete[1] with the intention of getting upon ground less emotional, and observed on the flyleaf "D.H. from I.A. In memory of the Hill of Stars." I looked appreciatively at the binding, and as soon as possible put it down.

"He was not bound to tell me," Dora asserted presently, in reply to my statement that the mare had somehow picked up a nail in the stable, and was laid up.

"You have been very good to him," I said. "I think he was."

"His reticence was due," she continued, as if defying contradiction, "to a simple dislike to bore one with his personal affairs."

"Was it?" I assented. My tone acknowledged with all humility that she was likely to know, and I did not deserve her doubtful glance.

"He could not certainly," she went on, with firmer decision, "have been in the least ashamed of his connection with Kauffer."

"He comes from a country where social distinctions are less sharp than they are in this idiotic place," I observed.

"Oh, if you think it is from any lack of recognition! His sensitiveness is beyond reason. He has met two or three men in the Military Department here — he was aware of the nicest shade of their patronage. But he does not care. To him life is more than a clerkship. He sees all round people like that. They are only figures in the landscape."

"Then," I said, "he is not at all concerned that nobody in this Capua[2] of ours knows him, or cares anything about him, or has bought a scrap of his work, except our two selves."

"That's a different matter. I have tried to rouse in him the feeling that it would be as well to be appreciated, even in Simla, and I think I've succeeded. He said, after those two men had gone away on Sunday, that he thought a certain reputation in the place where he lived would help anybody in his work."

"On Sunday? Do you mean between twelve and two?"

"Yes; he came and made a formal call. There was no reason why he shouldn't."

"Now that I think of it," I rejoined, "he shot a card on me too, at the Club. I was a little surprised. We didn't seem somehow to

---

1   *Aucassin and Nicolete*: a thirteenth-century romance written in prose and verse.
2   Capua: a town in southern Italy.

be on those terms. One doesn't readily associate him with any conventionality."

"There's no reason why he shouldn't," said Dora again, and with this vague comment we spoke of something else, both of us, I think, a little disquieted and dissatisfied that he had.

"I think," Dora said as I went away, "that you had better go up to the studio and tell him what you have told me. Perhaps it doesn't matter much, but I can't bear the thought of his not knowing."

"Come to Kauffer's in the morning and see the pictures," I urged; but she turned away, "Oh, not with you."

I found my way almost at once to Amy Villa, not only because I had been told to go there. I wanted, myself, certain satisfactions. Armour was alone and smoking, but I had come prepared against the contingency of one of his cigars. They were the cigars of the man who doesn't know what he eats. With sociable promptness I lighted one of my own. The little enclosed veranda testified to a wave of fresh activity. The north light streamed in upon two or three fresh canvases, the place seemed full of enthusiasm, and you could see its source, at present quiescent under the influence of tobacco, in Armour's face.

"You have taken a new line," I said, pointing to a file of camels, still half obscured by the dust of the day, coming along a mountain road under a dim moon. They might have been walking through time and through history. It was a queer, simple thing, with a world of early Aryanism[1] in it.

"Does that say anything? I'm glad. It was to me articulate, but I didn't know. Oh, things have been going well with me lately. Those two studies over there simply did themselves. That camp scene on the left is almost a picture. I think I'll put a little more work on it and give it a chance in Paris. I got in once, you know. Champ de Mars.[2] With some horses."

"Did you, indeed?" I said. "Capital." I asked him if he didn't atrociously miss the life of the Quarter, and he surprised me by saying that he never had lived it. He had been *en pension*[3] instead with a dear old professor of chemistry and his family at Puteaux,[4] and used

---

1 Aryanism: the Aryans were part of group of nomadic tribes who invaded India around 1500 B.C. Duncan associates the term "Aryan" with Indian pastoral life.
2 Champ de Mars: a park in Paris.
3 *en pension*: boarding.
4 Puteaux: a Parisian suburb.

to go in and out. A smile came into his eyes at the remembrance, and he told me one after the other idyllic little stories of the old professor and madame. Madame and the omelet — madame and the melon — M. Vibois and the maire;[1] I sat charmed. So long as we remained in France his humor was like this, delicate and expansive, but an accidental allusion led us across the Channel where he changed. He had no little stories of the time he spent in England. Instead he let himself go in generalizations, aimed, for they had a distinct animus, at English institutions and character, particularly as these appear in English society. I could not believe, from the little I had seen of him, that his experience of English society of any degree had been intimate; what he said had the flavor of Radical Sunday papers. The only original element was the feeling behind, which was plainly part of him; speculation instantly clamored as to how far this was purely temperamental and how far the result of painful contact. He himself, he said, though later of the Western States, had been born under the British flag of British parents — though his mother was an Irishwoman she came from loyal Ulster[2] — and he repeated the statement as if it in some way justified his attitude toward his fellow countrymen and excused his truculence in the ear of a servant of the empire which he had the humor to abuse. I heard him, I confess, with impatience, it was all so shabby and shallow, but I heard him out, and I was rewarded; he came for an illustration in the end to Simla. "Look," he said, "at what they call their 'Government House list'; and look at Strobo, Signor Strobo. Isn't Strobo a man of intelligence, isn't he a man of benevolence? He gave ten thousand rupees last week to the famine fund. Is Strobo on Government House list? Is he ever invited to dine with the Viceroy? No, because Strobo keeps a hotel![3] Look at Rosario — where does Rosario come in? Nowhere, because Rosario is a clerk, and a subordinate. Yet Rosario is a man of wide reading and a very accomplished fellow!"

It became more or less necessary to argue then, and the commonplaces with which I opposed him called forth a wealth of detail bearing most picturesquely upon his stay among us. I began to think he had never hated English rigidity and English snobbery until he came to Simla, and that he and Strobo and Rosario had

---

1   maire: the mayor.
2   loyal Ulster: a northern province of Ireland (part of which is now Northern Ireland) with strong ties to Great Britain. EN
3   keeps a hotel: Peliti's Grand Hotel, Simla.

mingled their experiences in one bitter cup. I gathered this by inference only, he was curiously watchful and reticent as to anything that had happened to him personally; indeed, he was careful to aver preferences for the society of "sincere" people like Strobo and Rosario, that seemed to declare him more than indifferent to circles in which he would not meet them. In the end our argument left me ridiculously irritated — it was simply distressing to see the platform from which he obtained so wide and exquisite a view of the world upheld by such flimsy pillars — and my nerves were not soothed by his proposal to walk with me to the Club. I could hardly refuse it, however, and he came along in excellent spirits, having effected the demolition of British social ideals, root and branch. His mongrel dog accompanied, keeping offensively near our heels. It was not even an honest pi, but a dog of tawdry pretensions with a banner-like tail dishonestly got from a spaniel. On one occasion I very nearly kicked the dog.

CHAPTER VII

"THE fact is," I said to Dora as we rode down to the gymkhana, "his personality takes possession of one. I constantly go to that little hut of his with intentions, benevolent or otherwise, which I never carry out."

"You mean," she answered, "that you completely forgot to reveal to him your hateful knowledge about Kauffer."

"On the contrary, I didn't forget it for a moment. But the conversation took a turn that made it quite impossible to mention."

"I can understand," Miss Harris replied softly, "how that might be. And it doesn't in the least matter," she went on triumphantly, "because I've told him myself."

My nerves must have been a trifle strung up at the time, for this struck me as a matter for offense. "You thought I would trample upon him" I exclaimed.

"No, no really. I disliked his not knowing it was known — *rien de plus*,"[1] she said lightly.

"What did he say?"

"Oh, not much. What should he say?"

"He might have expressed a decent regret on poor Kauffer's account," I growled. Dora did not reply, and a glance showed her frowning.

"I believe he apologized!" I cried, pushing, as it were, my advantage.

"He explained."

"Oh!"

"Of course he hasn't relished the position, and of course he didn't realize it before he came. Shall we trot?"

I was compelled to negative the idea of trotting, since we were descending quite the steepest pitch of the road down to Annandale. We went on at a walk, and it occurred to me, as my contemplative gaze fell on my own pig-skins, that we were, even for Simla, an uncommonly well-turned-out pair. I had helped to pick Dora's hack, and I allowed myself to reflect that he did my judgment credit. She sat him perfectly in her wrath — she was plainly angry — not a hair out of place. Why is it that a lady out of temper with her

---

1   *rien de plus*: nothing more.

escort always walks away from him? Is her horse sympathetic? Ronald, at all events, was leading by a couple of yards, when suddenly he shied, bounding well across the road.

The mare, whose manners I can always answer for, simply stopped and looked haughtily about for explanations. A path dropped into the road from the hillside; something came scrambling and stumbling down.

"Oh!" cried Dora, as it emerged and was Armour on his much enduring white pony, "how you frightened us!"

"Why don't you stick to the road, man?" I exclaimed. "It isn't usual to put ponies up and down these coolie tracks!"

He took no notice of this rather broad hint that I was annoyed, but fixed his eager, light, luminous eyes upon Dora.

"I'm sorry," he said, and added, "I did not expect to see you to-day!"

"Not till to-morrow," she returned. "You remember that we are sketching to-morrow?"

He looked at her and smiled slightly; and then I remember noticing that his full, arched upper lip seldom quite met its counterpart over his teeth. This gave an unpremeditated casual effect to everything he found to say, and made him look a dreamer at his busiest. His smile was at the folly of her reminder.

"I've just been looking for something that you would like," he said, "but it isn't much good hunting about alone. I see five times as much when we go together."

He and his pony barred the way; he had an air of leisure and of felicity; one would think we had met at an afternoon party.

"We are on our way," I explained, "to the gymkhana. Miss Harris is in one of the events. You did enter for the needle-threading race, didn't you, with Lord Arthur? I think we must get on."

A slow, dull red mounted to Armour's face and seemed to put out that curious light in his eyes.

"Is it far?" he asked, glancing down over the tree-tops. "I've never been there."

"Why," cried Dora, suddenly, "you've been down!"

"So you have," I confirmed her. "Your beast is damaged too."

"Oh, it was only a stumble," Armour replied; "I stuck on all right."

"Well," I said, "you had better get off now, as you didn't then, and look at your animal's near fore. The swelling's as big as a bun already."

Again he made me no answer, but looked intently and questioningly at Dora.

"Get off, Mr. Armour," she said, sharply, "and lead your horse home. It is not fit to be ridden. Good-by."

I have no doubt he did it, but neither of us were inclined to look back to see. We pushed on under the deodars, and I was indulgent to a trot. At the end of it Dora remarked that Mr. Armour naturally could not be expected to know anything about riding, it was very plucky of him to get on a horse at all, among these precipices; and I of course agreed.

Lord Arthur was waiting when we arrived, on his chestnut polo pony, but Dora immediately scratched for the brilliant event in which they were paired. Ronald, she said, was simply cooked with the heat. Ronald had come every yard of the way on his toes and was fit for anything, but Lord Arthur did not insist. There were young ladies in Simla, I am glad to say, who appealed more vividly to his imagination than Dora Harris did, and one of them speedily replaced her, a fresh-colored young Amazon who was staying at the Chief's. She wandered about restlessly over the dry turf for a few minutes, and then went and sat down in a corner of the little wooden Grand Stand and sent me for a cup of tea.

"Won't you come to the tent?" I asked a little ruefully, eying the distance and the possible collisions between, but she shook her head.

"I simply couldn't bear it," she said, and I went, feeling somehow chastened myself by the cloud that was upon her spirit.

I found her on my return regarding the scene with a more than usually critical eye, and a more than usually turned down lip. Yet it was exactly the scene it always was, and always, probably, will be. I sat down beside her and regarded it also, but more charitably than usual. Perhaps it was rather trivial, just a lot of pretty dresses and excited young men in white riding-breeches doing foolish things on ponies in the shortest possible time, with one little crowd about the Club's refreshment tent and another about the Staff's, while the hills sat round in an indifferent circle; but it appealed to me with a kind of family feeling that afternoon, and inspired me with tolerance, even benevolence.

"After all," I said, "it's mainly youth and high spirits — two good things. And one knows them all."

"And who are they to know?" complained Dora.

"Just decent young Englishmen and Englishwomen, out here on their country's business," I replied cheerfully; "with the marks of Oxford and Cambridge and Sandhurst and Woolwich on the men. Well-set-up youngsters, who know what to do and how to do it. Oh, I like the breed!"

"I wonder," said she, in a tone of preposterous melancholy, "if eventually I have got to marry one of them."

"Not necessarily," I said. She looked at me with interest, as if I had contributed importantly to the matter in hand, and resumed tapping her boot with her riding-crop. We talked of indifferent things and had long lapses. At the close of one effort Dora threw herself back with a deep, tumultuous sigh. "The poverty of this little wretched resort ties up one's tongue!" she cried. "It is the bottom of the cup; here one gets the very dregs of Simla's commonplace. Let us climb out of it."

I thought for a moment that Ronald had been too much for her nerves coming down, and offered to change saddles, but she would not. We took it out of the horses all along the first upward slopes, and as we pulled into breathe them she turned to me paler than ever.

"I feel better now," she said.

For myself I had got rid of Armour for the afternoon. I think my irritation with him about his pony rose and delivered me from the too insistent thought of him. With Dora it was otherwise; she had dismissed him; but he had never left her for a moment the whole long afternoon.

She flung a searching look at me. With a reckless turn of her head, she said, "Why didn't we take him with us?"

"Did we want him?" I asked.

"I think I always want him."

"Ah!" said I, and would have pondered this statement at some length in silence, but that she plainly did not wish me to do so.

"We might perfectly well have sent his pony home with one of our own servants — he would have been delighted to walk down."

"He wasn't in proper kit," I remonstrated.

"Oh, I wish you would speak to him about that. Make him get some tennis-flannels and riding-things."

"Do you propose to get him asked to places?" I inquired.

She gave me a charmingly unguarded smile. "I propose to induce you to do so. I have done what I could. He has dined with us several times, and met a few people who would, I thought, be kind to him."

"Oh well," I said, "I have had him at the Club too, with old Lamb and Colonel Hamilton. He made us all miserable with his shyness. Don't ask me to do it again, please."

"I've sent him to call on certain people," Dora continued, "and I've shown his pictures to everybody, and praised him and talked about him, but I can't go on doing that indefinitely, can I?"

"No," I said; "people might misunderstand."

"I don't think they would *mis*understand," replied this astonishing girl, without flinching. She even sought my eyes to show me that hers were clear and full of purpose.

"Good God!" I said to myself, but the words that fell from me were, "He is outside all that life."

"What is the use of living a life that he is outside of?"

"Oh, if you put it that way," I said, and set my teeth, "I will do what I can."

She held out her hand with an affectionate gesture, and I was reluctantly compelled to press it.

The horses broke into a trot, and we talked no more of Armour, or of anything, until Ted Harris joined us on the Mall.

I have rendered this conversation with Dora in detail because subsequent events depend so closely upon it. Some may not agree that it was basis enough for the action I thought well to take; I can only say that it was all I was ever able to obtain. Dora was always particularly civil and grateful about my efforts, but she gave me only one more glimpse, and that was enigmatic, of any special reason why they should be made. Perhaps this was more than compensated for by the abounding views I had of the situation as it lay with Ingersoll Armour, but of that, other persons, approaching the subject without prejudice, will doubtless judge better than I.

CHAPTER VIII

IT was better not to inquire, so I never knew to what extent Kauffer worked upon the vanity of ancient houses the sinful dodge I suggested to him; but I heard before long that the line of Armour's rejected efforts had been considerably diminished. Armour told me himself that Kauffer's attitude had become almost conciliatory, that Kauffer had even hinted at the acceptance of, and adhesion to, certain principles which he would lay down as the basis of another year's contract. In talking to me about it, Armour dwelt on these absurd stipulations only as the reason why any idea of renewal was impossible. It was his proud theory with me that to work for a photographer was just as dignified as to produce under any other conditions, provided you did not stoop to ideals which for lack of a better word might be called photographic. How he represented it to Dora, or permitted Dora to represent it to him, I am not so certain — I imagine there may have been admissions and qualifications. Be that as it may, however, the fact was imperative that only three months of the hated bond remained, and that some working substitute for the hated bond would have to be discovered at their expiration. Simla, in short, must be made to buy Armour's pictures, to appreciate them, if the days of miracle were not entirely past, but to buy them any way. On one or two occasions I had already made Simla buy things. I had cleared out young Ludlow's stables for him in a week — he had a string of ten — when he played polo in a straw hat and had to go home with sunstroke; and I once auctioned off all the property costumes of the Amateur Dramatic Society at astonishing prices. Pictures presented difficulties which I have hinted at in an earlier chapter, but I did not despair. I began by hauling old Lamb, puffing and blowing like a grampus, up to Amy Villa, filling him up all the way with denunciations of Simla's philistinism and suggestions that he alone redeemed it.

It is a thing I am ashamed to think of, and it deserved its reward.

Lamb criticized and patronized every blessed thing he saw, advised Armour to beware of mannerisms and to be a little less liberal with his color, and heard absolutely unmoved of the horses Armour had got into the Salon. "I understand," he said, with a benevolent wink, "that about four thousand pictures are hung every year at the Salon, and I don't know how many thousand are rejected. Let Mr. Armour get a picture accepted by the Academy. Then he will have something to talk about."

Neither did Sir William Lamb buy anything at all.

The experiment with Lady Pilkey was even more distressing. She gushed with fair appropriateness and great liberality, and finally fixed upon one scene to make her own. She winningly asked the price of it. She had never known anybody who did not understand prices. Poor Armour, the color of a live coal, named one hundred rupees.

"One hundred rupees! Oh, my dear boy, I can never afford that! You must, you must really give it to me for seventy-five. It will break my heart if I can't have it for seventy-five."

"Give me the pleasure," said Armour, "of making you a present of it. You have been so kind about everything, and it's so seldom one meets anybody who really cares. So let me send it to you." It was honest embarrassment; he did not mean to be impertinent.

And she did.

Blum, of the Geological Department — Herr Blüm in his own country — came up and honestly rejoiced, and at the end of an interminable pipe did purchase a little Breton bit that I hated to see go — it was one of the things that gave the place its air; but Blum had a large family undergoing education at Heidelberg, and exclaimed, to Armour's keenest anguish, that on this account he could not more do.

Altogether, during the months of August and September, persons resident in Simla drawing their income from Her Majesty, bought from the eccentric young artist from nowhere, living on Summer Hill, canvases and little wooden panels to the extent of two hundred and fifty rupees. Lady Pilkey had asked him to lunch — she might well! and he had appeared at three garden-parties and a picnic. It was not enough.

It was not enough, and yet it was, in a manner, too much. Pitiful as it was in substance, it had an extraordinary personal effect. Armour suddenly began to turn himself out well — his apparel was of smarter cut than mine, and his neckties in better taste. Little elegances appeared in the studio — he offered you Scotch in a Venetian decanter and Melachrinos from a chased silver box. The *farouche*[1] element faded out of his speech; his ideas remained as fresh and as simple as ever, but he gave them a form, bless me! that might have

---

1 *farouche*: sullen, unsociable.

been used at the Club. He worked as hard as ever, but more variously; he tried his hand at several new things. He said he was feeling
about for something that would really make his reputation.

In spite of all this his little measure of success made him more
contemptuous than before of its scene and its elements. He
declared that he had a poorer idea than ever of society now that
he saw the pattern from the smart side. That his convictions on this
head survived one of the best Simla tailors shows that they must
always have been strong. I think he believed that he was doing all
that he did do to make himself socially possible with the purpose
of pleasing Dora Harris. I would not now venture to say how far
Dora inspired and controlled him in this direction, and how far the
impulse was his own. The measure of appreciation that began to
seek his pictures, poor and small though it was, gave him, on the
other hand, the most unalloyed delight. He talked of the advice of
Sir William Lamb as if it were anything but that of a pompous old
ass, and he made a feast with champagne for Blum that must have
cost him quite as much as Blum paid for the Breton sketch. He
confirmed my guess that he had never in his life until he came to
Simla sold anything, so that even these small transactions were
great things to him, and the earnest[1] of a future upon which he
covered his eyes not to gaze too raptly. He mentioned to me that
Kauffer had been asked for his address — who could it possibly be?
— and looked so damped by my humorous suggestion that it was
a friend of Kauffer's in some other line who wanted a bill paid, that
I felt I had been guilty of brutality. And all the while the quality of
his wonderful output never changed or abated. Pure and firm and
prismatic it remained. I found him one day at the very end of
October, with shining eyes and fingers blue with cold, putting the
last of the afternoon light on the snows into one of the most dramatic hill pictures I ever knew him to do. He seemed intoxicated
with his skill, and hummed the "Marseillaise,"[2] I remember, all the
way to Amy Villa whither I accompanied him.

It was the last day of Kauffer's contract; and besides, all the
world, secretaries, establishments, hill captains, grass widows, shops,
and sundries, was trundling down the hill. I came to ask my young
friend what he meant to do.

"Do?" he cried. "Why eat, drink, and be merry! Kauffer has

---

1 earnest: foretaste.
2 the "Marseillaise": national anthem of France.

paid up, and his yoke is at the bottom of the sea. Come back and dine with me!"

The hour we spent together in his little inner room before dinner was served stands out among my strangest, loveliest memories of Armour. He was divinely caught up, and absurd as it is to write, he seemed to carry me with him. We drank each a glass of vermuth before dinner sitting over a scented fire of deodar branches, while outside the little window in front of me the lifted lines of the great empty Himalayan landscape faded and fell into a blur. I remembered the solitary scarlet dahlia that stood between us and the vast cold hills and held its color when all was gray but that. The hill world waited for winter; down a far valley we could hear a barking deer. Armour talked slowly, often hesitating for a word, of the joy there was in beauty and the divinity in the man who saw it with his own eyes. I have read notable pages that brought conviction pale beside that which stole about the room from what he said. The comment may seem fantastic, but it is a comment — I caressed the dog. The servant clattered in with the plates, and at a shout outside Armour left me. He came in radiant with Signor Strobo, also radiant and carrying a violin, for hotel-keeping was not the Signor's only accomplishment. I knew Strobo well; many a special dish had he ordered for my little parties; and we met at Armour's fireside like the genial old acquaintances we were. Another voice without and presently I was nodding to Rosario and vaguely wondering why he looked uncomfortable.

"I'm sorry," said Armour, as we sat down, "I've got nothing but beer. If I had known you were all coming, no vintage that crawls up the hill would have been good enough for me." He threw the bond of his wonderful smile round us as we swallowed his stuff, and our hearts were lightened. "You fellows," he went on nodding at the other two, "might happen any day, but my friend John Philips comes to me across aerial spaces; he is a star I've trapped — you don't do that often. Pilsener, John Philips, or Black?" He was helping his only servant by pouring out the beer himself, and as I declared for Black he slapped me affectionately on the back and said my choice was good.

The last person who had slapped me on the back was Lord Dufferin,[1] and I smiled softly and privately at the remem-

---

1 Lord Dufferin: Frederick Temple Blackwood, 1st Marquess of Dufferin and Ava, Governor-General of Canada 1872–78, afterwards Viceroy of India.

brance, and what a difference there was. I had resented Dufferin's slap.

We had spiced hump[1] and jungle-fowl and a Normandy cheese, everybody will understand that; but how shall I make plain with what exultation and simplicity we ate and drank, how the four candid selves of us sat around the table in a cloud of tobacco and cheered each other on, Armour always far in front turning handsprings as he went. Scraps come back to me, but the whole queer night has receded and taken its place among those dreams that insist at times upon having been realities. Rosario told us stories Kipling might have coveted of the under life of Port Said. Strobo talked with glorious gusto of his uncle the brigand. They were liberated men; we were all liberated men. "Let the direction go," cried Armour, "and give the senses flight, taking the image as it comes, beating the air with happy pinions." He must have been talking of his work; but I can not now remember. And what made Strobo say, of life and art, "I have waited for ten years and five thousand pounds — now my old violin says, 'Go, handle the ladle! Go, add up the account!'" And did we really discuss the chances of ultimate salvation for souls in the Secretariat? I know I lifted my glass once and cried, "I, a slave, drink to freedom!" and Rosario clinked with me. And Strobo played wailing Hungarian airs with sudden little shakes of hopeless laughter in them. I can not even now hear Naches without being filled with the recollection of how certain bare branches in me that night blossomed.

I walked alone down the hill and along the three miles to the Club, and at every step the tide sank in me till it cast me on my threshold at three in the morning, just the middle-aged shell of a Secretary to the Government of India that I was when I set forth. Next day when my head clerk brought me the files we avoided one another's glances; and it was quite three weeks before I could bring myself to address him with the dignity and distance prescribed for his station as "Mr." Rosario.

---

1 hump: the salted hump of Indian oxen. HJ

CHAPTER IX

I WENT of course to Calcutta for the four winter months. Harris and I were together at the Club. It was the year, I remember, of the great shindy[1] as to whether foreign consuls should continue to be made honorary members, in view of the sentiments some of them were freely reflecting from Europe upon the subject of a war in South Africa which was none of theirs. Certainly, feeling as they did, it would have been better if they had swaggered less about a club that stood for British Government; but I did not vote to withdraw the invitation. We can not, after all, take notice of every idle word that drops from Latin or Teutonic tongues;[2] it isn't our way; but it was a liverish cold weather on various accounts, and the public temper was short. I heard from Dora oftener, Harris declared, than he did. She was spending the winter with friends in Agra, and Armour, of course, was there too, living at Laurie's Hotel, and painting, Dora assured me, with immense energy. It was just the place for Armour, a sumptuous dynasty wrecked in white marble[3] and buried in desert sands for three hundred years; and I was glad to hear that he was making the most of it. It was quite by the way, but I had lent him the money to go there — somebody had to lend it to him — and when he asked me to decide whether he should take his passage for Marseilles or use it for this other purpose I could hardly hesitate, believing in him, as I did, to urge him to paint a little more of India before he went. I frankly despaired of his ever being able to pay his way in Simla without Kauffer, but that was no reason why he should not make a few more notes for further use at home, where I sometimes saw for him, when his desultory and experimental days were over and some definiteness and order had come into his work, a Bond Street exhibition.

I have not said all this time that I thought of Ingersoll Armour and Dora Harris together, because their connection seemed too

---

1 shindy: a row, commotion. OED
2 Latin or Teutonic tongues: Latin: used as a designation for the European peoples who speak languages descended from Latin; Teutonic: Of or pertaining to the group of languages allied to German (including Gothic, Scandinavian, Indo-Germanic, or Aryan family). OED
3 white marble: a reference to the Taj Mahal.

vague and fantastic and impossible to hold for an instant before a steady gaze. I have no wish to justify myself when I write that I preferred to keep my eyes averted, enjoying perhaps just such measure of vision as would enter at a corner of them. This may or may not have been immoral under the circumstances — the event did not prove it so — but for urgent private reasons I could not be the person to destroy the idyl, if indeed its destruction were possible, that flourished there in the corner of my eye. Besides, had not I myself planted and watered it? But it was foolish to expect other people, people who are forever on the lookout for trousseaux and wedding-bells, and who considered these two as mere man and maid, and had no sight of them as engaging young spirits in happy conjunction — it was foolish to expect such people to show equal consideration. Christmas was barely over before the lady with whom Miss Harris was staying found it her duty to communicate to Edward Harris the fact that dear Dora's charming friendship — she was sure it was nothing more — with the young artist — Mrs. Poulton believed Mr. Harris would understand who was meant — was exciting a good deal of comment in the station, and *would* dear Mr. Harris please write to Dora himself, as Mrs. Poulton was beginning to feel so responsible?

I saw the letter; Harris showed it to me when he sat down to breakfast with the long face of a man in a domestic difficulty, and we settled together whom we should ask to put his daughter up in Calcutta. It should be the wife of a man in his own department of course; it is to one's Deputy Secretary that one looks for succor at times like this; and naturally one never looks in vain. Mrs. Symons would be delighted. I conjured up Dora's rage on receipt of the telegram. She loathed the Symonses.

She came, but not at the jerk of a wire; she arrived a week later, with a face of great propriety and a smile of great unconcern. Harris, having got her effectually out of harm's way, shirked further insistence, and I have reason to believe that Armour was never even mentioned between them.

Dora applied herself to the gaieties of the season with the zest of a débutante; she seemed really refreshed, revitalized. She had never looked better, happier. I met her again for the first time at one of the Thursday dances at Government House. In the glance she gave me I was glad to detect no suspicion of collusion. She plainly could not dream that Edward Harris in his nefarious exercise of parental authority had acted upon any hint from me. It was rather sweet.

Out in the veranda, away from the blare of the Viceroy's band, she told me very delicately and with the most charming ellipses how Armour had been filling her life in Agra, how it had all been, for these two, a dream and a vision. There is a place below the bridge there, where the cattle come down from the waste pastures across the yellow sands to drink and stand in the low water of the Jumna, to stand and switch their tails while their herdsmen on the bank coax them back with "Ari!" "Ari!" "Ari!" long and high, faint and musical; and the minarets of Akbar's fort rise beyond against the throbbing sky and the sun fills it all. This place I shall never see more distinctly than I saw it that night on the veranda at Government House, Calcutta, with the conviction, like a margin for the picture, that its foreground had been very often occupied by the woman I profoundly worshiped and Ingersoll Armour. She told me that he had sent me a sketch of it, and I very much wished he hadn't. One felt that the gift would carry a trifle of irony.

"He has told me," she said once brusquely, "how good you have been to him."

"Is he coming to Simla again?" I asked.

"Oh yes! And please take it from me that this time he will conquer the place. He has undertaken to do it."

"At your request?"

"At my persuasion — at my long entreaty. They must recognize him — they must be taught. I have set my heart on it."

"Does he himself very much care?" I asked remembering the night of the thirty-first of October.

"Yes, he does care. He despises it, of course, but in a way he cares. I've been trying to make him care more. A human being isn't an orchid; he must draw something from the soil he grows in."

"If he were stable," I mused; "if he had a fixed ambition somewhere in the firmament. But his purpose is a will-o'-the-wisp."

"I think he has an ambition," said Miss Harris, into the dark.

"Ah! Then we must continue," I said — "continue to push from behind."

Dora did not reply. She is a person of energy and determination, and might have been expected to offer to cooperate gladly. But she didn't.

"He is painting a large picture for next season's exhibition," she informed me. "I was not allowed to see it or to know anything about it, but he declares it will bring Simla down."

"I hope not," I said, piously.

"Oh, I hope so. I have told him," Dora continued, slowly, "that a great deal depends on it."

"Here is Mrs. Symons," I was able to return, "and I am afraid she is looking for you."

March came, and the city lay white under its own dust. The electric fans began to purr in the Club, and Lent brought the flagging season to a full stop. I had to go that year on tour through the famine district with the Member, and we escaped, gasping, from the Plains about the middle of April. Simla was crimson with rhododendron blossoms, and seemed a spur of Arcady. There had been the usual number of flittings from one house to another, and among them I heard with satisfaction that Armour no longer occupied Amy Villa. I would not for the world have blurred my recollections of that last evening — I could not have gone there again.

"He is staying with Sir William Lamb," said Dora, handing me my cup of tea. "And I am quite jealous. Sir William, only Sir William, has been allowed to see the exhibition picture."

"What does that portend?" I said, thoughtfully.

"I don't know. Sir William was here yesterday simply swelling with his impression of it. He says it's the finest thing that has been done in India. I told you he would conquer them."

"You did," and without thinking I added, "I hope you won't be sorry that you asked him to." It must have been an inspiration.

Armour, those weeks before the exhibition, seemed invisible. Dora reported him torn with the incapacity of the bazaar frame-maker to follow a design, and otherwise excessively occupied, and there was no lack of demands upon my own time. Besides, my ardor to be of assistance to the young man found a slight damper in the fact that he was staying with Sir William Lamb. What competence had I to be of use to the guest of Sir William Lamb?

"I do not for a moment think he will be there," said Dora, on the day of the private view as we went along the Mall toward the Town Hall together. "He will not run with an open mouth to his success. He will take it from us later."

But he was there. We entered precisely at the dramatic moment of his presentation by Sir William Lamb to the Viceroy. He stood embarrassed and smiling in a little circle of compliments and congratulation. Behind him and a little to the left hung his picture, large and predominant, and in the corner of the frame was stuck the red ticket that signified the Viceroy's gold medal. We saw that, I think, before we saw anything else. Then with as little haste as was decent, considering His Excellency's proximity, we walked within range of the picture.

I am not particularly pleased, even now, to have the task of describing the thing. Its subject was an old Mahomedan priest with a green turban and a white beard exhorting a rabble of followers. I heard myself saying to Dora that it was very well painted indeed, very conscientiously painted, and that is certainly what struck me. The expression of the fire-eater's face was extremely characteristic; his arm was flung out with a gesture that perfectly matched. The group of listeners was carefully composed and most "naturally"; that is the only word that would come to me.

I glanced almost timidly at Dora. She was regarding it with a deep vertical line between her handsome brows.

"What — on earth — has he done with himself?" she demanded, but before I could reply Armour was by our side.

"Well?" he said, looking at Dora.

"It — it's very nice," she stammered, "but I miss *you*."

"She only means, you know," I rushed in, "that you've put in everything that was never there before. Accuracy of detail, you know, and so forth. 'Pon my word, there's some drawing in that!"

"No," said Dora, calmly, "what I complain of is that he has left out everything that was there before. But he has won the gold medal, and I congratulate him."

"Well," I said, uneasily, "don't congratulate me. I didn't do it. Positively I am not to blame."

"His Excellency says that it reminds him of an incident in one of Mrs. Steel's novels,"[1] said Armour, just turning his head to ascertain His Excellency's whereabouts.

"Dear me, so it does," I exclaimed, eagerly, "one couldn't name the chapter — it's the general feeling." I went on to discourse of the general feeling. Words came generously, questions with point, comments with intelligence. I swamped the situation and so carried it off.

"The Viceroy has bought the thing," Armour went on, looking at Dora, "and has commissioned me to paint another. The only restriction he makes is —— "

"That is shall be of the same size?" asked Dora.

---

1   Mrs. Steel's novels: Flora Annie Steel (1847-1929) lived in India
    (1868–89), where she worked as an architect, educationist, and writer.
    Well known as a writer of popular Anglo-Indian romances. RT

"That it must deal with some phase of native life."

Miss Harris walked to a point behind us, and stood there with her eyes fixed upon the picture. I glanced at her once; her gaze was steady, but perfectly blank. Then she joined us again, and struck into the stream of my volubility.

"I am delighted," she said, pleasantly, to Armour. "You have done exactly what I wanted you to do. You have won the Viceroy's medal, and all the reputation there is to win in this place. Come and dine to-night, and we will rejoice together. But wasn't it — for you — a little difficult?"

He looked at her as if she had offered him a cup, and then dashed it from his lips; but the occasion was not one, of course, for crying out.

"Oh no," he said, putting on an excellent face. "But it took a hideous time."

CHAPTER X

WITHIN a fortnight I was surprised and a little irritated to receive from Armour the amount of my loan in full. It was not in accordance with my preconceived idea of him that he should return it at all. I had arranged in my own mind that he should be governed by the most honest impulses and the most approved intentions up to the point of departure, but that he should never find it quite convenient to pay, and that in order to effect his final shipment to other shores I should be compelled to lend him some more money. In the far future, when he should be famous and I an obscure pauper on pension, my generous imagination permitted me to see the loan repaid; but not till then. These are perhaps stereotyped and conventional lines to conceive him on, but I hardly think that anybody who has followed my little account to this point will think them unjustifiable. I looked at his check with disgust. That a man turns out better than you expected is no reason why you should not be annoyed that your conception of him is shattered. You may be gratified on general grounds, but distinctly put out on personal ones, especially when your conception pointed to his inevitable removal. That was the way I felt.

The check stood for so much more than its money value. It stood for a possible, nay, a probable capacity in Armour to take his place in the stable body of society, to recognize and make demands, to become a taxpayer, a churchgoer, a house-holder, a husband. As I gazed, the signature changed from that of a gnome with luminous eyes who inhabited an inaccessible crag among the rhododendrons to that of a prosperous artist-bourgeois with a silk hat for Sundays. I have in some small degree the psychological knack, I saw the possibilities of the situation with immense clearness; and I cursed the check.

Coincidence is odious, tells on the nerves. I never felt it more so than a week later, when I read in the Pioneer[1] the announcement of the death of my old friend Fry, Superintendent of the School of Art in Calcutta. The paragraph in which the journal dismissed poor Fry to his reward was not unkind, but it distinctly implied that the removal of Fry should include the removal of his

---

1 the Pioneer: a daily newspaper published in Allahabad (1874-1931).

ideas and methods, and the substitution of something rather more up to date. It remarked that the Bengali student had been pinned down long enough to drawing plaster casts, and declared that something should be done to awake within him the creative idea. I remember the phrase, it seemed so directly to suggest that the person to awake it should be Ingersoll Armour.

I turned the matter over in my mind; indeed, for the best part of an hour my brain revolved with little else. The billet was an excellent one, with very decent pay and charming quarters. It carried a pension, it was the completest sort of provision. There was a long vacation, with opportunities for original effort, and I had heard Fry call the work interesting. Fry was the kind of man to be interested in anything that gave him a living, but there was no reason why a more captious spirit, in view of the great advantages, should not accommodate itself to the routine that might present itself. The post was in the gift of the Government of Bengal, but that was no reason why the Government of Bengal should not be grateful in the difficulty of making a choice for a hint from us. The difficulty was really great. They would have to write home and advertise in the Athenæum[1] — for some reason Indian Governments always advertise educational appointments in the Athenæum; it is a habit which dates from the days of John Company[2] — and that would mean delay. And then the result might be a disappointment. Might Armour not also be a disappointment? That I really could not say. A new man is always a speculation, and departments, like individuals, have got to take their luck.

The Viceroy was so delighted — everybody was so delighted — with the medal picture that the merest breath blown among them would secure Armour's nomination. Should I blow the breath? These happy thoughts must always occur to somebody. This one had occurred to me. Ten to one it would occur to nobody else, and last of all to Armour himself. The advertisement might already be on its way home to the Athenæum.

It would make everything possible. It would throw a very different complexion over the idyl. It would turn that interlacing wreath of laurels and of poppies into the strongest bond in the world.

---

1   the Athenæum: a journal of literature, science, and the arts, published in London, 1828-1921.
2   John Company: a colloquial way of referring to the East India Company. HB

I would simply have nothing to do with it.

But there was no harm in asking Armour to dine with me; I sent the note off by messenger after breakfast and told the steward to put a magnum of Pommery to cool at seven precisely. I had some idea, I suppose, of drinking with Armour to his eternal discomfiture. Then I went to the office with a mind cleared of responsibility and comfortably pervaded with the glow of good intentions.

The moment I saw the young man, punctual and immediate and a little uncomfortable about the cuffs, I regretted not having asked one or two more fellows. It might have spoiled the occasion, but it would have saved the situation. That single glance of my accustomed eye — alas! that it was so well accustomed — revealed him anxious and screwed up, as nervous as a cat, but determined, revealed — how well I knew the signs! — that he had something confidential and important and highly personal to communicate, a matter in which I could, if I only would, be of the greatest possible assistance. From these appearances twenty years had taught me to fly to any burrow, but your dinner-table offers no retreat; you are hoist, so to speak, on your own carving-fork. There are men, of course, and even women, who have scruples about taking advantage of so intimate and unguarded an opportunity, but Armour, I rapidly decided, was not one of these. His sophistication was progressing, but it had not reached that point. He wanted something — I flew instantly to the mad conclusion that he wanted Dora. I did not pause to inquire why he should ask her of me. It had seemed for a long time eminently proper that anybody who wanted Dora should ask her of me. The application was impossible, but applications nearly always were impossible. Nobody knew that better than the Secretary to the Government of India in the Home Department.

I squared my shoulders and we got through the soup. It was necessary to apologize for the fish. "I suppose one must remember," I said, "that it has to climb six thousand feet," when suddenly he burst out.

"Sir William Lamb tells me," he said, and stopped to swallow some wine, "that there is something very good going in Calcutta and that I should ask you to help me to get it. May I?"

So the miserable idea — the happy thought — had occurred to somebody else.

"Is there?" I said, with interest and attention.

"It's something in the School of Art. A man named Fry has died."

"Ah!" I said, "a man named Fry. He, I think, was Director of that institution." I looked at Armour in the considering, measuring way with which we suggest to candidates for posts that their fitness to fill them is not to be absolutely taken for granted. "Fry was a man of fifty-six," I said.

"I am thirty." He certainly did not look it, but years often fall lightly upon a temperament.

"It's a vile climate."

"I know. Is it too vile, do you think," he said anxiously, "to ask a lady to share?"

"Lots of ladies do share it," I replied, with amazing calmness; "but I must decline absolutely to enter into that."

My frown was so forbidding that he couldn't and didn't dare to go on. He looked dashed and disappointed; he was really a fool of an applicant, quite ready to retire from the siege on the first intimation that the gates were not to be thrown open at his approach.

"Do you think you would like teaching?" I asked.

"I can teach. Miss — my only pupil here has made capital progress."

"I am afraid you must not measure the Bengali art student by the standard of Miss Harris," I replied coldly. He *was* a fool. We talked of other things. I led him on to betray his ludicrous lack of knowledge of the world in various directions. At other times it had irritated me, that night it gave me the purest pleasure. I agreed with him about everything.

As he selected his smoke to go home with I said, "Send your application into the Director of Public Instruction, Bengal — Lamb will tell you how — and I'll see what I can do."

They were only too thankful to get him. As a student it seemed he had been diligent both in London and Paris; he possessed diplomas or some such things bearing names which were bound to have weight with a Department of Public Instruction anywhere. I felt particularly thankful for this, for I was committed to him if he had not a rag to show.

The matter was settled in three weeks, during which Armour became more and more the fashion in Simla. He was given every opportunity of experiment in the society of which he was about to become a permanent item. He dined out four or five times a week, and learned exactly what to talk about. He surprised me one day with a piece of news of my own department, which was a liberty of a very serious kind, but I forgave him upon finding that it was not true. He rode Lamb's weight-carriers, to cross which his short legs were barely adequate, and apart from this disadvantage he did not ride them badly. Only one thing marred the completeness of the transformation — he didn't dismiss the dog. The dog, fundamentally irreconcilable to any system of classification, was still and ever his companion. It was a suspicious circumstance if we had known; but we saw in it only a kind heart, and ignored it.

I saw little of Dora Harris at this time. Making no doubt that she was enjoying her triumph as she deserved, I took the liberty of supposing that she would hardly wish to share so intimate a source of satisfaction. I met them both several times at people's houses — certain things had apparently been taken for granted — but I was only one of the little circle that wondered how soon it might venture upon open congratulations. The rest of us knew as much, it seemed, as Edward Harris did. Lady Pilkey asked him point-blank, and he said what his daughter found to like in the fellow the Lord only knew, and he was glad to say that at the present he had no announcement to make. Lady Pilkey told me she thought it very romantic — like marrying a newspaper correspondent — but I pointed to the lifelong task, with a pension attached, of teaching fat young Bengalis to draw, and asked her if she saw extravagant romance in that.

They wrote up from Calcutta that they would like to have a look at Armour before making the final recommendation, and he left us, I remember, by the mail tonga[1] of the 3d of June. He dropped into my office to say good-by, but I was busy with the Member and could see nobody, so he left a card with "P.P.C."[2] on it. I kept the card by accident, and I keep it still by design, for the sake of that inscription.

Strobo had given up his hotel in Simla to start one in Calcutta. It never occurred to me that Armour might go to Strobo's; but it was, of course, the natural thing for him to do, especially as Strobo happened to be in Calcutta himself at the time. He went and stayed with Strobo, and every day he and the Signor, clad in bath-towels, lay in closed rooms under punkahs[3] and had iced drinks in the long tumblers of the East, and smoked and talked away the burden of the hours.

---

1 tonga: light cart.
2 P.P.C.: *pour prendre congé* (to take leave); written on cards, etc. OED
3 punkahs: fans, usually made from the leaf of the palmyra. EN

Strobo was in Calcutta to meet a friend, an Austrian, who was shortly leaving India in the Messagerie Maritimes steamer Dupleix after agreeable wanderings disguised as a fakir[1] in Tibet; and to this friend was attached, in what capacity I never thought well to inquire, a lady who was a Pole, and played and sang as well as Strobo fiddled. I believe they dined together every night, this precious quartette, and exchanged in various tongues their impressions of India under British control. "A houri[2] in stays,"[3] the lady who was a Pole described it. I believe she herself was a houri without them. And at midnight, when the south wind was cool and strong from the river, Strobo and Armour would walk up Chowringhee Road and look at the red brick School of Art from the outside in the light of the street lamps, as a preliminary to our friend's final acceptance of the task of superintending it from within.

We in Simla, of course, knew nothing of all this at the time; the details leaked out later when Strobo came up again. I began to feel some joyful anxiety when in a letter dated a week after Armour's arrival in Calcutta, the Director of Public Instruction wrote to inquire whether he had yet left Simla; but the sweet blow did not fall with any precision or certainty until the newspaper arrived containing his name immediately under that of Herr Vanrig and Mme. Dansky in the list of passengers who had sailed per S.S. Dupleix on the 15th of June for Columbo. There it was, "I. Armour," as significant as ever to two persons intimately concerned with it, but no longer a wrapping of mystery, rather a radiating center of light. Its power of illumination was such that it tried my eyes. I closed them to recall the outlines of the School of Art — it had been built in a fit of economy — and the headings of the last Director's report, which I had kindly sent after Armour to Calcutta. Perhaps that had been the last straw.

The real meaning of the task of implanting Western ideals in the Eastern mind rose before me when I thought of Armour's doing it — how they would dwindle in the process, and how he must go on handling them and looking at them withered and shrunken for twenty-odd years. I understood — there was enough left in me to

---

1 fakir: a Muslim or (rarely) Hindu religious mendicant or ascetic. EN
2 houri: a nymph of the Muslim Paradise; hence applied allusively to a voluptuously beautiful woman. OED
3 stays: a corset.

understand — Armour's terrified escape. I was happy in the thought of him sailing down the Bay.[1] The possibilities of marriage, social position, assured income, support in old age, the strands in the bond that held him, the bond that holds us all, had been untwisting, untwisting, from the 3d of June to the 15th. The strand that stood for Dora doubtless was the last to break, but it did not detract from my beatitude to know that even this consideration, before the Dupleix and liberty, failed to hold.

I kept out of Miss Harris's way so studiously for the next week or two that she was kind enough in the end to feel compelled to send for me. I went with misgivings — I expected, as may be imagined, to be very deeply distressed. She met me with a storm of gay reproaches. I had never seen her in better health or spirits. My surprise must have been more evident than I supposed or intended, for before I went away she told me the whole story. By that time she had heard from Ceylon,[2] a delicious letter with a pen-and-ink sketch at the top. I have it still; it infallibly brought the man back to me. But it was all over; she assured me with shining eyes that it was. The reason of her plainly boundless thankfulness that Armour had run away from the School of Art did not come to the surface until I was just going. Then I gathered that if he had taken the post she would have felt compelled, compelled by all she had done for him, to share its honors with him; and this, ever since at her bidding he had begun to gather such things up, was precisely what she had lost all inclination to do.

We were married the following October. We had a big, gorgeous official wedding, which we both enjoyed enormously. I took furlough, and we went home, but we found London very expensive and the country very slow; and with my K.C.S.I.[3] came the offer of the Membership,[4] so we went back to Simla for three perfectly unnecessary years, which we now look back upon with pleasure and regret. I fear that we, no more than Ingersoll Armour, were quite whole-hearted Bohemians; but I don't know that we really ever pretended to be.

---

1   the Bay: the Bay of Bengal.
2   Ceylon: now Sri Lanka.
3   K.C.S.I: Knight Commander of the Star of India. OED
4   Membership: senior government position.

Part IV

The Hesitation of Miss Anderson

CHAPTER I

WHEN it became known that Madeline Anderson had finally decided to go abroad for two years, her little circle in New York naturally talked a good deal, in review, about her curious reason for never having gone before. So much that happened afterward, so much that I am going to tell, depends upon this reason for not going before, that I also must talk about it and explain it; I could never bring it out just as we went along. It would have been a curious reason in connection with anybody, but doubly so as explaining the behavior of Miss Anderson, whose profile gave you the impression that she was anything but the shuttlecock of her emotions. Shortly, her reason was a convict, Number 1596, who, up to February in that year, had been working, or rather waiting, out his sentence in the State penitentiary. So long as he worked or waited, Madeline remained in New York, but when in February death gave him his quittance, she took her freedom too, with wide intentions and many coupons.

Earlier in his career Number 1596 had been known in New York society as Mr. Frederick Prendergast, and for a little while he was disapproved there on the score of having engaged himself to a Miss Anderson, Madeline Anderson, whom nobody knew anything about. There was her own little circle, as I have said, and it lacked neither dignity nor refinement, but I doubt whether any member of it was valeted from London, or could imply, in conversation, a personal acquaintance with Yvette Guilbert.[1] There is no need, however, to insist that there are many persons of comfortable income and much cultivation in New York, who would not be met by strangers having what are called the "best" introductions there. The best so often fails to include the better. It may be accepted that Madeline Anderson and her people were of these, and that she wondered sometimes during the brief days of her engagement what it would be like to belong to the brilliant little world about her that had its visiting list in London, Paris, or St. Petersburg, and was immensely entertained by the gaucheries of the great ones of the earth.

---

1 Yvette Guilbert: a French cabaret singer/performer (1865-1944). EN

Then came, with the most unexceptionable introductions, Miss Violet Forde, from a Sloane Square address, London. She came leaning on the arm of a brother, the only relative she had in the world, and so brilliant was the form of these young people that it occurred to nobody to imagine that it had the most precarious pecuniary foundation, must have faded and shriveled indeed, after another year or two of anything but hospitality as generous as that of New York. Well-nourished and undimmed, however, it concealed for them admirably the fact that it was the hospitality they were after, and not the bracing climate or the desire to see the fascinating Americans of London and Paris at home. New York found them agreeable specimens of high-spirited young English people, and played with them indefinitely. Miss Forde, when she sat imperturbably on a cushion in the middle of the floor after dinner and sang to a guitar the songs of Albert Chevalier, was an anomaly in English decorum that was as pleasing to observe as it was amusing to criticize.

The Americans she met delighted in drawing her out — it was a pastime that took the lead at dinner-parties, to an extent which her hostess often thought preposterous — and she responded with naïveté and vigor, perfectly aware that she was scoring all along the line. Upon many charming people she made the impression that she was a type of the most finished class of what they called "English society girls," that she represented the best they could do over there in this direction. As a matter of fact she might have sat to any of those "black and white" artists, who draw townish young women of London, saying cynical things to young men in the weekly papers. That was her type, and if you look for her picture there, you will see that her face was very accurately oval, with eyes that knew their value, and other features that didn't very much matter, except in so far as they expressed a very full conception of the satisfactions of this life, and a wide philosophy as to methods of obtaining them.

Frederick Prendergast was unacquainted with the popular pictures I have mentioned, having a very reasonable preference for the illustrated papers of his own country; otherwise — there is no telling — he might have observed the resemblance and escaped the State prison, whither he assuredly never would have gone had he married Madeline Anderson — as he fully intended to do when Miss Forde came over. He was worth at that time a great deal of money, besides being more personable than any one would have believed who knew him as "1596." His fiancée was never too obtrusively in evidence, and if Miss Forde thought of Miss Anderson with any scruple, it was probably to reflect that if she could not take care of these things she did not deserve to have them. This at all events was how her attitude expressed itself practically; and the upshot was that Miss Anderson lost them. There came a day when Frederick Prendergast, in much discomfort of mind, took to Violet the news that Madeline had brought their engagement to an end. She, Violet, gave him some tea, and they talked frankly of the absurd misconception of the relations between them upon which his dismissal was founded; and Prendergast went away much comforted and wholly disposed to respect Miss Anderson's startling wishes. She, with what both the others thought excellent taste, persuaded her mother and sister to move to Brooklyn; and so far as the thoroughfares and social theaters of New York were concerned, the city over the river might have been a nunnery which had closed its gates upon her. It was only in imagination that she heard Frederick Prendergast's wedding-bells when, two months later, he was united to Miss Forde in Grace Church, and that after the fact, their melody being brought to her inner sense next day by the marriage notice in the Tribune.

It would be painful, in view of what we know of Frederick Prendergast, to dwell upon what Madeline Anderson undeniably felt. Besides her emotions were not destructively acute, they only lasted longer than any one could have either expected or approved. She suffered for him as well; she saw as plainly as he did the first sordid consequences of his mistake the afternoon he came to solicit her friendship, having lost other claims; and it was then perhaps, that her responsibility in allowing Violet Forde to spoil his life for him began to suggest itself to her. Up to that time she had thought of the matter differently, as she would have said, selfishly. He was not permitted to come again; but he went away lightened, inasmuch as he had added his burden to hers.

When a year later the national credit involved that of Prendergast's firm, Madeline read financial articles in the newspapers with heavy concern, surprising her family with views on "sound money"; and when, shortly afterward, his partners brought that unhappy young man before the criminal courts for an irregular use of the firm's signature, which further involved it beyond hope of extrication, there was no moment of the day which did not find her, in spirit, beside him there.

The case dragged on through appeal, and the decision of the lower courts was not reversed. The day this became known the fact also transpired that poor Prendergast would never live to complete his ten years' term of imprisonment. He went to prison with hardly more than one lung, and in the most favorable physical condition to get rid of the other. Mrs. Prendergast wept a little over the installation, and assured Frederick that it was perfectly absurd; they were certain to get him out again; people always got people out again in America. She took him grapes and flowers once a week for about a month, and then she sailed for Europe. She put it about that her stay was to be as brief as was consistent with the transaction of certain necessary business in London; but she never came back, and Madeline Anderson had taken her place, in so far as the grapes and flowers were concerned, for many months, when the announcement of his wife's death reached Prendergast in an English paper published in Paris. About a year after that it began to be thought singular how he picked up in health, and Madeline's mother and sister occasionally romanced about the possibility of his recovering and marrying her after all — they had an enormous opinion of the artistic virtue of forgiveness — but it was not a contingency ever seriously contemplated by Miss Anderson herself. Her affection, pricked on by remorse, had long satisfied itself with the duties of her ministry. If she would not leave him until he died, it was because there was no one but herself to brighten the long day in the prison hospital for him, because she had thrown him into the arms of the woman who had deserted him, because he represented in her fancy her life's only budding toward the sun. Her patience lasted through six years, which was four years longer than any doctor had given Frederick Prendergast to live; but when one last morning she found an empty bed, and learned that Number 1596 had been discharged in his coffin, she rose from the shock with the sense of a task fully performed and a well-developed desire to see what else there might be in the world.

She announced her intention of traveling for a year or two with a maid, and her family expressed the usual acquiescence. It would help her, they said, to "shake it off"; but they said that to one another. They were not aware — and it would have spoiled an ideal for them if they had been — that she had shaken it off, quite completely, into Prendergast's grave.

This was the curious reason why Miss Anderson's travels were so long postponed.

CHAPTER II

IT was Madeline's fancy to enjoy the contrast between West and East in all its sharpness, so she and Brookes embarked at San Francisco for Yokohama.[1] Their wanderings in Japan were ideal, in spite of Brookes's ungrateful statement that she could have done with fewer eggs and more bacon; and Madeline prolonged the appeal of the country to her sense of humor and fantasy, putting off her departure for India from week to week. She went at last in March; and found herself down with fever at Benares[2] in the middle of one particularly hot April, two months after the last of her fellow travelers had sailed from Bombay, haunted on her baking pillow by pictorial views of the burning ghat and the vultures. The station doctor, using appalling language to her punkah-coolie,[3] ordered her to the hills; and thus it was that she went to Simla, where she had no intention of going, and where this story really begins.

Brookes has always declared that Providence in sending Miss Anderson to Simla had it in mind to prevent a tragedy; but as to that there is room for a difference of opinion: besides I can not be anticipated by Brookes.

"It's the oddest place imaginable, and in many ways the most delightful," Madeline wrote to her sister Adèle, "this microcosm of Indian official society withdrawn from all the world, and playing at being a municipality on three Himalayan mountain-tops. You can't imagine its individuality, its airy, unsubstantial, superior poise. How can I explain to you elderly gentlemen, whose faces express daily electric communication with the Secretary of State, playing tennis violently every single afternoon in striped flannels — writing letters of admonition to the Amir[4] all day long, and in the evening, with the assistance of yellow wigs and make-up sticks from the Calcutta hair-dresser, imagining that they produce things, poor dears, only a *little* less well done than is done at the Lyceum? Nothing is beyond them. I assure you

---

1   Yokahama: a city port in Japan.
2   Benares: now Varanasi, a city in northern India in Uttar Pradesh State on the northern bank of the Ganges River (home of temples of centre of learning). EN
3   punkah-coolie: person fanning. EN
4   the Amir: a commander. OED

they are contemplating at this moment The Second Mrs. Tanqueray.[1] The effect of remoteness from the world, I suppose, and the enormous mutual appreciation of people who have watched each other climb. For to arrive officially at Simla they have had to climb in more ways than one ... It is all so hilarious, so high-spirited, so young and yet, my word! what a cult of official dignity underlying! I saw a staff-officer in full uniform, red and white feathers and all, going to the birthday dinner at the Viceroy's the other evening in a perambulator — rickshaw, you know, such as they have in Japan. That is typical of the place. All the honors and dignities — and a perambulator to put them in — or a ridiculous little white-washed house made of mud and tin, and calling itself Warwick Castle, Blenheim, Abbotsford! They haven't a very good hold, these Simla residences, and sometimes they slip fifty yards or so down the mountain-side, but the chimneys (bad pun coming) are never any more out of drawing than they were before.

"Yet — never forget — the queer little place has a nobility, drawn I suppose from high standards of conduct in essentials.

" ...This matter of precedence is a bore for an outsider. I am very tired of being taken in to dinner by subalterns, because I have no 'official position.' Something of the kind was offered me, by the way, the other day, by a little gunner with red eyelids, in the Ordnance Department, named McDermott — Captain McDermott. He took my declining very cheerfully, said he knew Americans didn't like Englishmen, who hadn't been taught to pronounce their 'g's,' but hoped I would change my mind before the rains, when he was goin' down. Of course I sha'n't. The red eyelids alone .... I am living in a boarding-house precisely under the deodars, and have 'tiffin'[2] with Mrs. Hauksbee every day when neither of us are having it anywhere else. And I've been told the original of 'General Bangs,' 'that most immoral man.' You remember don't you the heliograph[3] incident — I needn't quote it. It really happened! and the General still lives, none the worse — perhaps rather better. Quite half the people seem materializations of Kipling, and it's very interesting; but one musn't say so if one wants to be popular. Talking of materializations, I saw the original of Crawford's

---

1 The Second Mrs. Tanqueray: a play (1893) by British playwright Arthur Wing Pinero.
2 'tiffin': a light meal, especially lunch. OED
3 heliograph: a signalling apparatus reflecting sunlight in flashes from a moveable mirror. OED

Mr. Isaacs, too, the other day. He used to be a diamond agent among the native princes when Crawford knew him. When I saw him he was auctioning off his collection of curios and things. These types of novelists look wonderfully little impaired; I suppose it's the dry air.

"P.S. — Brookes is also quite happy. She was much struck, on arriving, by an apparent anomaly in nature. 'Have you noticed, ma'am,' said she, 'how at this height all the birds are crows and monkeys?'"

Miss Anderson described Simla exhaustively in her letters to New York. She touched upon almost every feature, from Mrs. Mickie and Mrs. Gammidge, whose husbands were perspiring in the Plains, and nobody telling them anything, to the much larger number of ladies interested in the work of the Young Women's Christian Association; from the "type" of the Military Secretary to the Viceroy to that of Ali Buksh, who sold raw turquoises in a little carved shop in the bazaar. I should like to quote more of her letters, but if I did I should find nothing about Colonel Horace Innes, who represented — she often acknowledged to herself — her only serious interest. Miss Anderson took the world at its own light valuation as it came; but she had a scale of recognitions and acceptances, which she kept apart for the very few, and Innes had claimed a place in it the first time they met. It seems a trifle ungrateful that she should have left him out, since it was he who gave her a standard by which to measure the frivolity of Simla. He went to gymkhanas — if he knew she was going — but he towered almost pictorially above them; and when he talked to Madeline his shoulders expressed a resentment of possible interruptions that isolated him still further. I would not suggest that he was superior by conviction; he was only intent, whereas most of the other people were extremely diffused, and discriminating, while the intimacies of the rest were practically coextensive with Governmental House list. Neither, for his part, would he admit that the tone of Simla was as wholly flippant as I have implied. They often talked about it; he recognized it as a feature likely to compel the attention of people from other parts of the world; and one afternoon he asked her, with some directness, if she could see no tragedies underneath.

"Tragedies of the heart?" she asked. "Oh, I can not take them seriously. The emotion is so ephemeral! A woman came to tea with me three days ago, and made me her confessor. It was unexpected;

if it hadn't been, I wouldn't have asked her to tea. She was so unhappy that she forgot about the rouge, and it all came off on her handkerchief when she cried. The man likes somebody else better this season. Well, I gave her nougat and cheap cynicisms, and she allowed herself to be comforted! Why, the loves of kitchen-maids are more dignified."

They were riding on the broad four-mile road, blasted out of the rock, that winds round Jakko. The deodars stood thick above them, with the sunlight filtering through; a thousand feet below lay the little square fields, yellow and green, of the King of Koti. The purple-brown Himalayas shouldered the eye out to the horizon, and there the Snows lifted themselves, hardly more palpable than the drifted clouds, except for a gleam of ice in their whiteness. A low stone wall ran along the verge of the precipice, and, looking down, they saw tangled patches of the white wild rose of the Himalayas, waving and drooping over the abyss.

"I am afraid," said Innes, "you are not even upon the fringe of the situation."

"It's the situation as I see it."

"Then — excuse me — you do not see deep enough. That poor lady suffered, I suppose, to the extent of her capacity. You would not have increased it."

"I don't know. I should have preferred not to measure it."

"Besides, that was not quite the sort of thing I had in mind. I was thinking more of the — separations."

"Ah!" said Madeline.

"It's not fair to ask women to live much in India. Sometimes it's the children, sometimes it's ill health, sometimes it's natural antipathy to the place; there's always a reason to take them away."

"Yes," said Madeline, turning a glance of scrutiny on him. His face was impassive; he was watching mechanically for a chance to slay a teasing green spider-fly.

"That is the beginning of the tragedy I was thinking of. Time does the rest, time and the aridity of separations. How many men and women can hold themselves together with letters? I don't mean aging or any physical change. I don't mean change at all."

"No," said Madeline, and this time, though her curiosity was greater, she did not look at him.

"No. The mind could accustom itself to expect that, and so forestall the blow, if it really would be a blow, which I doubt. For myself, I'm pretty sure that nothing of that kind could have much effect upon one's feeling, if it were the real thing." He spoke practically to himself, as if he had reasoned this out many times.

"Oh, no!" said Madeline.

"But separation can do a worse thing than that. It can *reintroduce* people, having deprived them of their mutual illusion under which they married. If they lived together the illusion would go, I suppose, but custom and comfort would step in to prevent a jar. There never would be that awful revelation of indifference."

He stopped sharply, and the hope went through Madeline's mind that her face expressed no personal concern for him. There was a small red stain in the brown of his cheek as he looked at her to find out, and he added, "I've known — in Bombay — one or two bad cases of that. But, of course, it is the wife who suffers most. Shall we canter on?"

"In a minute," said Madeline, and he drew his rein again.

She could not let this be the last word; he must not imagine that she had seen, through the simple crystal of his convictions, the personal situation that gave them to him.

"Of course," she said, thoughtfully, "you know the Anglo-Indian world and I don't. You must have observed this that you speak of it; it sounds only too probable. And I confess it makes my little impression very vulgar and superficial." She turned her head and a candid smile to him. "All the same, I fancy that the people who are capable of suffering much that way are the exceptions. And — I don't care — I believe there is more cheap sentiment in this place than the other kind. What do you think I heard a woman say the other day at a tiffin-party? 'No man has touched my heart since I've been married,' she proclaimed, 'except my husband!' *At a tiffin*-party!"

She heard the relief in Innes's laugh and was satisfied.

"How does it happen," he said, "that women nowadays are critical of the world so young?"

"I shall be thirty in September, and we no longer look at society through a tambour-frame,"[1] she said, hardily.

"And I shall be forty-three next month, but hitherto I have known it to produce nothing like you," he returned, and if there was ambiguity in his phrase there was none in his face.

---

1 tambour-frame: a circular frame for holding fabric taut while it is being embroidered. OED

Miss Anderson made with her head her little smiling gesture — Simla called it very American — which expressed that all chivalrous speech was to be taken for granted and meant nothing whatever; and as they turned into the Ladies' Mile gave her horse his head, and herself a chance for meditation. She thought of the matter again that evening before her little fire of snapping deodar twigs, thought of it intently. She remembered it all with perfect distinctness; she might have been listening to a telephonic reproduction.

It was the most intimate glimpse Innes had given her of himself, and it brought her an excitement which she did not think of analyzing. She wrung from every sentence its last possibility of unconscious meaning, and she found when she had finished that it was eleven o'clock.

Then she went to bed, preferring not to call Brookes, with the somewhat foolish feeling of being unable to account for her evening. Her last reflection before she slept shaped itself in her mind in definite words.

"There are no children," it ran, "and her health has always been good, he says. She must have left him after that first six months in Lucknow, because of a natural antipathy to the country — and when she condescended to come out again for a winter he met the different lady he thinks about. With little hard lines around the mouth and common conventional habits of thought, full of subservience to his official superiors, and perfectly uninterested in him except as the source of supplies. But I don't know why I should *want* her to be so disagreeable."

As a matter of fact, Mrs. Innes, traveling at the moment with the mails from London to Bombay, was hastening to present to Miss Anderson features astonishingly different.

CHAPTER III

THE lady guests at Peliti's — Mrs. Jack Owen and the rest — were giving a tea in the hotel pavilion. They had the band, the wife of the Commander-in-Chief, the governess from Viceregal Lodge and one little Viceregal girl, three A.D.C.'s, one member of Council, and the Archdeacon. These were the main features, moving among a hundred or so of people more miscellaneous, who, like the ladies at Peliti's, had come up out of the seething Plains to the Paradise of the summer capital. The Pavilion overhung the Mall; looking down one could see the coming and going of leisurely Government peons in scarlet and gold, Cashmiri venders of great bales of embroideries and skins, big-turbaned Pahari[1] horse-dealers, chaffering in groups, and here and there a mounted Secretary-sahib[2] trotting to the Club. Beyond, the hills dipped blue and bluer to the plains, and against them hung a single waving yellow laburnum,[3] a note of imagination. Madeline Anderson was looking at it when Mrs. Mickie and Mrs. Gammidge came up with an affectionate observation upon the cut of her skirt, after which Mrs. Mickie harked back to what they had been talking about before.

"She's straight enough now, I suppose," this lady said.

"She goes down. But she gives people a good deal of latitude for speculation."

"Who is this?" asked Madeline. "I ask for information, to keep out of her way. I find I am developing the most shocking curiosity. I must be in a position to check it."

The ladies exchanged hardly perceptible glances. Then Mrs. Gammidge said, "Mrs. Innes," and looked as if, for the moment, at any rate, she would withhold further judgment.

"But you mustn't avoid the poor lady," put in Mrs. Mickie, "simply because of her past. It wouldn't be fair. Besides —— "

"Her past?" Madeline made one little effort to look indifferent, and then let the question leap up in her.

---

1 Pahari: an inhabitant of the lower ranges of the Himalayas. OED
2 Secretary-sahib: sahib was a respectful title used by Indians in addressing an Englishman or other European. OED
3 laburnum: small tree with yellow flowers.

"My dear," said Mrs. Gammidge, with brief impatience, "he married her in Cairo, and she was — dancing there. Case of chivalry, I believe, though there are different versions. Awful row in the regiment — he had to take a year's leave. Then he succeeded to the command, and the Twenty-third were ordered out here. She came with him to Lucknow — and made slaves of every one of them. They'll swear to you now that she was staying at Shepheard's with an invalid mother when he met her. And now she's accepted like everybody else; and that's all there is about it."

"There's nothing in that," said Madeline, determinedly, "to prove that she wasn't — respectable."

"N—no. Of course not," and again the eye of Mrs. Gammidge met that of Mrs. Mickle.

"Though, you see, love," added the latter lady, "it would have been nicer for his people — they've never spoken to him since — if she had been making her living otherwise in Cairo."

"As a barmaid, for instance," said Madeline, sarcastically.

"As a barmaid, for instance," repeated Mrs. Gammidge, calmly.

"But Simla isn't related to him — Simla doesn't care!" Mrs. Mickie exclaimed. "Everybody will be as polite as possible when she turns up. You'll see. You knew, didn't you, that she was coming out in the Caledonia?"

"No," said Madeline. She looked carefully where she was going to put her coffee-cup, and then she glanced out again at the laburnum hanging over the plains. "I — I am glad to hear it. These separations you take so lightly out here are miserable, tragic."

The other ladies did not exchange glances this time. Miss Anderson's change of tone was too marked for comment which she might have detected.

"Colonel Innes got the telegram this morning. She wired from Brindisi," Mrs. Gammidge said.

"Does he seem pleased?" asked Mrs. Mickie, demurely.

"He said he was afraid she would find it very hot coming up here from Bombay. And, of course, he is worried about a house. When a man has been living for months at the Club —— "

"Of course, poor fellow! I do love that dear old Colonel Innes, though I can't say I know him a bit. He won't take the trouble to be nice to me, but I am perfectly certain he must be the dearest old thing inside of him. Worth any dozen of these little bow-wows that run round after rickshaws," said Mrs. Mickie, with candor.

"I think he's a ridiculous old glacier," Mrs. Gammidge remarked and Mrs. Mickie looked at Madeline and said, "Slap her!"

"What for?" asked Miss Anderson, with composure. "I dare say he is — occasionally. It isn't a bad thing to be, I should think, in Indian temperatures."

"I guess you got it that time, dear lady," said Mrs. Mickie to Mrs. Gammidge, as Madeline slipped toward the door.

"Meant to be cross, did she? How silly of her! If she gives her little heart away like that often, people will begin to make remarks."

"The worst of that girl is," Mrs. Mickie continued, "that you never can depend upon her. For days together she'll be just as giddy and jolly as anybody and then suddenly she'll give you a nasty superior bit of ice down the back of your neck like that. I've got her coming to tea to-morrow afternoon," Mrs. Mickie added, with sudden gloom, "and little Lord Billy and all that set are coming. They'll throw buns at each other — I know they will. What, in Heaven's name, made me ask her?"

"Oh, she'll have recovered by then. You must make allowance for the shock we gave her, poor dear. Consider how you would feel if Lady Wordley suddenly appeared upon the scene, and demanded devotion from Sir Frank."

"She wouldn't get it," Mrs. Mickie dimpled candidly. "Frank always loses his heart and his conscience at the same time. But you don't suppose there's anything serious in this affair? Pure pretty platonics, I should call it."

Mrs. Gammidge lifted her eyebrows. "I dare say that is what they imagine it. Well, they're never in the same room for two minutes without being aware of it, and their absorption when they get in a corner — I saw her keep the Viceroy waiting, the other night after dinner, while Colonel Innes finished a sentence. And then she was annoyed at the interruption. Here's Kitty Vesey, lookin' *such* a dog! Hellow, Kitty! where did you get that hat, where did you get that tile?[1] But that wasn't the color of your hair last week, Kitty!"

"Don't feel any kind of a dog" — Mrs. Vesey's pout, though becoming, was genuine. "I'm in a perfectly furious rage, my dears, and I'm going home to cry, just as soon as I've had an ice. What do you think — they won't let me have Val for Captain Wynne's part in The Outcast Pearl — they say he's been tried before, and he's a stick. Did you ever hear of such brutes? They want me to act with Major Dalton, and he's *much* too old for the part."

---

1 tile: a hat. OED

"Kitten," said Mrs. Mickie, with conviction, "Valentine Drake on the stage would be fatal to your affection for him."

"I don't care, I won't act with anybody else — I'll throw up the part. Haven't I got to make love to the man? How am I to play up to such an unkissable-looking animal as Major Dalton? I shall *certainly* throw up the part."

"Don't do anything rash, Kitty. If you do, they'll probably offer it to me, and I warn you I won't give it back to you."

"Oh, refuse it, like a dear! I am dying to put them in a hole. It's jealousy, that's what it is. Good-by, Mrs. Jack, I've had a lovely time. Val and I have been explaining our affection to the Archdeacon, and he says it's perfectly innocent. We're going to get him to put it on paper to produce when Jimmy sues for a divorce, aren't we, Val?"

"You're not going?" said Mrs. Jack Owen.

"Oh, yes, I must. But I've enjoyed myself awfully, and so had everybody I've been talking to. I say, Mickie, dear — about to-morrow afternoon — I suppose I may bring Val?"

"Oh, dear, yes," Mrs. Mickie replied. "But you must let me hold his hand."

"I don't know which of you is the most ridiculous," Mrs. Owen remarked; "I shall write to both your husbands this very night," but as the group shifted and left her alone with Mrs. Gammidge, she said she didn't know whether Mrs. Vesey would be quite so chirpy three weeks hence. "When Mrs. Innes comes out," she added in explanation; "oh, yes, Valentine Drake is quite her property. My own idea is that Kitty won't be in it."

Where the road past Peliti's dips to the Mall Madeline met Horace Innes. When she appeared in her rickshaw he dismounted, and gave the reins to his syce.[1] She saw in his eyes the look of a person who has been all day lapsing into meditation, and rousing himself from it. "You are very late," she said as he came up.

"Oh, I'm not going; at least, you are just coming away, aren't you? I think it is too late. I'll turn back with you."

"Do," she said, and looked at his capable, sensitive hand as he laid it on the side of her little carriage. Miss Anderson had not the accomplishment of palm-reading, but she took general manual impressions. She had observed Colonel Innes's hand before, but it

---

1 syce: groom. OED

had never offered itself so intimately to her inspection. That, perhaps, was why the conviction seemed new to her, as she thought "He is admirable — and it is all there."

When they got to the level Mall he kept his hold, which was a perfectly natural and proper thing for him to do, walking alongside; but she still looked at it.

"I have heard your good news," she said, smiling congratulation at him.

"My good news? Oh, about my wife, of course. Yes, she ought to be here by the end of the month. I thought of writing to tell you when the telegram came, and then I — didn't. The files drove it out of my head, I fancy."

"Heavy day?"

"Yes," he said, absently. They went along together in an intimacy of silence, and Madeline was quite aware of the effort with which she said:

"I shall look forward to meeting Mrs. Innes."

It was plain that his smile was perfunctory, but he put it on with creditable alacrity.

"She will be delighted. My wife is a clever woman," he went on, "very bright and attractive. She keeps people very well amused."

"She must be a great success in India, then."

"I think she is liked. She has a tremendous fund of humor and spirits. A fellow feels terribly dull beside her sometimes."

Madeline cast a quick glance at him, but he was only occupied to find other matters with which he might commend his wife.

"She is very fond of animals," he said, "and she sings and plays well — really extremely well."

"That must be charming," murmured Madeline, privately iterating, "He doesn't mean to damn her — he doesn't mean to damn her." "Have you a photograph of her?"

"Quantities of them," he said, with simplicity.

"You have never shown me one. But how could you?" she added in haste; "a photograph is always about the size of a door nowadays. It is simply impossible to keep one's friends and relations in a pocketbook as one used to do."

They might have stopped there, but some demon of persistence drove Madeline on. She besought help from her imagination; she was not for the moment honest. It was an impulse — an equivocal impulse — born doubtless of the equivocal situation, and it ended badly.

"She will bring something of the spring out to you," said Madeline — "the spring in England. How many years is it since you have seen it? There will be a breath of the cowslips about her, and in her eyes the soft wet of the English sky. Oh, you will be very glad to see her." The girl was well aware of her insincerity, but only dimly of her cruelty. She was drawn on by something stronger than her sense of honesty and humanity, a determination to see, to know, that swept these things away.

Innes's hand tightened on the rickshaw, and he made at first no answer. Then he said:

"She has been staying in town, you know."

There was just a quiver of Madeline's eyelid; it said nothing of the natural rapacity behind. This man's testimony was coming out in throes, and yet — it must be said — again she probed.

"Then she will put you in touch again," she cried; "you will remember when you see her all the vigor of great issues and the fascination of great personalities. For a little while, anyway, after she comes, you will be in a world — far away from here — where people talk and think and live."

He looked at her in wonder, not understanding, as indeed how could he?

"Why," he said, "you speak of what *you* have done"; and before the truth of this she cast down her eyes and turned a hot, deep red, and had nothing to say.

"No," he said, "my wife is not like that."

He walked along in absorption, from which he roused himself with resentment in his voice.

"I can not leave such a fabric of illusion in your mind. It irritates me that it should be there — about anybody belonging to me. My wife is not in the least what you imagine her. She has her virtues, but she is — like the rest. I can not hope that you will take to her, and she won't like you either — we never care about the same people. And we shall see nothing of you — nothing. I can hardly believe that I am saying this of my own wife, but — I wish that she had stayed in England."

"Mrs. Mickie!" cried Madeline to a passing rickshaw, "what are you rushing on like that for? Just go quietly and peaceably along with us, please, and tell us what Mrs. Vesey decided to do about her part in The Outcast Pearl. I'm dining out to-night — I must know." And Mrs. Mickie was kind enough to accompany them all the rest of the way.

Miss Anderson dined out, and preferred to suppose that she had no time to think until she was on her way home along the empty road round Jakko at eleven o'clock that night. Then it pleased her to get out of her rickshaw and walk. There was an opulent moon, the vast hills curving down to the plains were all gray and silvery, and the deodars overhead fretted the road with dramatic shadows. About her hung the great stillness in a mighty loneliness in which little Simla is set, and it freed her from what had happened, so that she could look at it and cry out. She actually did speak, pausing in the little pavilion on the road where the nurse-maids gather in the daytime, but very low, so that her words fell round her even in that silence, and hardly a deodar was aware. "I will not go now," she said. "I will stay and realize that he is another woman's husband. That should cure me if anything will — to see him surrounded by the commonplaces of married life, that kind of married life. I will stay till she comes and a fortnight after. Besides, I want to see her — I want to see how far she comes short." She was silent for a moment, and the moonlight played upon her smile of quiet triumph. "He cares too," she said; "he cares too, but he doesn't know it, and I promise you one thing, Madeline Anderson, you won't help him to find it out. And in five weeks I will go away and leave my love where I found it — on a mountain-top in the middle of Asia!"

CHAPTER IV

MADELINE did her best to make certain changes delicately, imperceptibly, so that Innes would not, above all things, be perplexed into seeking for their reason. The walks and rides came to a vague conclusion, and Miss Anderson no longer kept the Viceroy or anybody else waiting, while Innes finished what he had to say to her in public, since his opportunities for talking to her seemed to become gradually more and more like everybody else's. So long as she had been mistress of herself she was indifferent to the very tolerant and good-natured gossip of the hill capital; but as soon as she found her citadel undermined, the lightest kind of comment became a contingency unbearable. In arranging to make it impossible, she was really over-considerate and over-careful. Her soldier never thought of analyzing his bad luck or searching for motive in it. To him the combinations of circumstances that seemed always to deprive him of former pleasures were simply among the things that might happen. Grieving, she left him under that impression for the sake of its expediency, and tried to make it by being more than ever agreeable on the occasions when he came and demanded a cup of tea, and would not be denied. After all, she consoled herself, no situation was improved by being turned too suddenly upside down.

She did not wholly withdraw his privilege of taking counsel with her, and he continued to go away freshened and calmed, leaving her to toss little sad reflections into the fire, and tremulously wonder whether the jewel of her love had flashed ever so little behind her eyes. They both saw it a conspicuous thing that as those three weeks went on, neither he nor she alluded even remotely to Mrs. Innes, but the fact remained, and they allowed it to remain.

Nevertheless, Madeline knew precisely when that lady was expected, and as she sauntered in the bazaar one morning, and heard Innes's steps and voice behind her, her mind became one acute surmise as to whether he could possibly postpone the announcement any longer. But he immediately made it plain that this was his business in stopping to speak to her. "Good morning," he said, and then, "My wife comes to-morrow." He had not told her a bit of personal news, he had made her an official communication, as briefly as it could be done, and he would have raised his hat and gone on without more words if Madeline had not thwarted him. "What a stupidity for him to be haunted by afterward!" was the essence of the thought that visited her; and she put out a detaining hand.

"Really! By the Bombay mail, I suppose — no, an hour or so late; private tongas are always as much as that behind the mail."

"About eleven, I fancy. You — you are not inclined for a canter round Summer Hill before breakfast?"

"I am terrified of Summer Hill. The Turk always misbehaves there. Yesterday he got one leg well over the khud[1] — I *was* thankful he had four. Tell me, are you all ready for Mrs. Innes — everything in the house? Is there anything I can do?"

"Oh, thanks very much! I don't think so. The house isn't ready, as a matter of fact, but two or three people have offered to put us up for a day or so until it is. I've left it open till my wife comes, as I dare say she has already arranged to go to somebody. What are you buying? Country tobacco, upon my word! For your men? That's subversive of all discipline!"

The lines on his face relaxed; he looked at her with fond recognition of another delightful thing in her.

"You give sugar-cane to your horses," she declared; "why shouldn't I give tobacco to mine? Good-by; I hope Mrs. Innes will like 'Two Gables.' There are roses waiting for her in the garden, at all events."

"Are there?" he said. "I didn't notice. Good-by, then."

He went on to his office thinking of the roses, and that they were in his garden, and that Madeline had seen them there. He thought that if they were good roses — in fact, any kind of roses — they should be taken care of, and he asked a Deputy Assistant Inspector-General of Ordnance whether he knew of a gardener that was worth anything.

"Most of them are mere coolies," said Colonel Innes, "and I've got some roses in this little place I've taken that I want to look after."

Next day Madeline took Brookes, and The Amazing Marriage, and a lunch-basket, and went out to Mashobra, where the deodars shadow hardly any scandal at all, and the Snows come, with perceptible confidence, a little nearer.

---

1 khud: a deep ravine or chasm; a precipitous cleft or descent in a hill-side. OED

"They almost step," she said to Brookes, looking at them, "out of the realm of the imagination."

Brookes said that they did indeed, and hoped that she hadn't by any chance forgotten the mustard.

"The wind is keen off the glaciers over there — anybody would think of a condiment," Miss Anderson remarked in deprecation, and to this Brookes made no response. It was a liberty she often felt compelled to take.

The Snows appealed to Madeline even more than did Carintha, Countess of Fleetwood, to whose fortunes she gave long pauses while she looked across their summits at renunciation, and fancied her spirit made strong and equal to its task. She was glad of their sanctuary; she did not know where she should find such another. Perhaps the spectacle was more than ever sublime in its alternative to the one she had come away to postpone the sight of; at all events it drove the reunion of the Inneses from her mind several times for five minutes together, during which she thought of Horace by himself, and went over, by way of preparation for her departure, all that had come and gone between them. There had been luminous moments, especially as they irradiated him, and she dwelt on these. There was no reason why she should not preserve in London or in New York a careful memory of them.

So the lights were twinkling all up and down and round about Simla when she cantered back to it and it was late when she started for the Worsleys, where she was dining. One little lighted house looked much like another perched on the mountain-side, and the wooden board painted "Branksome Hall, Maj.-Gen. T.P. Worsley, R.E.," nailed to the most conspicuous tree from the main road, was invisible in the darkness. Madeline arrived in consequence at the wrong dinner-party, and was acclaimed and redirected with much gaiety, which gave her a further agreeable impression of the insouciance of Simla, but made her later still at the Worsleys. So that half the people were already seated when she at last appeared, and her hostess had just time to cry, "My dear, we thought the langurs[1] must have eaten you! Captain Gordon, you are not to be abandoned after all. You know Miss Anderson?" when she found herself before her soup.

---

1 langurs: long-tailed monkeys. OED

Captain Gordon heard her account of herself with complacence, and declared, wiping his mustache, that a similar experience had befallen him only a fortnight before.

"Did you ever hear the story of that absent-minded chap, Sir James Jackson, who went to the *right* dinner-party by mistake?" he asked, "and apologized like mad, by Jove! and insisted he couldn't stay. The people nearly had to tie him down in his — " Captain Gordon stopped, arrested by his companion's sudden and complete inattention.

"I see a lady," interrupted Madeline, with odd distinctness, "curiously like somebody I have known before." Her eyes convinced themselves, and then refused to be convinced of the inconceivable fact that they were resting on Violet Prendergast. It was at first too amazing, too amazing only. Then an old forgotten feeling rose in her bosom; the hand on the stem of her wine-glass grew tense. The sensation fell away; she remembered her emancipation, the years arose and reassured her during which Violet Prendergast, living or dead, had been to her of absolutely no importance. Yet there was a little aroused tremor in her voice as she went on, "She is on the General's right — he must have taken her in. Can you see from where you are sitting?"

"These narrow oval tables are a nuisance that way, aren't they? You don't know who you're dining with till the end of the function. Oh! I see — that's Mrs. Innes, just out, and fresh as paint, isn't she? The Colonel" — Captain Gordon craned his head again — "is sitting fourth from me on this side."

"Mrs. Innes! Really!" said Madeline. "Then — then of course I must be mistaken."

She removed her eyes almost stealthily from the other woman's face and fixed them on the pattern of the table-cloth. Her brain guided her clearly through the tumult of her perception, and no emotion could be observed in the smiling attention which she gave to Captain Gordon's account of the afternoon's tandem racing; but there was a furious beating in her breast, and she thought she could never draw a breath long enough to control it. It helped her that there was food to swallow, wine to drink, and Captain Gordon to listen to; and under cover of these things she gradually, consciously, prepared herself for the shock of encounter which should be conclusive. Presently she leaned a little forward and let her glance, in which no outsider could see the steady recognition, rest upon the lady on the General's right, until that person's agreeable blue eyes wandered down the table and met it. Perhaps Madeline's own eyelids fluttered a little as she saw the sudden stricture in the face that received her message, and the grimace with which it uttered, pallid with apprehension, its response to a pleasantry of General Worsley's. She was not consummate in her self-control, but she was able at all events to send the glance traveling prettily on with a little casual smile for an intervening friend, and bring it back to her dinner-roll without mischief. It did not adventure again; she knew, and she set herself to hold her knowledge, to look at it and understand it, while the mechanical part of her made up its mind about the entrées, and sympathized with Captain Gordon on his hard luck in having three ponies laid up at once. She did not look again, although she felt the watching of the other woman, and was quite aware of the moment at which Mrs. Innes allowed herself the reprieve of believing that at the Worsley's dinner-party at least there would be no scandal. The belief had its reflex action, doing something to calm her. How could there be — scandal — she asked herself, and dismissed with relief the denunciations which crowded vague but insistent in her brain. Even then she had not grasped the salient points of the situation; she was too much occupied with its irony as it affected her personally; her impressions circled steadily round the word "twice" and the unimaginable coincidence. Her resentment filled her, and her indignation was like a clear flame behind her smiling face. Robbed twice, once in New York and — oh! preposterous — the second time in Simla! Robbed of the same thing by the same hand! She perceived in the shock of it only a monstrous fatality, a ludicrously wicked chance. This may have been due to the necessity of listening to Captain Gordon.

At all events it was only as she passed Colonel Innes on her way to the drawing-room and saw ahead of her the very modish receding back of Mrs. Innes that she realized other things — crime and freedom.

It was the reversion of power; it brought her a great exultation. She sat down under it in a corner, hoping to be left alone, with a white face and shining eyes. Power and opportunity and purpose — righteous purpose!

The circumstances had come to her in a flash; she brought them up again steadily and scrutinized them. The case was absolutely clear. Frank Prendergast had been dead just seven months. Colonel Innes imagined himself married four years. Violet Prendergast was a bigamist, and Horace Innes had no wife.

That was the marvelous transcendent fact; that was what lifted her and carried her on great pulsing waves that rolled beyond the walls of the little fripperied[1] drawing-room and its collection of low-necked women, out into her life, which had not these boundaries. She lived again in a possible world. There was no stone wall between herself and joy.

The old Mussulman[2] butler who offered her coffee looked at her with aroused curiosity — here was certainly a memsahib[3] under the favor of God — and as she stirred it, the shadow that Violet Prendergast had thrown upon her life faded out of her mind in the light that was there. Then she looked up and met that lady's vivid blue eyes. Mrs. Innes's color had not returned, but there was a recklessness in the lines of her mouth, in the way she held her chin, expressing that she had been reflecting on old scores, and anticipated the worst. Meeting this vigilance Miss Anderson experienced a slight recoil. Her happiness, she realized, had been brought to her in the hands of ugly circumstance.

"And so melodramatic," she told herself. "It is really almost vulgar. In a story I should have no patience with it." But she went on stirring her coffee with a little uncontrollable smile.

A moment later she had to contemplate the circumstance that her hostess was addressing her. Mrs. Innes wished to be introduced. Mrs. Innes, incarnate, conscious sensation, was smiling at her, saying that she must know so great a friend of her husband's. He made so few friends, and she was so grateful to anybody who was good to him. Eyes and voice tolerably in rein, aware of the situation at every point, she had a meretricious daring; and it occurred to Madeline, looking at her, that she was after all a fairly competent second-class adventuress. She would not refuse the cue. It would make so little difference.

"On the contrary, I am tremendously indebted to Colonel Innes. He has been so very kind about ponies and jhampanies[4] and things. Simla is full of pitfalls for a stranger, don't you think?" And Miss Anderson, unclosing her fan, turned her reposeful head a little in the direction of three married schoolgirls voluble on her left.

---

1 fripperied: full of knick-knacks. OED
2 Mussulman: a Muslim.
3 memsahib: a respectful designation for a European married woman in India. OED
4 jhampanies: a jhampan is an enclosed chair, carried by four men, used in the hill country of India; jhampanies refers to the bearers of the jhampan. OED

"Not when you get to know the language. You must learn the language; it's indispensable. But of course it depends on how long you mean to stay."

"I think I will learn the language," said Madeline.

"But General Worsley told me you were leaving Simla in a fortnight."

"Oh no. My plans are very indefinite; but I shall stay much longer than that."

"It is Miss Anderson, isn't it? — Miss Madeline Anderson, of New York — no, Brooklyn?"

Madeline looked at her. "Did not the General say so?" she said.

"Yes, he did. But one likes to make quite sure."

"I can understand that."

Mrs. Innes leaned forward with one elbow on her knee.

It was not a graceful attitude, but it gave the casual air to the conversation which was desirable.

"What are you going to do?" she said.

"My plans are as indefinite as possible, really," Madeline returned. "I may spend the cold weather in Calcutta, or go into camp with the Dovedells — I should like that."

"Mrs. Innes," cried the nearest schoolgirl, "we are coming tomorrow to see all the lovely things in your boxes, may we?"

"Do, duckies. But mind, no copying of them by durzies[1] in the veranda. They're all Paris things — Coulter's — and you know he doesn't copy well, does he? Oh, dear! here are the men — they always come too soon, don't they? So glad to have had even a little chat, Miss Anderson. I'll come and see you to-morrow. You know newcomers in India always make the first calls. I shall find you at home, sha'n't I?"

"By all means," Madeline said.

Mrs. Innes crossed the room, crying out that the heat was perfectly absurd for Simla, it must be cooler outside; and as Captain Valentine Drake followed her into the semi-darkness of the veranda, the three married schoolgirls looked at each other and smiled.

"Don't be naughty," said Captain Gordon, leaning over the sofa from behind. "They're very dear friends, and they've been separated for two years."

---

1 durzies: a durzi is an Indian tailor. OED

Madeline heard this as plainly as they did. She noted disdainfully how it all fell in.

"How absent you are to-night!" Horace Innes exclaimed, when Miss Anderson had asked him a trivial question for the third time. "Hush!" she said. "Mrs. Scallepa is going to sing"; and as Mrs. Scallepa sang she let her eyes play over him with a light in them so tender, that once catching it he felt a sudden answering throb, and looked again; but after that her eyes were on the floor.

"We are staying here," he said, a quarter of an hour later, as he saw her into her rickshaw; "and I think I must see you to your quarters. It's very dark, and there is an ugly little slip half-way between this and the Mall."

He ran up-stairs to get his coat and stick, and a white face like an apparition suddenly hung itself on the edge of Madeline's rickshaw-hood.

"Don't tell him to-night," it said, hoarsely.

"Are you ready, Colonel Innes? Then good night, everybody," cried Madeline.

She was not at all sure that she would not tell Horace Innes "to-night."

CHAPTER V

"MY wife," said Colonel Innes, "is looking extremely well."

"She seems so, indeed," Madeline replied.

"She is delighted with 'Two Gables.' Likes it better, she says, than any other house we could have got."

"What a good thing!"

"It was a record trip for the Caledonia, thirteen days from Brindisi to Bombay. Was she telling you about the voyage?"

"No," said Madeline, impatiently, "she didn't mention it. How shall I tell the men to put down the hood, please? A rickshaw is detestable with the hood up — stifling! Thanks. I beg your pardon. The Caledonia made a good run?"

"Thirteen days. Wonderful weather, of course, which was luck for Violet. She is an atrocious sailor."

Madeline fancied she heard repose and reassurance in his voice. Her thought cried, "It is not so bad as he expected!" We can not be surprised that she failed to see in herself the alleviation of that first evening.

"She has brought quantities of things for the house with her," Innes went on, "as well as three dachshund puppies," and he laughed. "Wouldn't you like one? What can we do with three — and the terrier, and Brutus?"

"Oh, thank you, no."

How could he laugh? How could he speak pleasantly of these intimate details of his bondage? How could he conceive that she would accept ——

"Already she has arranged four dinner-parties! It will be a relief not to have to think of that sort of thing — to be able to leave it to her."

"Mrs. Innes must have great energy. To drive all the way up from Kalka by noon and appear at a dinner-party at night — wonderful!"

"Oh, great energy," Horace said.

"She will take you everywhere — to all the functions. She will insist on your duty to society."

Madeline felt that she must get him somehow back into his slough of despond. His freedom paralyzed her. And he returned with a pathetic change of tone.

"I suppose there is no alternative. Violet is very good about being willing to go alone, or with somebody else; but I never think it quite fair on one's wife to impose on her the necessity of going about with other men."

"Mrs. Worsley introduced us after dinner," said Madeline.

She kept disparagement out of her mind, but he could not help perceiving aloofness.

"Yes?"

The monosyllable told her sensitive ear that while he admitted her consideration in going on with the subject, he was willing to recognize that there was no more to say, and have done with it. She gathered up her scruples and repugnances in a firm grasp. She would not let him throw his own shadow, as an effectual obstacle, between himself and liberty.

"I am going to ask you something," she said; "it might come naturally enough from another man with whom your friendship was as candid as it is with me; but there is an awkwardness in it from a woman. You must believe I have a good reason. Will you tell me about your first meeting with Mrs. Innes, when — when you became engaged?"

She knew she was daring a good deal; but when a man's prison is to be brought down about his ears, one might as well begin, she thought, at the foundation.

For a moment Innes did not speak, and then his words came slowly.

"I find it difficult," he said, "to answer you. How can it matter — it is impossible. I suppose you have heard some story, and it is like you to want to be in a position to negative it. Ignore it instead. She has very successfully championed herself. Believe nothing to her disadvantage that may be said about that — that time. I was pleased to marry her, and she was pleased to marry me. But for God's sake don't let us talk about it!"

As he spoke Madeline saw the vivid clearness of the situation grow blurred and confused. It was as if her point of view had suddenly changed and her eyes failed her. Her eager impulse had beat less and less strongly from the Worsley's door; now it seemed to shrink away in fetters. Her eyes filled with vaguely resentful tears, which sprang, if she could have traced them, from the fact that the man she loved was loyal to his own mistake, and the formless premonition that he might continue to be. She contorted her lip to keep her emotion back, and deliberately turned away from a matter in which she was not mistress, and which contained ugly possibilities of buffeting. She would wait a little; and though consideration for Violet Prendergast had nothing to do with it, she would not tell him to-night.

"I am sorry," she said; and, after a moment, "Did I tell you that I have changed my plans?"

"You are not going so soon?" She took all the comfort there was in his eagerness.

"I am not going at all for the present. I have abandoned my intentions and my dates. I mean to drift for a little while. I have been too — too conscientious."

"Are you quite serious — do you mean it?"

"Indeed I do."

"And in less than a fortnight you will not go out of one's life. You will stay on — you summer day! It's hard to believe in luck like that. I sent a poor devil of a sepoy[1] a reprieve last week — one knows now how he must have felt about it."

"Does it make all that difference?" Madeline asked, softly.

"It makes a difference," he answered, controlling his words, "that I am glad you can not conceive, since that would mean that your life has been as barren as mine." He seemed to refrain from saying more, and then he added, "You must be careful when you plant your friendship that you mean it to stay, and blossom. It will not come easily up by the roots, and it will leave an ugly hole."

He was helping her out of her rickshaw, and as they followed the servant who carried her wraps the few yards to the door, she left her hand lightly on his arm. It was the seal, he thought, of her unwritten bond that there should be no uprooting of the single flower he cherished; and he went back almost buoyantly because of it to the woman who had been sitting in the sackcloth and ashes of misfortune, turning over the expedients for which his step might make occasion.

By the time the monkeys began to scramble about the roof in the early creeping of the dawn among the deodars, Madeline had groped her way to a tolerably clear conception of what might happen. The impeding circumstance everywhere, it must be acknowledged, was Frederick Prendergast's coffin. The case, had convict No. 1596 been still alive and working out his debt to society, would have been transcendentally simple, she told herself. Even a convict has a right — a prospective right — to his wife, and no honest man should be compelled to retain a criminal's property. This was an odd reflection, perhaps, to be made by Madeline Anderson, but the situation as a whole might be described as curious. And there was no doubt about the coffin.

---

1 sepoy: an Indian soldier under British rule. OED

CHAPTER VI

THE veranda of which Miss Anderson's little sitting-room claimed its section hung over the road, and it seemed to her that she heard the sound of Mrs. Innes's arrival about ten minutes after breakfast. On the contrary, she had spent two whole hours contemplating, with very fixed attention, first the domestic circumstances of Colonel Horace Innes and their possible development, and then, with a pang of profoundest acknowledgment, the moral qualities which he would bring to bear upon them. She was further from knowing what course she personally intended to pursue than ever, when she heard the wheels roll up underneath; and she had worked herself into a state of sufficient detachment from the whole problem to reflect upon the absurdity of a bigamist rattling forth to discuss her probable ruin in the fanciful gaiety of a rickshaw. The circumstance had its value though; it lightened all responsibility for the lady concerned. As Madeline heard her jump out and give pronounced orders for the securing of an accompanying dachshund, it did not seem to matter so particularly what became of Violet Prendergast.

Mrs. Innes's footsteps came briskly along the veranda. Madeline noted that there was no lagging. "Number seven," she said aloud; as she passed other doors, "Number eight — number nine! Ah! there you are." The door was open. "I wouldn't let them bring up my card for fear of some mistake. How do you do? Now please don't get up — you look so comfortable with your book. What is it? Oh, yes, of course, *that*. People were talking about it a good deal when I left London, but I haven't read it. Is it good?"

"I like it," said Madeline. She half rose as Mrs. Innes entered; but as the lady did not seem to miss the ceremony of greeting, she was glad to sink back in her chair.

"And how do you like Simla? Charming in many ways, isn't it? A little too flippant, I always say — rather *too* much champagne and silliness. But awfully bracing."

"The Snows are magnificent," Madeline said, "when you can see them. And there's a lot of good work done here."

"Aren't they divine? I did nothing, absolutely nothing, my first season but paint them. And the shops — they're not bad, are they, for the size of the place? Though to-day, upon my soul, there doesn't seem to be a yard of white spotted veiling among them."

"That is annoying," said Madeline, "if you want spotted veiling."

"Isn't it? Well" — Mrs. Innes took a deep breath — "you *didn't* tell him last night?"

"N—no," said Madeline, with deliberation.

"I *was* grateful. I knew I could rely upon you not to. It would have been too cruel when we had only just been reunited — dear Horace would have had to sleep in the —— "

"Pray —— "

"Well, Horace is the soul of honor. Is your ayah[1] in there?" Mrs. Innes nodded toward the bedroom door. "You can not imagine what long ears she has."

"I have no ayah. There is only Brookes"; and as that excellent woman passed through the room with a towel over her arm, Madeline said, "You can go now, Brookes, and see about that alpaca. Take the rickshaw; it looks very threatening."

"Maid! You *are* a swell! There are only four genuine maids in Simla that I know of — the rest are really nurse-girls. What a comfort she must be! *The* luxury of all others that I long for; but, alas! army pay, you know. I did once bring a dear thing out with me from Nice — you should have seen Horace's face."

"I couldn't very well go about quite alone; it would be uncomfortable."

"Except that you Americans are so perfectly independent."

"On the contrary. If I could order about a servant the way an Englishwoman does —— "

"Say you are not going to tell him! I've got such a lot of other calls to make," exclaimed Mrs. Innes. "Dear Lady Bloomfield won't understand it if I don't call to-day, especially after the baby. What people in that position want with more babies I can not comprehend. Of course you haven't noticed it, but a baby is such a shock to Simla."

"Don't let me keep you," Madeline said, rising.

"But you haven't promised. Do promise, Miss Anderson. You gain nothing by telling him, except your revenge; and I should think by this time you would have forgiven me for taking Frederick away from you. He didn't turn out so well! You can't still bear me malice over that convict in Sing Sing."

"For his sake, poor fellow, I might."

"Coming along I said to myself, 'She *can* score off me badly, but surely she doesn't want to so much as all that.' Besides, I really only

---

1 ayah: an Indian nurse or maidservant. OED

took your leavings, you know. You threw poor Fred Prendergast over."

"I am not prepared to discuss that," Madeline said, at no pains to smooth the curve out of her lip.

"Then I thought, 'Perhaps — you never can tell with people — she will think it her *duty* to make a fuss.'"

"That is a possible point of view."

"I know. You think I'm an imposter on society and I ought to be exposed, and I suppose you could shut every door in Simla against me if you liked. But you are a friend of my husband's, Miss Anderson. You would not turn his whole married life into a scandal and ruin his career?"

"Ruin his career?"

"Of course. Government is awfully particular. It mayn't be his fault in the least, but no man is likely to get any big position with a cloud over his domestic affairs. Horace would resign, naturally."

"Or take long leave," Mrs. Innes added to herself, but she did not give Madeline this alternative. A line or two of nervous irritation marked themselves about her eyes, and her color had faded. Her hat was less becoming than it had been, and she had pulled a button off her glove.

"Besides," she went on quickly, "it isn't as if you could do any good, you know. The harm was done once for all when I let him think he'd married me. I thought then — well, I had to take it or leave it — and every week I expected to hear of Frederick's death. Then I mean to tell Horace myself, and have the ceremony over again. He couldn't refuse. And all these years it's been like living on a volcano, in the fear of meeting New York people. Out here there never are any, but in England I dye my hair, and alter my complexion."

"Why did you change your mind," Madeline asked, "about telling Colonel Innes?"

"I haven't! Why should I change my mind? For my own protection, I mean to get things put straight instantly — when the time comes."

"When the times," Madeline repeated; and her eyes, as she fixed them on Mrs. Innes, were suddenly so lightened with a new idea that she dropped the lids over them as she waited for the answer.

"When poor Frederick does pass away," Mrs. Innes said, with an air of observing the proprieties. "When they put him in prison it was a matter of months, the doctors said. That was one reason why

I went abroad. I couldn't bear to stay there and see him dying by inches, poor fellow."

"Couldn't you?"

"Oh, I couldn't. And the idea of the hard labor made me *sick*. But it seems to have improved his health, and now — there is no telling! I sometimes believe he will live out his sentence. Should you think that possible in the case of a man with half a lung?"

"I have no knowledge of pulmonary disease," Madeline said. She forced the words from her lips and carefully looked away, taking this second key to the situation mechanically, and for a moment groping with it.

"What arrangement did you make to be informed about — about him?" she asked, and instantly regretted having gone so perilously near provoking a direct question.

"I subscribe to the New York World. I used to see lots of things in it — about the shock the news of my death gave him —— "

A flash of hysterical amusement shot into Mrs. Innes's eyes, and she questioned Madeline's face to see whether it responded to her humor. Then she put her own features straight behind her handkerchief and went on.

"And about his failing health, and then about his being so much better. But nothing now for ages."

"Did the World tell you," asked Miss Anderson, with sudden interest, "that Mr. Prendergast came into a considerable fortune before — about two years ago?"

Mrs. Innes's face turned suddenly blank. "How much?" she exclaimed.

"About five hundred thousand dollars, I believe. Left him by a cousin. Then you didn't know?"

"That must have been Gordon Prendergast — the engineer!" Mrs. Innes said, with excitement. "Fancy that! Leaving money to a relation in Sing Sing! Hadn't altered his will, I suppose. Who could possibly," and her face fell visibly, "have foreseen such a thing?"

"No one, I think," said Madeline, through a little edged smile. "On that point you will hardly be criticized."

Mrs. Innes, with clasped hands, was sunk in thought. She raised her eyes with a conviction in them which she evidently felt to be pathetic.

"After all," she said, "there is something in what the padres say about our reaping the reward of our misdeeds in this world — some of us, anyway. If I had stayed in New York —— "

"Yes?" said Madeline. "I shall wake up presently," she reflected, "and find that I have been dreaming melodrama." But that was a fantastic underscoring of her experience. She knew very well she was making it.

Mrs. Innes, again wrapped in astonished contemplation, did not reply. Then she jumped to her feet with a gesture that cast fortunes back into the lap of fate.

"One thing is certain," she said; "I can't do anything *now*, can I?"

Madeline laid hold of silence and made armor with it. At all events, she must have time to think.

"I decline to advise you," she said, and she spoke with a barely perceptible movement of her lips only. The rest of her face was stone.

"How unkind and unforgiving you are! Most people would think the loss of a hundred thousand pounds about punishment enough for what I have done. You don't seem to see it. But on top of that you won't refuse to promise not to tell Horace?"

"I will not bind myself in any way whatever."

"Not even when you know that the moment I hear of the — death I intend to — to ——— "

"Make an honest man of him? Not even when I know that."

"Do you want me to go down on my knees to you?"

Madeline glanced at the flowered fabric involved and said, "I wouldn't, I think."

"And this is to hang over me the whole season? I shall enjoy nothing — absolutely *nothing*." The blue eyes were suddenly eclipsed by angry tears, which the advent of a servant with cards checked as suddenly.

"Good-by, then, dear," cried Mrs. Innes, as if in response to the advancing rustle of skirts in the veranda. "So glad to have found you at home. Dear me, has Trilby made her way up — and I gave such particular orders! Oh, you *naughty* dog!"

CHAPTER VII

FROM the complication that surged round Miss Anderson's waking hours one point emerged, and gave her a perch for congratulation. That was the determination she has shown in refusing to let Frederick Prendergast leave her his money, or any part of it.

It has been said that he had outlived her tenderness, if not her care, and this fact, which she never found it necessary to communicate to poor Frederick himself, naturally made his desire in the matter sharply distasteful. She was even unaware of the disposition he had made of his ironical fortune, a reflection which brought her thankfulness that there was something she did not know. "If I had let him do it," she thought, "I should have felt compelled to tell her everything, instantly. And think of discussing it with her!" This was quite a fortnight later, and Mrs. Innes still occupied her remarkable position only in her own mind and Madeline's, still knowing herself the wife of 1596 and of 1596 only, and still unaware that 1596 was in his grave. Simla had gone on with its dances and dinners and gymkhanas quite as if no crucial experience were hanging over the heads of three of the people one met "everywhere," and the three people continued to be met everywhere, although only one of them was unconscious. The women tried to avoid each other without accenting it, exchanging light words only as occasion demanded, but they were not clever enough for Mrs. Gammidge and Mrs. Mickie, who went about saying that Mrs. Innes's treatment of Madeline Anderson was as ridiculous as it was inexplicable. "Did you ever know her to be jealous of anybody before?" demanded Mrs. Mickie, to which Mrs. Gammidge responded, with her customary humor, that the Colonel had never, in the memory of the oldest inhabitant, been known to give her occasion.

"Well," declared Mrs. Mickie, "if friendships — *unsentimental* friendships — between men and women are not understood in Simla, I'd like to be told what is understood."

Between them they gave Madeline a noble support, for which — although she did not particularly require it, and they did not venture to offer it in so many words — she was grateful. A breath of public criticism from any point of view would have blown over the toppling structure she was defending against her conscience. The siege was severe and obstinate, with an undermining conviction ever at work that in the end she would yield; in the end she would go away, at least as far as Bombay or Calcutta, and from there send to Mrs. Innes the news of her liberation. It would not be necessary, after all, or even excusable, to tell Horace. His wife would do that quickly enough — at least, she had said she would. If she didn't — well, if she didn't nothing would be possible but another letter, giving *him* the simple facts, she, Madeline, carefully out of the way of his path of duty — at all events, at Calcutta or Bombay. But there was no danger that Mrs. Innes would lose the advantage of confession, of throwing herself on his generosity — and at this point Madeline usually felt her defenses against her better nature considerably strengthened, and the date of her sacrifice grow vague again.

Meanwhile, she was astonished to observe that, in spite of her threat to the contrary, Mrs. Innes appeared to be enjoying herself particularly well. Madeline had frequent occasion for private comment on the advantages of a temperament that could find satisfaction in dancing through whole programs at the very door, so to speak, of the criminal courts; and it can not be denied that this capacity of Mrs. Innes's went far to increase the vacillation with which Miss Anderson considered her duty toward that lady. If she had shown traces of a single hour of genuine suffering, there would have been an end to Madeline's hesitation. But beyond an occasional watchful glance at conversations in which she might be figuring dramatically, and upon which she instantly turned her back as soon as she was perceived, Mrs. Innes gave no sign even of preoccupation. If she had bad half-hours, they occurred between the teas and tennises, the picnics, riding-parties, luncheons, and other entertainments, at which you could always count upon meeting her; and in that case they must have been short. She looked extremely well, and her admirable frocks gave an accent even to "Birthday" functions at Viceregal Lodge, which were quite hopelessly general. If any one could have compelled a revelation of her mind, I think it would have transpired that her anxieties about Capt. Valentine Drake and Mrs. Vesey gave her no leisure for lesser ones. These for a few days had been keen and indignant — Captain Drake had so far forgotten himself as to ride with Mrs. Vesey twice since Mrs. Innes's arrival — and any display of poverty of spirit was naturally impossible under the circumstances. The moment was a critical one; Captain Drake seemed inclined to place her in the category of old, unexacting friends — ladies who looked on and smiled, content to give him tea on rainy days, and call him by his Christian name, with perhaps the privilege of a tapping finger on his shoulder, and an occasional order about a rickshaw. Mrs. Violet was not an introspective person, or she might have discovered here that the most stable part of her self-respect was her *exigence*[1] with Captain Drake. She found out quickly enough, however, that she did not mean to discard it. She threw herself, therefore — her fine shoulders and arms, her pretty clothes, her hilarity, her complexion, her eye-lashes, and all that appertained to her — into the critical task of making other men believe, at Captain Drake's expense, that they were quite as fond of her as he was. Mrs. Vesey took opposite measures, and the Club laid bets on the result.

The Club was not prepossessed by Captain Drake. He said too little and he implied too much. He had magnificent shoulders, which he bent a great deal over secluded sofas, and a very languid interest in matters over which ordinary men were enthusiastic. He seemed to believe that if he smiled all the way across his face, he would damage a conventionality. His clothes were unexceptionable, and he always did the right thing, though bored by the necessity. He was good-looking in an ugly way, which gave him an air of restrained capacity for melodrama, and made women think him interesting. Somebody with a knack of disparagement said that he was too much expressed. It rather added to his unpopularity that he was a man whom women usually took with preposterous seriousness — all but Kitty Vesey, who charmed and held him by her outrageous liberties. When Mrs. Vesey chaffed him, he felt picturesque. He was also aware of inspiring entertainment for the lookers-on, with the feeling at such times that he, too, was an amused spectator. This was, of course, their public attitude. In private there was sentiment, and they talked about the tyranny of society, or delivered themselves of ideas suggested by works of fiction which everybody simply *had* to read.

For a week Mrs. Innes looked on, apparently indifferent, rather apparently not observing; and an Assistant Secretary in the Home Department began to fancy that his patience in teaching the three dachshund puppies tricks was really appreciated. He was an on-coming Assistant Secretary, with other conspicuous parts, and hitherto his time had been too valuable to spend upon ladies' dachshunds. Mrs. Innes had selected him well. There came an evening when, at a dance at the Lieutenant-Governor's, Mrs. Innes was so absorbed in what the Assistant Secretary was saying to her, as she

---

1 *exigence:* exactingness.

passed on his arm, that she did not see Captain Drake in the corridor at all, although he had carefully broken an engagement to walk with Kitty Vesey that very afternoon, as the beginning of the gradual and painless reform in her direction. His unrewarded virtue rose up and surprised him with the distinctness of its resentment; and while his expression was successfully amused, his shoulders and the back of his neck, as well as the hand on his mustache, spoke of the discipline which promised to be efficient. Reflection assured him that discipline was after all deserved, and a quarter of an hour later found him wagging his tail, so to speak, over Mrs. Innes's program in a corner pleasantly isolated. The other chair was occupied by the Assistant Secretary. Captain Drake represented an interruption, and was obliged to take a step toward the nearest lamp to read the card. Three dances were rather ostentatiously left, and Drake initialed them all. He brought back the card with a bow, which spoke of dignity under bitter usage, together with the inflexible intention of courteous self-control, and turned away.

"Oh, if you please, Captain Drake — let me see what you've done. All those? But ——— "

"Isn't it after eleven, Mrs. Innes?" asked the Assistant Secretary, with a timid smile. He was enjoying himself, but he had a respect for vested interests, and those of Captain Drake were so well known that he felt a little like a buccaneer.

"Dear me, so it is!" Mrs. Innes glanced at one of her bracelets. "Then, Captain Drake, I'm sorry" — she carefully crossed out the three "V.D.'s" — "I promised all the dances I had left after ten to Mr. Holmcroft. Most of the others I gave away at the gymkhana — really. Why weren't you there? That Persian tutor again! I'm afraid you are working too hard. And what did the Rani[1] do, Mr. Holmcroft? It's like the Arabian Nights, only with real jewels ——— "

"Oh, I say, Holmcroft, this is too much luck, you know. Regular sweepstakes, by Jove!" And Captain Drake lingered on the fringe of the situation.

"Perhaps I have been greedy," said the Assistant Secretary, deprecatingly. "I'll ——— "

"Not in the very least! That is," exclaimed Mrs. Violet, pouting, "if *I'm* to be considered. We'll sit out all but the waltzes, and you shall tell me official secrets about the Rani. She put us up once, she's a delicious old thing. Gave us string beds to sleep on and gold plate to

1 Rani: a raja's wife or widow; a Hindu queen. OED

eat from, and swore about every other word. She had been investing in Government paper, and it had dropped three points. 'Just my damn luck!' she said. Wasn't it exquisite? Captain Drake —— "

"Mrs. Innes —— "

"I don't want to be rude, but you're a dreadful embarrassment. Mr. Holmcroft won't tell you official secrets!"

"If she would only behave!" thought Madeline, looking on, "I would tell her — indeed I would — at once."

Colonel Innes detached himself from a group of men in mess dress as she appeared with the Worsleys, and let himself drift with the tide that brought them always together.

"You are looking tired — ill," she said, seriously, as they sought the unconfessed solace of each other's eyes. "Last night it was the Commander-in-Chief's, and the night before the dance at Peliti's. And again to-night. And you are not like those of us who can rest next morning — you have always your heavy office work!" She spoke with indignant, tender reproach, and he gave himself up to hearing it. "You will have to take leave and go away," she insisted, foolishly.

"Leave! Good heavens, no! I wish all our fellows were as fit as I am. And —— "

"Yes?" she said.

"Don't pity me, dear friend. I don't think it's good for me. The world really uses me very well."

"Then it's all right, I suppose," Madeline said, with sudden depression.

"Of course it is. You are dining with us on the eighth?"

"I'm afraid not, I'm engaged."

"Engaged again? Don't you *want* to break bread in my house, Miss Anderson?" She was silent, and he insisted, "Tell me," he said.

She gave him instead a kind, mysterious smile.

"I will explain to you what I feel about that some day," she said; "some day soon. I can't accept Mrs. Innes's invitation for the eighth, but — but Brookes and I are going to take tea with the fakir's monkeys on the top of Jakko to-morrow afternoon."

"Anybody else, or only Brookes?"

"Only Brookes." And she thought she had abandoned coquetry!

"Then may I come?"

"Indeed you may."

"I really don't know," reflected Madeline, as she caught another glimpse of Mrs. Innes vigorously dancing the reel opposite little Lord Billy in his Highland uniform, with her hands on her flowered-satin hips, "that I am behaving very well myself."

CHAPTER VIII

HORACE INNES looked round his wife's drawing-room as if he were making an inventory of it, carefully giving each article its value, which happened, however, to have nothing to do with rupees. Madeline Anderson had been saying something the day before about the intimacy and accuracy with which people's walls expressed them, and though the commonplace was not new to him, this was the first time it had ever led him to scan his wife's. What he saw may be imagined, but his only distinct reflection was that he had no idea that she had been photographed so variously or had so many friends who wore resplendent Staff uniforms. The relation of cheapness in porcelain ornaments to the lady's individuality was beyond him, and he could not analyze his feelings of sitting in the midst of her poverty of spirit. Indeed, thinking of his ordinary unsusceptibility to such things, he told himself sharply that he was adding an affectation of discomfort to the others that he had to bear; and that if Madeline had not given him the idea it would never have entered his mind. The less, he mused, that one had to with finicking[1] feelings in this world the better. They were well enough for people who were tolerably conditioned in essentials — he preferred this vagueness, even with himself, in connection with his marriage — otherwise they added pricks. Besides he had that other matter to think of.

He thought of the other matter with such obvious irritation that the butler coming in to say that the "English water"[2] was finished, and how many dozen should he order, put a chair in its place instead, closed the door softly again, and went away. It was not good for the dignity of butlers to ask questions of any sort with a look of that kind under the eyebrows of the sahib. The matter was not serious, Colonel Innes told himself, but he would prefer by comparison to deal with matters that were serious. He knew Simla well enough to attach no overwhelming importance to things said about women at the Club, where the broadest charity prevailed underneath, and the idle comment of the moment had an intrinsic value as a distraction rather than a reflective one as a criticism.

---

1 finicking: refined, dainty, fastidious OED
2 the "English water": soda-water.

This consideration, however, was more philosophical in connection with other men's wives. He found very little in it to palliate what he had overheard, submerged in the Times of India, that afternoon. And to put an edge on it, the thing had been said by one of his own juniors. Luckily the boy had left the room without discovering who was behind the Times of India. Innes felt that he should be grateful for having been spared the exigency of defending his wife against a flippant word to which she had very probably laid herself open. He was very angry, and it is perhaps not surprising that he did not pause to consider how far his anger was due to the humiliating necessity of speaking to her about it. She was coming at last though; she was in the hall. He would get it over quickly.

"Good-by!" said Mrs. Innes at the door. "No, I can't possibly let you come in to tea. I don't know how you have the conscience after drinking three cups at Mrs. Mickie's, where I had no business to take you! To-morrow? Oh, all right, if you want to *very* badly. But I won't promise you strawberries — they're nearly all gone."

There was the sound of a departing pony's trot, and Mrs. Innes came into the drawing-room.

"Good heavens, Horace! what are you sitting there for like a — like a ghost? Why didn't you make a noise or something, and why aren't you at office? I can't tell you how you startled me."

"It is early," Colonel Innes said. "We are neither of us in the house, as a rule, at this hour."

"Coincidence!" Violet turned a cool, searching glance on her husband, and held herself ready. "I came home early because I want to alter the lace on my yellow bodice for to-night. It's too disgusting as it is. But I was rather glad to get away from Mrs. Mickie's lot. So rowdy!"

"And I came because I had a special reason for wanting to speak to you."

Mrs. Violet's lips parted, and her breath, in spite of herself, came a little faster.

"As we are dining out to-night, I thought that if I didn't catch you now I might not have another opportunity — till to-morrow morning."

"And it's always a pity to spoil one's breakfast. I can tell from your manner, *mon ami*, it's something disagreeable. What have I been and gone and done?"

She was dancing, poor thing, in her little vulgar way, on hot iron. But her eyes kept their inconsistent coolness.

"I heard something to-day which you are not in the way of hearing. You have — probably — no conception that it could be said."

"Then she has been telling other people. *Absolutely* the worst thing she could do!" Mrs. Innes exclaimed privately, sitting unmoved, her face a little too expectant.

"You won't be prepared for it — you may be shocked and hurt by it. Indeed, I think there is no need to repeat it to you. But I must put you on your guard. Men are coarser, you know, than women; they are apt to put their own interpretation —— "

"What is it?"

There was a physical gasp, a sharpness in her voice that brought Innes's eyes from the floor to her face.

"I am sorry," he said, "but — don't overestimate it, don't let it worry you. It was simply a very impertinent — a very disagreeable reference to you and Mr. Holmcroft, I think, in connection with the Dovedells' picnic. It was a particularly silly thing as well, and I am sure no one would attach any importance to it, but it was said openly at the Club, and —— "

"Who said it?" Mrs. Innes demanded.

A flood of color rushed over her face. Horace marked that she blushed.

"I don't know whether I ought to tell you, Violet. It certainly was not meant for your ears."

"If I'm not to know who said it, I don't see why I should pay any attention to it. Mere idle rumor —— "

Innes bit his lip.

"Captain Gordon said it," he replied.

"Bobby Gordon! *Do* tell me what he said! I'm dying to know. Was he very disagreeable? I *did* give his dance away on Thursday night."

Innes looked at her with the curious distrust which she often inspired in him. He had a feeling that he would like to put her out of the room into a place by herself, and keep her there.

"I won't repeat what he said." Colonel Innes took up the Saturday Review.

"Oh, do, Horace! I particularly want to know."

Innes said nothing.

"Horace! Was it — was it anything about Mr. Holmcroft being my Secretariat baa-lamb?"

"If you adorn your guess with a little profanity," said Innes, acidly, "you won't be far wrong."

Mrs. Violet burst into a peal of laughter.

"Why, you old goose!" she articulated, behind her handkerchief; "he said that to *me*."

Innes laid down the Saturday Review.

"To you!" he repeated; "Gordon said it to you!"

"Rather!" Mrs. Violet was still mirthful. "I'm not sure that he didn't call poor little Holmie something worse than that. It's the purest jealousy on his part — nothing to make a fuss about."

The fourth skin which enables so many of us to be callous to all but the relative meaning of careless phrases had not been given to Innes, and her words fell upon his bare sense of propriety.

"Jealous," he said, "of a married woman? I find that difficult to understand."

Violet's face straightened out.

"Don't be absurd, Horace. These boys are always jealous of somebody or other — it's the occupation of their lives! I really don't see how one can prevent it."

"It seems to me that a self-respecting woman should see how. Your point of view in these matters is incomprehensible."

"Perhaps," Violet was driven by righteous anger to say, "you find Miss Anderson's easier to understand."

Colonel Innes's face took its regimental disciplinary look, and, though his eyes were aroused, his words were quiet with repression.

"I see no reason to discuss Miss Anderson with you," he said. "She has nothing to do with what we are talking about."

"Oh, don't you, really! Hasn't she, indeed! I take it you are trying to make me believe that compromising things are said about Mr. Holmcroft and me at the Club. Well, I advise you to keep your ears open a little more, and listen to the things said about you and Madeline Anderson there. But I don't suppose you would be in such a hurry to repeat them to *her*."

Innes turned very white, and the rigidity of his face gave place to a heavy dismay. His look was that of a man upon whom misfortune had fallen out of a clear sky. For an instant he stared at his wife. When he spoke his voice was altered.

"For God's sake!" he said, "let us have done with this pitiful wrangling. I dare say you can take care of yourself; at all events, I only meant to warn you. But now you must tell me exactly what you mean by this that you have said — this — about —— "

"The fat's in the fire," was Mrs. Innes's reflection.

"Certainly, I'll tell you —— "

"Don't shout, please!"

"I mean simply that all Simla is talking about your affair with Miss Anderson. You may imagine that because you are fifteen years older than she is things won't be thought of, but they are, and I hear it's been spoken about at Viceregal Lodge. I *know* Lady Bloomfield has noticed it, for she herself mentioned it to me. I told her I hadn't the slightest objection, and neither have I, but there's an old proverb about people in glass houses. What are you going to do?"

Colonel Innes's expression was certainly alarming, and he had made a step toward her that had menace in it.

"I am going out," he said, and turned and left her to her triumph.

CHAPTER IX

SHE — Violet — had unspeakably vulgarized it, but it must be true — it must be, to some extent, true. She may even have lied about it, but the truth was there, fundamentally, in the mere fact that it had been suggested to her imagination. Madeline's name, which had come to be for him an epitome of what was finest and most valuable, most to be lived for, was dropping from men's lips into a kind of abyss of dishonorable suggestion. There was no way out of it or around it. It was a cloud which encompassed them, suddenly blackening down.

There was nothing that he could do — nothing. Except, yes, of course — that was obvious, as obvious as any other plain duty. Through his selfishness it had a beginning; in spite of his selfishness it should have an end. That went without saying. No more walks or rides. In a conventional way, perhaps — but nothing deliberate, designed — and never alone together. Gossip about flippant married women was bad enough, but that it should concern itself with an unprotected creature like Madeline was monstrous, incredible. He strode fiercely into the road round Jakko, and no little harmless snake, if it had crawled across his path, would have failed to suffer a quick fate under the guidance of his imagination. But there was nothing for him to kill, and he turned upon himself.

The sun went down into the Punjab and left great blue-and-purple hill worlds barring the passage behind him. The deodars sank waist deep into filmy shadow, and the yellow afterlight lay silently among their branches. A pink-haunched monkey lopading[1] across the road with a great show of prudence seemed to have strayed into an unfamiliar country, and the rustling twigs behind him made an episode of sound. The road in perpetual curve between its little stone parapet and the broad flank of the hill rose and fell under the deodars; Innes took its slopes and its steepnesses with even, unslackened stride, aware of no difference, aware of little indeed except the physical necessity of movement, spurred on by a futile instinct that the end of his walk would be the end of his trouble — his amazing, black, menacing trouble. A pony's trot behind him struck through the silence like percussion-caps; all

---

1 lopading: loping (from the verb "to lope").

Jakko seemed to echo with it; and it came nearer — insistent, purposeful — but he was hardly aware of it until the creature pulled up beside him, and Madeline, slipping quickly off, said —

"I'm coming too."

He took off his hat and stared at her. She seemed to represent a climax.

"I'm coming too," she said. "I'm tired of picking flies off the Turk, and he's really unbearable about them to-night. Here, syce." She threw the reins to the man and turned to Innes with a smile of relief. "I would much rather do a walk. Why — you want me to come too, don't you?"

His face was all one negative, and under the unexpectedness of it and the amazement of it her questioning eyes slowly filled with sudden, uncontrollable tears, so that she had to lower them, and look steadily at the hoof-marks in the road while she waited for his answer.

"You know how I feel about seeing you — how glad I always am," he stammered. "But there are reasons ―― "

"Reasons?" she repeated, half audibly.

"I don't know how to tell you. I will write. But let me put you up again ―― "

"I will not," Madeline said, with a sob. "I won't be sent home like a child. I am going to walk, but — but I can quite well go alone." She started forward, and her foot caught in her habit so that she made an awkward stumble and came down on her knee. In rising she stumbled again, and his quick arm was necessary. Looking down at her, he saw that she was crying bitterly. The tension had lasted long, and the snap had come when she least expected it.

"Stop," Innes said, firmly, hardly daring to turn his head and ascertain the blessed fact that they were still alone. "Stop instantly. You shall not go by yourself." He flicked the dust off her habit with his pocket-handkerchief. "Come, please; we will go on together." Her distress seemed to make things simple again. It was as if the cloud that hung over them had melted as she wept, and lifted, and drifted a little further on. For the moment, naturally, nothing mattered except that she should be comforted. As she walked by his side shaken with her effort at self-control, he had to resist the impulse to touch her. His hand tingled to do its part in soothing her, his arm ached to protect her, while he vaguely felt an element of right, of justice, in her tears; they were in a manner his own. What he did was to turn and ask the syce following if he had loosened the Turk's saddle-girths.

"I shall be better — in a moment," Madeline said, and he answered, "Of course"; but they walked on and said nothing more until the road ran out from under the last deodar and round the first bare boulder that marked the beginning of the Ladies' Mile. It lay rolled out before them, the Ladies' Mile, sinuous and gray and empty, along the face of the cliff; they could see from one end of it to the other. It was the bleak side of Jakko; even tonight there was a fresh springing coldness in it blowing over from the hidden snows behind the rims of the nearer hills. Madeline held up her face to it, and gave herself a moment of its grateful discipline.

"I have been as foolish as possible," she said, "as foolish as possible. I have distressed you. Well, I couldn't help it — that is all there is to be said. Now if you will tell me — what is in your mind —what you spoke of writing — I will mount again and go home. It doesn't matter — I know you didn't mean to be unkind." Her lip was trembling again, and he knew it, and dared not look at it.

"How can you ask me to tell you — miserable things!" he exclaimed. "How can I find the words? And I have only just been told — I can hardly myself conceive it —— "

"I am not a child in her teens that my ears should be guarded from miserable things. I have come of age, I have entered into my inheritance of the world's bitterness with the rest. I can listen," Madeline said. "Why not?"

He looked at her with grave tenderness. "You think yourself very old, and very wise about the world," he said; "but you are a woman, and you will be hurt. And when I think that a little ordinary forethought on my part would have protected you, I feel like the criminal I am."

"Don't make too much of it," she said, simply. "I have a presentiment —— "

"I'll tell you," Innes said, slowly; "I won't niggle about it. The people of this place — idiots! — are unable to believe that a man and a woman can be to each other what we are."

"Yes?" said Madeline. She paused beside the parapet and looked down at the indistinct little fields below, and the blurred masses of white wild roses waving midway against the precipice.

"They can not understand that there can be any higher plane of intercourse between us than the one they know. They won't see — they can't see — that the satisfaction we find in being together is of a different nature."

"I see," said Madeline. She had raised her eyes, and they sought the solemn lines of the horizon. She looked as if she saw something infinitely lifted above the pettiness he retailed to her. "So they say — good God, why should I tell you what they say!" It suddenly flashed upon him that the embodiment of it in words would be at once, from him, sacrilegious and ludicrous. It flashed upon him that her natural anger would bring him pain, and if she laughed — it would be as if she struck him. He cast about him dumb and helpless while she kept her invincibly quiet gaze upon the farther hills. She was thinking that this breath of gossip, now that it had blown, was a very slight affair compared with Horace Innes's misery — which he did not seem to understand. Then her soul rose up in her, brushing everything aside, and forgetting, alas! the vow it had once made to her.

"I think I know," she said. "They are indeed foolish. They say that we — love each other. Is not that what they say?"

He looked in amazement into her tender eyes and caught at the little mocking smile about her lips. Suddenly the world grew light about him, the shadows fled away. Somewhere down in the valley, he remembered afterward, a hill-flute made music. When he spoke it was almost in a whisper, lest he should disturb some newly perceived lovely thing that had wings, and might leave him. "Oh, Madeline," he said, "is it true?" She only smiled on in gladness that took no heed of any apprehension, any fear or scruple, and he himself keeping his eyes upon her face, said, "It is true."

So they stood for a little time in silence while she resisted her great opportunity. She resisted it to the end, and presently beckoned to the syce, who came up leading the pony. Innes mounted her mechanically and said, "Is that all right?" as she put her foot in the stirrup, without knowing that he had spoken.

"Good-by," she said; "I am going away — immediately. It will be better. And listen — I have known this for weeks — and I have gone on seeing you. And I hope I am not any more wicked than I feel. Good-by."

"Good-by," he said, taking his hand from the pony's neck, and she rode buoyantly away. He, turning to breast the road again, saw darkness gathering over the end of it, and drawing nearer.

At eleven o'clock next morning Brookes rose from her packing to take a note addressed to her mistress from the hand of a messenger in the Imperial red and gold. It ran:

"DEAR MISS ANDERSON — I write to tell you that I have obtained three weeks' leave, and I am going into the interior to shoot, starting this afternoon. You spoke yesterday of leaving Simla almost immediately. I trust you will not do this, as it would be extremely risky to venture down to the Plains just now. In ten days the rains will have broken, when it will be safe. Pray wait till then.

Yours sincerely,

HORACE INNES."

Involuntarily the letter found its way to Madeline's lips, and remained there until she saw the maid observing her with intelligence.

"Brookes," she said, "I am strongly advised not to start until the rains break. I think, on the whole, that we won't."

"Indeed, miss," returned Brookes, "Mrs. Sergeant Simmons told me that it was courting cholera to go — and nothing short of it. I must say I'm thankful."

CHAPTER X

A WEEK later Colonel Innes had got his leave, and had left Simla for the snow-line by what is facetiously known as "the carriage road to Tibet." Madeline had done as she was bidden, and was waiting for the rains to break. Another day had come without them. To write and tell Innes, to write and tell Violet, to go away and leave the situation as she found it; she had lived and moved and slept and awakened to these alternatives. At the moment she slept.

It was early, very early in the morning. The hills all about seemed still unaware of it, standing in the grayness compact, silent, immutable, as if they slept with their eyes open. Nothing spoke of the oncoming sun, nothing was yet surprised. The hill world lifted itself unconscious in a pale solution of daylight, and only on the sky-line, very far away, it rippled into a cloud. The flimsy town clinging steeply roof above roof to the slope, mounting to the saddle and slipping over on the other side, cut the dawn with innumerable little lines and angles all in one tone like a pencil drawing.

There was no feeling in it, no expression. It had a temporary air in that light, like trampled snow, and even the big Secretariat buildings that raised themselves here and there out of the huddling bazaar looked trivial, childish enterprises in the simple revelation of the morning. A cold silence was abroad, which a crow now and then vainly tried to disturb with a note of tentative enterprise, forced, premature. It announced that the sun would probably rise, but nothing more. In the little dark shops of the wood-carvers an occasional indefinite figure moved, groping among last night's tools, or an old woman in a red sari washed a brass dish over the shallow open drain that ran past her door. At the tonga terminus, below the Mall, a couple of coughing syces, muffled in their blankets, pulled one of these vehicles out of the shed. They pushed it about sleepily, with clumsy futility; nothing else stirred or spoke at all in Simla. Nothing disturbed Miss Anderson asleep in her hotel.

A brown figure in a loin-cloth, with a burden, appeared where the road turned down from the Mall, and then another, and several following. They were coolies, and they carried luggage.

The first to arrive beside the tonga bent and loosed the trunk he brought, which slipped from his back to the ground. The syces looked at him, saying nothing, and he straightened himself against the wall of the hillside, also in silence. It was too early for conversation. Thus did all the others.

When the last portmanteau had been deposited, a khaki-colored heap on the shed floor rose up as a broad-shouldered Punjabi driver, and walked round the luggage, looking at it.

"And you, owls' brethren," he said, with sarcasm, addressing the first coolie, "you have undertaken to carry these matter fifty-eight kos[1] to Kalka, have you?"

"Ná,"[2] replied the coolie, stolidly, and spat.

"How else, then, is it to be taken?" the driver cried, with anger in his argument. "Behold the memsahib has ordered but one tonga, and a fool-thing of an ekka.[3] Here is work for six tongas! What reason is there in this?"

The coolie folded his naked arms, and dug in the dust with an unconcerned toe.

"I, what can I do?" he said. "It is the order of the memsahib."

Ram Singh grunted and said no more. A rickshaw was coming down from the Mall, and the memsahib was in it.

Ten minutes later the ponies stood in their traces under the iron bar, and the lady sat in the tonga behind Ram Singh. Her runners, in uniform, waited beside the empty rickshaw with a puzzled look, at which she laughed, and threw a rupee to the head man.

The luggage was piled and corded on three ekkas behind, and their cross-legged drivers, too, were ready.

"Chellao!"[4] she cried, crisply, and Ram Singh imperturbably lifted the reins. The little procession clanked and jingled along the hillside, always tending down, and broke upon the early gray melancholy with a forced and futile cheerfulness, too early, like everything else. As it passed the last of Simla's little gardens, spread like a pocket-handkerchief on the side of the hill, the lady leaned forward and looked back as if she wished to impress the place upon her memory. Her expression was that of a person going forth without demur into the day's hazards, ready to cope with them, yet there was some regret in the backward look.

"It's a place," she said aloud, "where *everybody* has a good time!"

---

1   kos: miles.
2   Ná: No.
3   ekka: a small one-horse vehicle. OED
4   "*Chellao!*": "Go on!"

Then the Amusement Club went out of sight behind a curve; and she settled herself more comfortably among her cushions, and drew a wrap round her to meet the chill wind of the valley. It was all behind her. The lady looked out as the ponies galloped up to the first changing-place, and, seeing a saddled horse held by a syce, cramped herself a little into one corner to make room. The seat would just hold two.

Ram Singh salaamed,[1] getting down to harness the fresh pair, and a man put his face in at the side of the tonga and took off his hat.

"Are you all right?" he said. His smile was as conscious as his words were casual.

"Quite right. The ayah was silly about coming — didn't want to leave her babies or something — so I had to leave her behind. Everything else is either here or in the ekkas."

"The brute! Never mind — they're not much use in a railway journey. You can pick up another at Bombay. Then I suppose I'd better get in."

"I suppose you better had. Unless you think of walking," she laughed, and he took the place beside her.

Ram Singh again unquestioningly took up the reins.

"Nobody else going down?"

"Not another soul. We might just as well have started together."

"Oh, well, we couldn't tell. Beastly awkward if there had been anybody."

"Yes," she said, but thrust up her under lip indifferently.

Then, with the effect of turning to the business in hand, she bent her eyes upon him understandingly and smiled in frank reference to something that had not been mentioned. "It's good-by to Simla, isn't it?" she said. He smiled in response and put his hand upon her firm, round arm, possessively, and they began to talk.

Ram Singh, all unaware, kept his horses at their steady clanking downward gallop, and Simla, clinging to the hilltops, was brushed by the first rays of the sun.

It came a gloriously clear morning; early riders round Jakko saw the real India lying beyond the outer ranges, flat and blue and pictured with forests and rivers like a map. The plains were pretty and interesting in this aspect, but nobody found them very attractive. Sensitive people liked it better when the heat mist veiled them and

---

1   salaamed: bowed.

it was possible to look abroad without a sudden painful thought of contrasting temperatures. We may suppose that the inhabitants of Paradise sometimes grieve over their luck. Even Madeline Anderson, whose heart knew no constriction at the remembrance of brother or husband at some cruel point in the blue expanse, had come to turn her head more willingly the other way, toward the hills rolling up to the snows, being a woman who suffered by proxy, and by observation, and by Rudyard Kipling.

On this particular morning, however, she had not elected to do either. She slept late instead, and was glad to sleep. I might as well say at once that on the night before she had made up her mind, had brought herself to the point, and had written to Mrs. Innes, at "Two Gables," all the facts, in so far as she was acquainted with them, connected with Frederick Prendergast's death. She was very much ashamed of herself, poor girl; she was aware that, through her postponement, Horace Innes would now see his problem in all its bitterness, make his choice with his eyes wide open. If it had only happened before he knew — anything about her!

She charged herself with having deliberately waited, and then spent an exhausting hour trying to believe that she had drifted unconsciously to the point of their mutual confession. Whatever the truth was, she did not hesitate to recognize a new voice in her private counsels from that hour, urging her in one way or another to bring matters to an end. It was a strong instinct; looking at the facts, she saw it was the gambler's. When she tried to think of the ethical considerations involved she saw only the chances. The air seemed to throb with them all night; she had to count them finally to get rid of them.

Brookes was up betimes, however, and sent off the letter. It went duly, by Surnoo, to Mrs. Innes at "Two Gables." Madeline woke at seven with a start, and asked if it had gone, then slept again contentedly. So far as she was concerned the thing was finished. The breakfast gong had sounded, and the English mail had arrived before she opened her eyes again upon the day's issues; she gave it her somewhat desultory attention while Brookes did her hair. There was only one scrap of news. Adèle mentioned in a postscript that poor Mr. Prendergast's money was likely to go to a distant relative, it having transpired that he died without leaving a will.

"She is sure, absolutely sure," Madeline mused, "to answer my letter in person. She will be here within an hour. I shall have this to tell her, too. How pleased she will be! She will come into it all, I suppose — if she is allowed. Though she won't be allowed, that is if —" But there speculation began, and Madeline had forbidden herself speculation, if not once and for all, at least many times and for fifteen minutes.

No reasonable purpose would be served by Mrs. Innes's visit, Madeline reflected, as she sat waiting in the little room opening on the veranda; but she would come, of course she would come. She would require the satisfaction of the verbal assurance; she would hope to extract more details; she would want the objectionable gratification of talking it over.

In spite of any assurance, she would believe that Madeline had not told her before in order to make her miserable a little longer than she need be; but, after all, her impression about that did not particularly matter. It couldn't possibly be a pleasant interview, yet Madeline found herself impatient for it.

"Surnoo," she said of her messenger, "must be idling on his way back in the bazaar. I must try to remember to fine him two pice. Surnoo is incorrigible."

She forgot, however, to fine Surnoo. The pad of his bare feet sounded along the veranda almost immediately, and the look in his Pahari eyes was that of expected reproach, and ability to defend himself against it.

He held out two letters at arm's-length, for as he was expected to bring only one there was a fault in this; and all his domestic traditions told him that he might be chastened. One was addressed to Madeline in Mrs. Innes's handwriting; the other, she saw with astonishment, was her own communication to that lady, her own letter returned. Surnoo explained volubly all the way along the veranda, and in the flood of his unknown tongue Madeline caught a sentence or two.

"The memsahib was not," said Surnoo. Clearly he could not deliver a letter to a memsahib who was not. "Therefore," Surnoo continued, "I have brought back your honor's letter, and the other I had from the hand of the memsahib's runner, the runner with one eye, who was on the road to bring it here. More I do not know, but it appears that the memsahib has gone to her father and mother in Belaat,[1] being very sorrowful because the Colonel-sahib has left her to shoot."

"The letter will tell me," Madeline said to herself, fingering it. "Enough, Surnoo."

---

1 Belaat: England.

The man went away, and Madeline closed and locked the door of her sitting-room. The letter would tell her — what? She glanced about her with dissatisfaction, and sought the greater privacy of her bedroom, where also she locked the door and drew the muslin curtain across the window. She laid the letter on the dressing-table and kept her eyes upon it while she unfastened, with trembling hands, the brooch at her neck and the belt at her waist. She did one or two other meaningless things, as if she wanted to gain time, to fortify her nerves even against an exhibition before herself.

Then she sat down with her back toward the light and opened the letter. It had a pink look and a scented air. Even in her beating suspense Madeline held it a little farther away from her, as she unfolded it, and it ran:

"DEAR MISS ANDERSON — What will you say, I wonder, and what will Simla say, when you know that Captain Drake and I have determined to *disregard conventionalities*, and live henceforward only for one another! I am all packed up, and long before this meets your eye we shall have taken the step which society condemns, but which I have a feeling that you, knowing my storm-tossed history, will be broad-minded enough to sympathize with, at least to some extent. That is the reason I am writing to you rather than to any of my own chums, and also of course to have the satisfaction of telling you that I no longer care what you do about letting out the secret of my marriage to Frederick Prendergast. I am now *above and beyond it*. Any way you look at it, I do not see that I am much to blame. As I never have been Colonel Innes's wife there can be no harm in leaving him, though if he had ever been sympathetic, or understood me the *least little bit*, I might have felt bound to him. But he has never been able to evoke the finer parts of my nature, and when this is the case marriage is a mere miserable fleshly failure. You may say, 'Why try it a third time?' — but my union with Val will be different. I have never been fond of the opposite sex — so far as that goes I should have made a very good nun — but for a long time Valentine Drake has been the only man I cared to have come within a mile of me, and lately we have discovered that we are absolutely necessary to each other's existence on the higher plane. I don't care much what Simla thinks, but if you happen to be talking about it to dear Lady Bloomfield, you might just mention this. Val has eight hundred a year of his own, so it is perfectly practicable. Of course, he will send in his papers. *Whatever happens*, Val and I will never bind ourselves in any way. We both think it wrong and enslaving. I have nothing more to add, except that I am depending on you to explain to Simla that I never was Mrs. Innes.

"Yours sincerely,

"VIOLET PRENDERGAST.

"P.S. — I have written to Horace, telling him everything about everything, and sent my letter off to him in the wilds by a runner. If you see him you might try and smooth him down. I don't want him coming after Val with a revolver."

Madeline read this communication through twice. Then quietly and deliberatingly she lay down upon the bed, and drew herself out of the control of her heart by the hard labor of thought. When she rose, she had decided that there were only two things for her to do, and she began at once to do them, continuing her refuge in action. She threw her little rooms open again, and walked methodically round the outer one, collecting the odds and ends of Indian fabrics with which she had garnished it.

As the maid came in, she looked up from folding them.

"I have news, Brookes," she said, "that necessitates my going home at once. No, it is not bad news, but — important. I will go now and see about the tonga. We must start to-morrow morning."

Brookes called Surnoo, and the rickshaw[1] came round.

Madeline looked at her watch.

"The telegraph office," she said; "and as quickly as may be."

As the runners panted over the Mall, up and down and on, Madeline said to herself, "She shall have her chance. She shall choose."

The four reeking Paharis pulled up at the telegraph office, and Madeline sped up the steps. There was a table, with forms printed "Indian Telegraphs," and the usual bottle of thickened ink and pair of rusty pens. She sat down to her intention as if she dared not let it cool; she wrote her message swiftly, she had worded it on the way.

"*To* MRS. INNES,
  Dak Bungalow,   *From* M. ANDERSON,
  Solon.   Simla.

"Frederick Prendergast died on January 7th, at Sing Sing. Your letter considered confidential if you return. Prendergast left no will.

"M. ANDERSON."

---

1 rickshaw: a two-wheeled vehicle drawn by one or more people. OED

"Send this 'urgent,' Babu," she said to the clerk, "and repeat it to the railway station, Kalka. Shall I fill up another form? No? Very well."

At the door she turned and came back.

"It is now eleven o'clock," she said. "The person I am telegraphing to is on her way down to get to-night's train at Kalka. I am hoping to catch her half-way at Solon. Do you think I can?"

"I think so, madam. Oyess! It is the custom to stop at Solon for tiffin. The telegram can arrive there. All urgent telegram going very quick."

"And in any case," said Madeline, "it can not fail to reach her at Kalka?"

"Not possible to fail, madam."

"She will have her chance," she said to herself, on her way to the post-office to order her tonga. And with a little nauseated shudder at the thought of the letter in her pocket, she added, "It is amazing. I should have thought her too good a woman of business!" After which she concentrated her whole attention upon the necessities of departure. Her single immediate apprehension was that Horace Innes might, by some magic of circumstances, be transported back into Simla before she could get out of it. That such a contingency was physically impossible made no difference to her nerves, and to the last Brookes was the hurrying victim of unnecessary promptings.

The little rambling hotel of Kalka, where the railway spreads out over the plains, raises its white-washed shelter under the very walls of the Himalayas. Madeline, just arrived, lay back in a long wicker chair on the veranda, and looked up at them as they mounted green and gray and silent under the beating of the first of the rains. Everywhere was a luxury of silence, the place was steeped in it, drowned in it. A feeding cow flicked an automatic tail under a tree. Near the low mud wall that strolled irresolutely between the house and the hills leaned a bush with a few single pink roses; their petals were floating down under the battering drops. A draggled bee tried to climb to a dry place on a pillar of the veranda. Above all, the hills, immediate, towering, all gray and green, solidly ideal, with phantasies of mist. Everything drippingly soft and silent. Suddenly the venetian blind that hung before the door of a bedroom farther on swayed out before a hand variously ringed to emit a lady in a pink lawn dress with apt embroideries. Madeline's half-closed eyes opened very wide, and for an instant she and the lady, to whom I must once more refer as Mrs. Innes, confronted each other. Then Mrs. Innes's countenance expanded, and she took three or four light steps forward.

"Oh, you dear thing!" she exclaimed. "I thought you were in Simla! Imagine you being here! Do you know you have *saved* me!"

Madeline regarded her in silence, while a pallor spread over her face and lips, and her features grew sharp with a presage of pain.

"Have I?" she stammered. She could not think.

"Indeed you have. I don't know how to be grateful enough to you. Your telegram of yesterday reached me at Solon. We had just sat down to tiffin. Nothing will ever shake my faith in Providence again! My dear, *think* of it — after all I've been through, my darling Val — and one hundred thousand pounds!"

"Well?"

"Well — I stayed behind there last night, and Val came on here and made the necessary arrangements, and —— "

"Yes?"

"And we were married this morning. Good heavens! what's the matter with you! Here — oh, Brookes! Water, salts — anything!"

Brookes, I know, would think that I should dwell at greater length upon Miss Anderson's attack of faintness in Kalka, and the various measures which were resorted to for her succor, but perhaps the feelings and expedients of any really capable lady's-maid under the circumstances may be taken for granted. I feel more seriously called upon to explain that Colonel Horace Innes, shortly after these last events, took two years' furlough to England, during which he made a very interesting tour in the United States with the lady who now bears his name by inalienable right. Captain and Mrs. Valentine Drake are getting the most that is to be had out of Frederick Prendergast's fortune with courage in London and the European capitals, where Mrs. Drake is sometimes mentioned as a lady with a romantic past. They have not returned to Simla, where the situation has never been properly understood. People have always supposed that Mrs. Drake ran away that June morning with her present husband, who must have been tremendously fond of her to have married her "after the divorce." She is also occasionally mentioned in undertones as "the first Mrs. Innes." All of which we know to be quite erroneous, like most scandal.

Mrs. Mickie and Mrs. Gammidge, in retirement, are superintending the education of their children in Bedford, where it is cheap and practical. They converse when they meet about the iniquitous prices of dressmakers and the degeneracy of the kind of cook obtainable in England at eighteen pounds a year. Mrs. Gammidge has grown rather portly and very ritualistic. They seldom speak of Simla, and when they do, if too reminiscent a spark appears in Mrs. Mickie's eye, Mrs. Gammidge changes the subject. Kitty Vesey still fills her dance cards at Viceregal functions, though people do not quote her as they used to, and subalterns imagine themselves vastly witty about her color, which is unimpaired. People often commend her, however, for her good nature to *débutantes*, and it is admitted that she may still ride with credit in "affinity stakes" — and occasionally win them.

THE END

Appendix A: Excerpts from
A Social Departure

[These excerpts chronicle Duncan's trip around the world with her friend Lily Lewis. Here Duncan describes their visit to the same historic sites visited by the characters in *A Mother in India* (the Taj Mahal, etc.), and thus provides us with a good sense of Duncan's own reactions to the places she describes in her short story.]

XXXV

OF that first night we were in Agra, I remember only a strange, fierce, confused picture. It was too late after dinner for any of the guide-book sights, so we took a *ticca-gharri* from the hotel and drove down into the city. On the way, set back somewhere among trees and gardens, we saw suggestions of scattered English bungalows, but these were few and did not obtrude themselves. We found Agra as "native" of India as Tokio had been of Japan. Darkness was settling down over the masses of low-walled houses and narrow streets; but every squalid little open shop, chiefly holding tinselled gew-gaws, sent a flood of light into the road, which was full of people and cattle, and the gaudy little chariots, high, two-wheeled, fantastically painted, the shape of an old woman's poke bonnet, they call *ekkas*. Bullocks were harnessed to them, and wildly gesticulating black figures drove them, swinging long whips and uttering strange cries. The town seemed in a hubbub, the crowd surged in one direction — a mad grotesque crowd of men and women, boys and girls, in white and yellow and crimson scraps of drapery, gold glittering on their arms, silver at their ankles, jewels flashing in their nostrils. They crowded about our *gharri* and stared in; the children and beggars formed close about us demanding backsheesh. We were going with the crowd, and it became so dense that we could not turn. The driver struck out with his whip indiscriminately, and the syce behind used what we imagined to be voluble profanity, which scattered and silenced them for a moment; but immediately they closed in again more importunate than before. Presently we reached the end of the street, where the struggling mass was thickest and the uproar most deafening. Looking out, we saw a star-lit sky and palms waving against it. Under these a façade of duskily lighted houses, latticed and balconied, white and pink and yellow. The excited crowd swayed in front, waving torches, and from its midst into the semi-darkness rose, lofty and grotesque, and in some sort majestic, the head and neck of a camel ridden by two or three natives beating drums. The syce came round to the *gharri* window. "See!" he shouted, "nautch!" He turned the horse so that we saw at one side, on a sort of platform among the trees, two huge and hideous figures, blood red and grinning, for which we knew no better name than idols. Behind these something seemed to be going on. The syce invited us to descend, but we felt several degrees more comfortable in our *gharri* in that multitude. So, as we would not go to the nautch, the nautch came to us. The crowd parted, and a slender girl came through, with slow steps and passes, the drums and conches and flageolets playing with redoubled din and fury. She put her hands on her hips and looked at us. Her face was painted, and there was a charcoal addition to her eyelashes. Her features were delicately cut, and she was draped with much decency and some art; but there was a look of unutterable depravity in her round eyes, bold through their softness. We showed her a rupee and she began to dance for us.

The famous nautch! Orthodocia and I watched it begin with all the qualms and thrills that accompany a deliberate impropriety of behaviour; for many times we had heard of its iniquity, and now to witness it, alone — impromptu! But the qualms and thrills departed, one by one, leaving our consciences reprieved. For her performance was nothing more extraordinary than a succession of wrigglings and contortions, of putting one foot before and the other behind, of crossing her arms on her breast, or locking her fingers above her head. The crowd watched breathlessly, apparently with intense enjoyment, but our sense of the grace of motion was not cultivated to stand more than a very little of it, with the heat and the noise and the smells; and we were glad to escape from the inferno of which the girl with her bangles seemed the central figure and the climax.

We would not go to see the Taj, we decided next morning after breakfast, until the starlight of the early evening with the prospect of the moon at nine o'clock. After a certain point in a trip round the world one grows extremely nice about one's new sensations, most particular as to the circumstances one obtains them under. It is a sort of epicureanism of the imagination. At first one bolts things, as it were. And we knew that the Taj was the crown and glory of India, that all Indian vistas led up to it and melted away in it, that it had been the source of more extravagance of language in the people we had met who were going round the world the other way than anything else the guide-books had provided them with. We felt, therefore, that the Taj demanded a selection of circumstances and some preparation of the emotions. Orthodocia suggested dieting, but I thought it would do to abstain from any violent form of sight-seeing during the day and pass it in a state of anticipation. So we went for a quiet drive to the Fort.

Akbar built the Fort, I find in Orthodocia's note-book — but Baedeker or Murray will tell you the same thing — one of the old conquering Moguls that left their art and religion all over India. He built it nearly three hundred years ago, of red sandstone many feet thick, and made it run half a mile along the high river-bank of the Jumna and a quarter of a mile in toward the town. India, Orthodocia remarks under this head, is not a country of old architectural monuments. It has added no Sphinx to the problems of modern humanity. (I *shall* enjoy telling you about Orthodocia and one we have!) Its peoples, she says, meaning India, builded for their time as a general thing, and the wave of the next century obliterated the traces of the last. So,

> "Akbar's red bulwarks, shutting treasures in
> With league-long ramp of sandstone,"

gather more than their rightful share of interest and colour and feeling, as a survival showing exceptional breadth of conception and power of achievement. I'm not absolutely sure that Orthodocia is right about this; but I'm much obliged to her for the paragraph, which reads well. There is a good deal more of it; but when one is given an inch one doesn't always like to take an ell, and perhaps she will want to print it herself.

But Akbar builded and Victoria occupies. As we drove through the wide space in the tremendous walls where the iron gates used to be, a red-coated "Tommy" lounging on guard at either side stood up very straight and importantly; and inside in an asphalt quadrangle we saw the careful white parallelograms of a British tennis-court. The roads inside the Fort were smooth and hard and wide; the sunlight lying in broad white masses over them and over the tiled roofs and shining domes that Akbar's Mussulman successors had gathered within it. Our driver, with the pertinacity of his kind, stopped half a dozen times at places which he knew all right-minded tourists wished to inspect; but we confused his notions of the desires of the *sahib-lok* by declining to get out, and entirely upset them by sending him off when we reached the heart of the Fort — the scene of the extravagant domesticity of Akbar and Jahan and the rest — and strolling away through the curious old red place by ourselves.

We climbed innumerable shallow steps, glad of both topee and umbrella in the merciless sun, and then we were in a labyrinth of narrow winding passages and wide pillared chambers. A friendly hand painted on the walls pointed the way through for Europeans, or we should probably have been inspecting the household arrangements of Shah Jahan and his family still. It showed us first to the "Dwan-i-Am," that autocrat's Hall of Audience, and we entered a great roofless chamber as big as a London square, rows of pillars with arches between running along three sides of it. The sky shone blue overhead; the sun lay in a blinding square in the middle, lizards ran over the walls. The pillars had been painted in distemper once in curious designs, blue and red and yellow and green; but this early artistic effort had been obscured by a later one. The more modern artist had produced broader effects, one might say. He had a free hand, too, his massing was admirable, and there was no inequality in his treatment. He had stood sublimely on a step-ladder and dipped his brush in that pigment exalted in domestic economy all the world over — whitewash. The local authorities had done it in honour of some visiting dignitary years ago; then the Prince of Wales came, and the British Resident tried to let him see the pattern underneath, but the genius [of] the pail-artist was still more *en évidence* than that of his predecessor. This is a mark of esteem, Orthodocia found out somewhere, still very popular in native India. For any guest of consideration the Rajah will whitewash all over — his house, his stables, his temples, any antiquities on the premises he thinks the stranger may be interested in, his record, his grandmother. It is ennobling, but monotonous in general effect.

We followed the hand, and it showed us into a wide empty raised terrace, columned like the other, looking into the garden, with a great black marble slab in it that once upheld Shah Jahan's golden throne and flashed back the stones that were set therein. Here he must have sat magnificently in his gold-embroidered robes inwrought with jewels, and heard petitions and dispensed justice, and looked upon slaves, and received tribute, and watched the feats of his courtier horsemen, and listened to the laughter of his dark-eyed harem peeping through the *grilles* in the wall above his head. The hand led on, and we found ourselves in a maze of dusty corridors and twisted stairs, with here and there a mysterious windowless cell-like room that suggested what domestic insubordination must have meant in the establishment of Shah Jahan. We went through one of them gingerly enough, for it had been let to a family extremely resentful of intrusion — a thousand or so of Indian wild bees. If they had decided to put their minds to it they could have stung us to death in half an hour, but their attention was entirely occupied with their own affairs.

There seemed to be nobody in the place but an occasional native who followed us furtively in the hope of backsheesh. To such as these Orthodocia would turn with an air of majesty and say imperatively "Jow!" I have not the least idea of the meaning of "Jow!" I don't much think Orthodocia had either, and I am convinced that the natives had not; but usually when she had said it three times they went away.

The old pile was full of surprises. We stepped out once upon an open passage that ran along the top of the wall of the Fort. Little round-pillared balconies jutted out of this, and we sat down on the floor of one of these and looked away across below us at one of the most exquisitely-blended scenes one could find in the world. The sky was shimmering white at the horizon, growing bluer towards its dome. The Jumna slept among its sands and gave back the sky colour with scarcely a ripple. The river-bed lay in its windings — all pale grays and saffron-yellows, flat and wide, and across it came an endless train of slow-moving desultory cattle, that seemed accents of the colour about them, so perfectly the sand-tints were deepened and enriched in their soft dusky bodies. The drivers strolled and gossiped by the way, black-faced at this distance, white-turbaned, crimson-sashed. Along the shore the trees grew thickly, and out of them white domes and towers rose up. Closer below us lay the great ditch of the Fort, then an outer wall; and sheer seventy feet down from our little balcony a tiny enclosed court full of palms and mango trees, and long rank grass, once made beautiful for the pleasaunce of the ladies who sat round their lord where we were sitting then, now abandoned to snakes and lizards, and the little swift green parrots that flew in and out in the sun like straight large-headed arrows about their noisy business.

And all this we saw framed in the red sandstone pillars of the little balcony the Shahs had built with never a thought of us — entering into our part of the inheritance barbarism has handed down to civilisation the world over.

We left it all — the inlaid "Dwan-i-Khas," the bathing-house of mirrors, the chambers with long-necked holes in the walls where the slender-armed ladies of the zenana kept their jewels safely; the whole quaint old place with its naïve grandeur and odd little tender bits of sentiment, feeling a certain gentle regret that did not attach to many scenes more pretentious and splendid. As we traced our way out again by more terraces and steps, we found in the heart of it still another garden, close-walled and impenetrable; and high perched where no tourist foot might profane, we caught a glimpse of the flame spires of the three-domed white marble "Gem Mosque" — "Naginah Musjid" — where the beautiful Persians that ruled the Shahs with love's uncertain sceptre, entered the presence of Allah and swayed dreamily toward Mecca on their prayer carpets, and clasped their little henna-stained red palms in petition that they might bring sons, not daughters, to their lords.

We found a *gharri* to take us back whose driver simply declined to pass the Pearl Mosque. He spoke no English, and we no Hindustani; and though Orthodocia said "Jow!" in her best manner several times, it had not the least effect upon him. He remained entirely unmoved, and so did we. He presented an impassive, impenetrable back to our entreaties; he evidently knew our duty as well as his own, and was not going to have either shirked. So, as it was extremely warm sitting in a *ticca-gharri* in the March sun of the North-West Provinces of India, to say nothing of the heat of the argument, we succumbed. I find in Mr. Murray's valuable "Handbook" several columns of facts and statistics about the "Moti Musjid" — the Pearl Mosque — but none of them seem to aid my memory much. I cannot remember, for instance, that I observed the "trihedral projection" of the gateway, though it must have been there, or that there were fifty-eight pillars with twelve-sided shafts on square bases in the cloisters. But nobody who has ever entered this loveliest of sanctuaries can forget its sweet, cool purity, broad floor, slender pillars, arched colonnades; every inch one's eye can make its own covered with glistening white marble, veined in gray and blue. We walked between long shadowy rows of pillars, under engrailed arches, on a platform raised somewhat above the great square central floor, and bounding it on three sides. Only this colonnade was roofed. The sun slanted dazzling white upon the marble floor and the tank for pious ablutions, and the old sun-dial in the corner, except for which the place would have been utterly empty. We wandered about it with a curious baffling sense of its meaninglessness. Wholly without incident, or sign, or emblem, it represented so high a religious abstraction that the Western eye lost sight of it, and perceived only beauty for the sake of the beautiful. The guide-book told us that "they worshipped in the Western part." From the opposite colonnade we could see three swelling white marble domes above this Western part, fair against the blue, and on the inner side a row of graceful minarets. We crossed the shining floor, the click of our footsteps sounding loud and clear through the emptiness of the place, to see why they worshipped in the Western part; and we found the marble walls of the colonnade to be divided into panels, with flower wreaths sculptured on them in exquisite workmanship. We found at the end three doorways, too, one open, the others filled up with lattices of marble wonderfully cut. Beyond the open door were dusty passages and stairs that hinted so strongly of scorpions that we gave up our search for the Mussulman's religious idea in that direction.

We could not find it anywhere, but the pale, cool loveliness of the mosque itself —

> "That gem
> Of Holy places named the House of Pearl
> Moti-Musjid, where Archangels might pray
> And miss no grace of heaven, no purity!"

was enough to satisfy much deeper ascetic curiosity than possessed our nomad souls.

And so I have come to the end of the chapter before evening fell at the close of the day in Agra, and brought the stars that helped us to see that dream-wonder of the world, the Taj.

XXXVI

It came about this way, as of course you know, that the world has the Taj.

The Taj is a Queen's tomb, the most beautiful tomb of the most beautiful queen that ever, when her queenship crumbled away into the dust of common humanity, needed sepulchring like her subjects. The beauty of the queen lives in the beauty of the tomb, for without the immortalisation of the Taj, Arjamand Banu would have died like other "dark stars" of the Orient, and when her lord, who only knew her face, followed her to another Paradise, her memory would have vanished from the palaces and pleasure grounds he made for her, and none of us perhaps would have known her name. But Shah Jahan, who called this lovely Persian wife of his "Mumtaz-i-Mahal" — "Chosen of the Palace". — exalted her above all the rest in his love while she lived and his grief when she died, and thought her last wish for a tomb that would tell the world of her, when she lay in his arms "that ill day in the camp at Burhanpur," a light thing and easily fulfilled. So the Taj was conceived and begun, in a garden of roses and palms, on the right bank of the Jumna, high above its floods; and the queen was buried in the garden, where the bulbuls and the koils sang over her until it was finished.

From his lonely palace chamber in the Fort, with the blue river winding a mile between, Shah Jahan watched the wonderful white dome swelling and its four guardian towers rising to be the world's memorial of his love; and found more pleasure there than in the soft eyes of all from whom Arjamand had been the "Chosen." For seventeen years he watched it, teaching Arjamand's sons and daughters their mother's immortality, while the marble and the sandstone and the jewels came by toiling men and straining cattle "over a thousand wastes, a hundred hills," to perfect the symmetry and the grandeur and the inner loveliness of this most worshipful work that man has left upon the earth — the Taj. Then Shah Jahan died also, and was buried beside his queen, so that the great tomb tells of them both. Yet when one sees it, it seems eloquent only of her who desired it, and who was so dear a queen that her desire evoked it.

In the sweet, cool starlight that comes like a sudden benediction when the sun is gone in India, we drove to see the Taj. It was a long drive from Agra's one hotel, perched high in midtown, along a dusty, wide, red road that wound through the native bazaars and beyond the Fort, and past the shadowy bungalows where the mem-sahibs ruled. We met patient Indian cattle with their beautiful eyes and intelligent, confiding faces, and gaudy *ekkas* and pariah dogs and water-carriers, and now and then a group of white-draped natives or a trio of British "Tommies," but the drive had not many incidents, and I remember only the coolness and silence of it, and our eagerness. The driver stopped at last beneath some trees by the road-side, and we looked to the left and found ourselves before the high dark archway of the outer court. In a state of mental breathlessness we jumped from the *gharri* and went in. Was that the Taj? — that great majestic semi-dome of sandstone, arched and pillared, and written high on all its arches and pillars in white marble letters with stately script from the Koran — rising between massive walls adorned with graceful cupolas, and standing there before us in that mysterious light like a portal to all the East! For a moment we thought so, and felt the sensation of an ideal turned upside down. But if we could have read the Toghra text it would have said to us, "Enter God's Garden," even as it bade the poet enter who sat "with Sa'di" there, as you have learned; and we would have known that this was only the screen of the Taj and the gate of Arjamand's garden. We could not read the Toghra text, but a dusky figure stole out from some lurking-place beneath, touched its forehead with the palm of its hand, and, pointing inwards, broke the stillness, saying "Sala'am! — The Taj!" Then the figure crept back into the shadows, and we went in together.

After the throbbing heat of the day, after the clattering *ekkas* and the crowded bazaars, we stood in a garden, all softly, tenderly green and full of silence, stretching into filmy darkness everywhere. Ghostly marble paths interlaced under the palms and the pipal trees; the stars could just tell the difference between the red roses and the yellow ones. The day would have shown us aloes and tulip-trees and waxen frangipanni,

> "Sheets of fiery Indian marigolds,
>   Moon-flowers and shell-flowers, crimson panoply
>   Of the silk cottons and soft lilac lights,
>   Where sunbeams sift through bougainvilleas."

But in this sweet half-light we saw only the glamour of the garden, hiding in its arbours, straying across its paths. Rather, perhaps, we felt it, for as we stood there in our places in the long list of those whose feet have entered the portals of Arjamand, we had eyes only for the strange dream-thing that the garden made sanctuary for, rising phantasmal at its further end, beyond the roses and above the palms. The dropping of water came through the odorous air, and at our feet we saw the stars in a still, dark, glistening stretch, broken here and there by lily pads, troubled here and there where the fountain jets played, lying between the wide white marble pavements we stood upon. The pavements clove the garden, and led, the glistening water-tank always between, the roses shadowing over, and lines of dark mourning thuja trees on either side, by a long glimmering vista to the threshold of the dream-thing. We followed it with uncertain, quiet, timid footfalls; we could not be sure that it would suffer itself to be approached, or that a fugitive glance would find it on returning.

We reached wide, shallow steps and climbed them. Then we were on a sandstone platform, "a thousand feet each way," and closer to the phantasy, which curiously remained. So close, we could see that it rested lightly upon a great white marble level, that came down by many steps into the garden — steps that one might ascend, and so learn of a surety that the Taj was real. But for the moment we did not ascend them, preferring there in the sensuous mystery of that starlit Indian place, where was no voice or step but ours, the feeling of trespassing upon some old enchanted ground, that might vanish at any backward wand wave from before our eyes and under our feet.

The great tomb rose before us like a shapen cloud in the pallor of the starlight. It seemed to advance, it seemed to recede, it seemed to stand still. Here and there the pure whiteness of its swelling dome almost broke into a gleam, but never quite. The gleam would have fixed it — given it substance and surface, and it had not these. Whether a creation of the heavens above or the earth beneath, it hung poised between — a wonder unfamiliar to either. The great white dome lifted itself between two lesser domes, among attendant minarets, and the understructure that seemed to grow out of its snowy base to meet and support them, shaped like a square, "the angles shorn," was broken by a lovely lofty Saracenic arch in the middle, and another in each upspringing face. And from every corner of the broad white field it rested on sprang the slenderest pale minaret far towards the stars. Then trees, the bamboos and the palms, and out of the darkness of these the gentle glimmering curves of the shrine-mosques on either side. But no talk of plinths or arches, and no comparison — the world has nothing remotely like it — can make you see the Taj as we saw it there in the silent starlight of Shah Jahan's garden, the fountains rippling quietly in his marble watercourses, a drowsy bird stirring in his grieving thuja trees, the air a dream of perfume from the flowers that Arjamand loved. For the marvel and the spell of it lie over and beyond any conception of architecture. We did not think until afterwards of the beauty of the design, or the skill of the workmen, or the splendour of the material. Nobody does.

"You see it with the heart, before the eyes
Have time to gaze!"

And to that subtler consciousness which receives it the Taj tells
its own untranslatable story of Love and Death, and that strange
brooding infinity, the shadow of whose wings falls over both Love
and Death, which is the soul of the world. One may set down the
majesty, the tenderness, the ideality of the Taj, and there seem to be
no more words for this untold story. But that is because one is not
the poet who sat with Sa'di there. He, with the wisdom of poets,
calls it —

> "A passion and a worship and a faith
> Writ fast in alabaster, so that earth
> Hath nothing anywhere of mortal toil
> So fine wrought, so consummate, so supreme,
> So, beyond praise, Love's loveliest monument
> As what, in Agra, upon Jumna's bank
> Shah Jahan builded for his lady's grave."

Behind us, as we sat there mute with the marvel of it, and behind
the furthest, duskiest palms at the garden's verge, had come a deepening yellow sky-rift; and there presently the slow beauty of the moon
came up. It touched the gold finial of the fair white central dome, it
crept down the curving sides, it reached the lesser domes and tipped
the minarets — downward the sweet revelation spread, lovingly, gra-
ciously, marking the stern desolateness of the thuja trees, leaving pale
flickering lights among the rose thickets. And as it lifted itself wan to
the moon, with all its delicate traceries and inlayings, and bearing high
scrolls of strange characters we knew to mean reverence to Allah and
submission, we saw the Taj as the shrine of a tender human grief. And
we fell to talking of Arjamand and of her Emperor's love.

★　★　★

We sat there a long time, so long that a figure crouched on a
lower step rose and stole up to us, and pointed down one of the
paths and said something which we knew to mean, "The Presence
is there!" thinking that we awaited some sahib who was our escort.
We had no words with which to tell him that we were alone, so he
crept back and watched. And presently, as a quick silent black shadow fell across the path, he started forward again.

"The Presence comes!" he said.

The shadow stopped before us and removed its hands from its pockets. "So it is you two!" the shadow's personality observed, taking off his hat. "I thought you ought to turn up soon, in the ordinary course of things." And Orthodocia said a great deal more than she knew in her little cry, "*Jack!*"

"Yes!" he admitted, and then those extraordinary young people, wholly forgetting the Taj and the palms, and the roses, and the moon, forgetting everything except their two precious selves and the fact that they were profoundly interested in one another, said "How do you do?" and shook hands with all the circumstance that might have been expected of them in Mayfair! It was too utterly absurd, and in contemplating the absurdity of it I did not observe that Mr. Jack Love entirely forgot to shake hands with me till afterward. Orthodocia informed me later that there was nothing at all extraordinary about our meeting him in that particular spot of that particular corner of the North-West Provinces of India (meaning that there was nothing at all extraordinary in *her* meeting him there), that it seemed to her altogether natural and a thing to be expected there of all places, as soon as he appeared; but nobody would have gathered this from the elaborately proper, but somewhat disjointed conversation that followed. And after Orthodocia had inquired tenderly and particularly for the Assiniboian Aunt, and made a few other references equally suitable to the time and place, she was inquired of as to whether she had seen the South-Eastern minaret yet; and they both prayed me to go with them to look at it. Whereupon I told them, with a fine inward scorn, that the Taj was all I wanted to see to-night, thank you, and they went away into the glamour of Arjamand's rose garden together.

Then, I remember, there stole out into the night from a spot in that garden place where the shadows were thickest and the moonlight fairest, a low sweet dropping melody, that fell, and ceased, and throbbingly fell again. It was the Bulbul singing to the Rose. If we may believe the poet he sang in Persian:

> "Sweet, ever sweeter, sweetest Love hath been
> *Shirin, shirintar,* and *shirintarin!*"

And the Rose understood. And it seemed to me, although I was not versed in Persian, that I also understood.

★   ★   ★

"Well?" said I to Orthodocia an hour later, in the privacy of our apartment, inquiringly.

"Well?" she returned, with a transient defiance of my right to interrogate, and an inclination to tears.

"Do you mean to say that he *didn't*?" — for I saw that the situation had to be taken by the horns, and with decision.

"I th — th — think he was *going to*," my friend replied from the depths of her pillow, "but we qua — qu — quarrelled again!"

"Crops this time?" I asked, ironically, "or freight rates, or the duty on binders and reapers?"

"None of them," said my friend, sitting up suddenly, with spirit and indignation. "The tendencies of the age!"

"Which of you disapproved?"

"*He* did! and I think it was *extremely impertinent* of him. A person needn't *say* straight out what he means to make you understand very well! And if he didn't mean the tendency of girls to travel by themselves, why did he say he had been thinking about it ever since he saw us at Corona? And why did he think proper to start round the world the other way to meet us, and help us out of imaginary difficulties, and protect us from imaginary dangers, *pure* imagination —— "

"Did he come for that?" I asked.

"He — he *insinuated* that he did."

"It was a long way to come — for that, Orthodocia," I remarked thoughtfully.

"I know it was!" rather miserably. "Don't you see that's just the *thing* of it! When one knows the motive to be — unobjectionable — one can't resent the — the covert criticism of the act. I defy *you* to do it! I found it simply impossible; so I ignored it! But I *was* angry! So I told him — very politely and blandly, and *quite* ignoring his argument — what a delightful trip we'd had so far, and how kind everybody'd been; and he said yes, he had no doubt of it; and that made me simply *furious*, so I said — not taking the slightest notice of what was in his mind — what a relief it was not to have a man bothering about the luggage labels, and feeling injured because he's kept waiting — which is all Uncle Robert ever did on the Continent; and then I distinctly saw him smile, and he changed the subject. Now, if there *is* an aggravating thing, it's to have one's subject changed that way! And he's at the club, and I know he means to call to-morrow afternoon, and I never told him we had to leave by the midday train to catch the *Oriental* at Bombay, and I *forbid* your doing it, and — well, that's all!"

"I can remember," I said, "a few occasions upon which I would have been — glad of a man."

"So can I!" returned my friend instantly; "but you wouldn't had had me *admit* it!"

"On the whole," I said, "perhaps it's as well that you didn't. It is difficult to say what the result might have been."

I could see very plainly next morning by her eyelids that Orthodocia's stern resolution had dissolved in the night, so I sent a note privately to the club with an intimation of our departure. The bearer came back in half an hour to say that the sahib had gone forth with some other sahibs, and would not be back till two o'clock. So I did not tell Orthodocia that I had violated her commands, and together we went again, in the full glory of the sunlight, to see the Taj. Indeed, in flat disobedience to Murray's "Handbook," we bestowed no thought or care upon Futtehpur Sikri, the deserted city, or Sikandarah with its sculptures, or the tomb of Itimud Dowlah, "Light of the World," but jealously gave all the few hours we had left in Agra to Shah Jahan and Arjamand, grieving only that we could not learn the beauty of the Taj in the Eastern dawning, and under the soft long shadows of the waning day. What we would not see by impotent torch-light that first night in the garden — the interior of the Taj where the cenotaphs are — we saw the next day, entering under the Saracenic arch and standing beneath the wonderful white dome. There we noted how exquisite the marble was, with its delicate veinings of rose and blue, that closed so tenderly far above our heads. How marvellous the many lattices, all wrought in marble, that so refined the Indian sun into a mystery of luminous twilight, falling gravely all about us on the texts from the Koran, and the jasper and the onyx, the crystal and the chalcedony, the jade and the lazulite, that twined in flower-fancies over and around the tomb of Arjamand. So that she

> "Who loved her garden lieth now
>   Wrapped in a garden."

But far most wonderful, most eloquent, most full of sweetest mystery, was the Voice of the Dome, a Voice that took up our lightest word, carried it to the coping-stone, and then sent it down, down, down, exquisitely softened and attuned, till the echo seemed to die away in the tomb, as if it had gone to talk with the queen there. Orthodocia lingered behind here, saying nothing, and as I turned to wait for her just outside the inner portal I heard the sweetest murmurings falling about her. She had evoked them herself, and she did not know I heard, so I shall not tell you the burden of them. But if ever you are in love, she advised me afterward, and want a faithful word about it, go to the Taj and ask Queen Arjamand.

So we gathered a red rose each in the garden, Orthodocia for the rose and I for the sweet sake of my friend, and came away.

★   ★   ★

In the daytime they sell you slabs of marble in the outer court, inlaid in the manner of the cenotaphs, and loquats, yellow and luscious, and pictures of the Emperor and of Mumtaz-i-Mahal, which I shall borrow from Orthodocia to adorn this chapter with. And there are many whose forefathers bowed before Shah Jahan who now demand backsheesh of the pilgrim stranger, with other afflictions, all of which vanish when the stars come out. Therefore I adjure you, when you go to Agra, see the Taj by starlight, but look to it that your visit be upon no occasion of festivity, for I have it upon excellent authority that the Taj is then glorified by magnesium light and — ah, the atrocity! — the *band plays there!*

Appendix B: Excerpts from The Crow's Nest

[Duncan wrote *The Crow's Nest* in Simla while undergoing treatment for tuberculosis. The treatment required her to spend all of her time outdoors (night and day), hence the British title, *On the Other Side of the Latch.* These excerpts provide some interesting and often humorous examples of Duncan's personal experiences and views of life in Simla. Duncan calls her husband Tilgath-Pileser.]

Chapter XIII, 149-62

I have had a morning of domestic details with the Average Woman. I don't quite know whether one ought to write about such things, or whether one ought to draw a veil; I have not yet formed a precise opinion as to the function of the commonplace in matter intended for publication. But surely no one should scorn domestic details, which make our universal background and mainstay of existence. Theories and abstractions serve to adorn it and to give us a notion of ourselves: but we keep them mostly for lectures and sermons, the monthly reviews, the original young man who comes to tea. All would be glad to shine at odd times, but the most luminous demonstration may very probably be based upon a hatred of cold potatoes and a preference for cotton sheets. And of course no one would dare to scorn the average woman; she is the backbone of society. Personally I admire her very humbly, and respect her very truly. For many of us, to become an average woman is an ambition. I think I will go on.

Besides, Thalia interrupted us, and Thalia will always lend herself to a chapter.

The Average Woman is not affectionate but she is solicitous, and there was the consideration of my original situation and my tiresome health. Then she perceived that I had a garden and that it was a pretty garden. I said, indifferently, that people thought so; I knew it was a subject she would not pursue unless she were very much encouraged, and there was no reason at all why she should pursue it; she would always be a visitor in such a place, whereas there were many matters which she could treat with familiar intelligence. I was quite right; she wandered at once into tins of white enamel, where it seemed she had already spent several industrious hours.

We sympathized deeply over the extent to which domestic India was necessarily enamelled, though I saw a look of criticism cross her face when I announced that I hoped one day to be rich enough not to possess a single article painted in that way — not a chair, not a table. I think she considered my declaration too impassioned, but she did not dissent from it. That is a circumstance one notes about the Average Woman: she never dissents from anything. She never will be drawn into an argument. One could make the most wild and whirling statement to her, if one felt inclined, and it is as likely as not that she would say "Yes indeed," or "I think so too," and after a little pause of politeness go on to talk about something else. I can't imagine why one never does feel inclined.

We continued to discuss interior decoration, and I learned that she was preparing a hearth seat for her drawing-room, one of those low square arrangements projecting into the room before the fire, upon which two ladies may sit before dinner and imagine they look picturesque, while the rest of the assembled guests, from whom they quite cut off the cheerful blaze, wonder whether they do. The Average Woman declared that she could no longer live without one.

"As time goes on one notices that fewer and fewer average women can," I observed absently, and hastily added, "I mean, you know, that of course very portly ladies — "

"Oh, I *see*," said she. "No, of course not."

"So long," I went on, pursuing the same train of thought, "as one can sit down readily upon a hearth seat, and especially so long as one can clasp one's knees upon it, one is not even middle-aged. To clasp one's knees is really to hug one's youth."

"I had *such* a pretty one in Calcutta," said the Average Woman. "So cosy it looked. Everybody admired it."

"But in Calcutta," I exclaimed with astonishment, "it is always so hot — and there are no fireplaces."

"Oh, that didn't matter," replied she triumphantly, "I draped the mantelpiece. It looked just as well." And yet there are people who say that the Average Woman has no imagination.

"Talking of age," she continued, "how old do you suppose Mrs. —— is? Somebody at tiffin yesterday *who knew the family* declared that she could not be day under thirty-seven. I should not give her more than thirty-five myself. My husband says thirty-two."

"About a person's age," I said, "what can another person's husband know?"

"What *should* you say?" she insisted. I am sorry to have to underline so much, but you know how the average woman talks in italics. It is as if she wished to make up in emphasis — but I will not finish that good-natured sentence.

"Oh," said I, "you cannot measure Mrs. ———'s age in years! She is as old as Queen Elizabeth and as young as the day before yesterday. Parts of her date from the Restoration and parts from the advent of M. Max Nordau — " At that moment Thalia arrived. "And that is the age of all the world," I finished.

"We were wondering," said the Average Woman, "how old Mrs. ——— is."

"*You* were wondering," I corrected her.

"What does it matter?" said Thalia, which was precisely what I should have expected her to say. What *does* it matter? Why should the average woman excite herself so greatly about this particularly small thing? How does it bear upon the interest or the attractiveness or the value of any woman to know precisely how many years she counts between thirty and forty, at all events to another of her sex? Yet to the average woman it seems to be the all-important fact, the first thing she must know. She is *enragée* to find it out, she will make the most cunning enquiries and take the most subtle means. Much as I appreciate the average woman, I have in this respect no patience with her. It is as if she would measure the pretensions of all others by recognized rule of thumb with a view to discovering the surplus claim and properly scoring it down. It is surely a survival from days when we were much more feminine than we are now; but it is still very general, even among married ladies, for whom, really, the question might have an exhausted interest.

"What does it matter?" said Thalia. "I see your fuchsias, like me, have taken advantage of a fine day to come out. What a lot you've got!"

"Yes," I said, without enthusiasm, "they were here when we came."

"Oh, don't you like them?" exclaimed the Average woman, "I think the fuchsia such a graceful, pretty flower."

"It is graceful and it is pretty," I assented. There are any number of fuchsias, as Thalia said, standing in rows along the paling under the potato-creeper; the last occupant must have adored them. They remain precisely in the pots in which these were originally cherished. Knowing that the first thing I do for a flower I like is to put it in the ground where it has room to move its feet and stir about at night, and take its share in the joys of the community, Tiglath-Pileser says compassionately of the fuchsia, "It is permitted to occupy a pot;" but I notice that he does not select it for his button-hole notwithstanding.

Thalia looked at me suspiciously. "What have you got against it?" she demanded, and the Average Woman chorussed, "Now tell us."

I fixed a fuchsia sternly with my eye. "It's an affected thing," I said. "Always looking down. I think modesty can be an overrated virtue in a flower. It is also like a ballet-dancer, flaunting short petticoats, which doesn't go with modesty at all. I like a flower to be sincere; there is no heart, no affection, no sentiment about a fuchsia."

Thalia listened to this diatribe with her head a little on one side.

"You are *full* of prejudices," said she, "but there is something in this one. Nobody could say 'My love is like a fuchsia.'"

"It depends," I said; "there are ladies not a hundred miles from here who thrill when they are told that they walk like the partridge and shine like the moon. I shouldn't care about it myself."

"No, indeed," said the Average Woman. "That bit beyond the mignonette seems rather empty. What are you going to put in there?"

"Oh, nothing," I said.

"I don't know," remarked Thalia combatively, "when there are so many beautiful things in the world, why you should discriminate in favour of nothing?"

"Yes, why?" said the Average Woman.

"Well," I replied defiantly, "that's my spare bedroom. You've got to have *some*-where to put people. I don't like the feeling that every border is fully occupied and not a square inch available for any one coming up late in the season."

You can see that Thalia considers that while we are respected for our virtues our weaknesses enable us to enjoy ourselves. She accepts them as an integral and intentional part of us and from some of them she even extracts a contemplative pleasure. The Average Woman looks down upon such things and I did not dare to encounter her glance of reserved misunderstanding.

Thalia smiled. I felt warmed and approved. "Alas!" said she, "my garden is all spare bedrooms." She lives, poor dear, on the other side of the Jakko and has to wait till September for her summer. "I see you keep it aired and ready."

As a matter of fact Atma had freshly turned the earth. I hold to that in the garden; it seems to me a parallel to good housekeeping. The new-dug mould makes a most enhancing background; and an empty bed, if it is only freshly made, offers the mind as much pleasure as a gay parterre. It is the sense, I suppose, of effort expended and care taken, and above all it is a stretch of the possible, a vista beyond the realized present which is as valuable in a garden as it is in life. Oh no, not as valuable. In life it is the most precious thing, and it is sparingly accorded. Thalia has it, I know, but I looked at the Average Woman in doubt. Thalia, whatever else she does, will have high comedy always for her portion, and who can tell in what scenes she will play or at what premières she will assist? But the Average Woman, — can one not guess at the end of ten years what she will be talking about, what she will have experienced, what she will have done? I looked at the Average Woman and wondered. She was explaining to Thalia the qualities of milk tea. I decided that she was probably happier than Thalia, and that there was no need whatever to be sorry for her. She stayed a long time; I think she enjoyed herself; and when she went away of course we talked about her.

We spoke in a vein of criticism, and I was surprised to learn that the thing about the Average Woman to which Thalia took most exception was her husband. I had always found the poor patient creatures entirely supportable, and I said so. "Oh, yes," replied Thalia impatiently, "in themselves they're well enough. But didn't you hear her? '*George adores you in "Lady Thermidore."*' Now that annoys me."

"Does it?" said I. "Why shouldn't George adore you in *Lady Thermidore* if he wants to, especially if he tells his wife?"

"That's exactly it," said Thalia. "If he really did he wouldn't tell her. But he doesn't. She just says so in order to give herself the pleasure of imagining that I am charmed to believe that George — her George — "

"I see," I said, sympathetically.

"They are always offering their husbands up to me like that," continued Thalia, gloomily. "They expect me, I suppose, to blush and simper. As if I hadn't a very much better one of my own!"

"They think it the highest compliment they can pay you."

"Precisely. That's what is so objectionable. And besides it's a mistake."

"I shall never tell you that Tiglath-Pileser adores you," I stated.

"My dear, I have known it for ages!" said Thalia, *en se sauvant*, as they do in French novels.

Perhaps the Average Woman is a little tiresome about her husband. She is generally charged with quoting him overmuch. I don't think that; his opinions are often useful and nearly always sensible, but she certainly assumes a far too general interest for him as a subject upon which to dwell for long periods. Average wives of officials are much more distressingly affected in this way than other ladies are; it is quite a local peculiarity of bureaucratic centres. They cherish the delusion, I suppose, that in some degree they advance the interests of these unfortunate men by a perpetual public attitude of adoration, but I cannot believe it is altogether the case. On the contrary, I am convinced that the average official husband himself would find too much zeal in the recounting of his following remarkable traits. His obstinate and absurd devotion to duty. "In *my* husband the Queen has a good bargain!" His remarkable youth for the post he holds, — I remember a case where my budding affection for the wife of an Assistant Secretary was entirely checked by this circumstance. The compliments paid him by his official superiors, those endless compliments. And more than anything perhaps, his extraordinary and deplorable indifference to society. "I simply can*not* get my husband out; I am positively ashamed of making excuses for him." When her husband is served up to me in this guise I feel my indignation rising out of all proportion to its subject, always an annoying experience. Why should I be expected to accept his foolish idea that he is superior to society, and admire it? Why should I be assumed to observe with interest whether he comes out; why indeed, so far as I am concerned, should he not eternally stay in?

It comes to this that one positively admires the woman who has the reticence to let her husband make his own reputation.

What offends one, I suppose, is the lack of sincerity. A very different case is that of the simple soul who says, "Tom will not allow me to have it in the house," or "Jim absolutely refuses to let me know her." One hears that with the warm thrill of mutual bondage; one has one's parallel ready — the tyranny I could relate of Tiglath-Pileser! The note of grievance is primitive and natural; but the woman who butters her husband in friendly council, what excuse has she?

★   ★   ★

Who indeed should care to hear about every day as it goes on under a conifer in a garden, when that garden — let me keep it back no longer — is a mere patch on a mountain top of the Himalayas? Not even India down below there, grilling in the sun which is not quite warm enough here — that would be easy with snakes and palm-trees and mangoes and chutneys all growing round, ready and familiar; but Simla, what is Simla? An artificial little community which has climbed eight thousand feet out of the world to be cool. Who ever leaves Charing Cross for Simla? Who among the world's multitudes ever casts an eye across the Rajputana deserts to Simla? Does Thomas Cook know where Simla is? No; Simla is a geographical expression, to be verified upon the map and never to be thought of again, and a garden in Simla is a vague and formless fancy, a possibility, no more.

★   ★   ★

There is a right side and a wrong side to the mountain of Simla, for it was a mountain eight thousand feet high and equally important long before it became the summer headquarters of the Government of India, and a possible pin-point on the map. These mountains run across the tip of India, you will remember, due east and west, so that if you live on one of them you are very apt to live due north or south. On the south side you look down, on a clear day, quite to the plains, if that is any advantage; you see the Punjab lying there as flat as the palm of your hand and streaked with rivers, and the same sun that burns all India bakes down upon you. On the north side you have turned your back on Hindostan and sit upon the borders of Thibet, a world of mountains bars your horizon, a hermit Mahatma might abide with you in his ashes and have his meditations disturbed by no thought of missionaries or income tax. Your prospect is all blue and purple with a wonderful edge sometimes of white; cool winds blow out of it and fan your roses on the hottest day. Out there is no-man's-land, where the coolies come from, or perhaps the country of a little king who wears his crown embroidered on his turban, and in India who recks of little kings? Out there are no Secretariats, no Army Headquarters, no precedence, probably very little pay, but the vast blue freedom of it! And all expanded, all extended just at your front door.

★   ★   ★

It was an event this morning when Thalia came whisking along the Mall in her rickshaw and turned in here. The Mall, I should mention, is the only road in Simla that has a name. It is a deplorably inappropriate name, it makes you think of sedan-chairs and elderly beaux and other things that have never appeared upon the Himlayas, and it was doubtless given in derision, but it has stuck fast like many another poor old joke until at last people take it seriously and forget that it ever pretended to be humorous. I don't even know whether it is more fashionable to live upon the Mall than elsewhere, or whether one can claim to live upon it when it runs past one's attic windows like an elevated railway; but we have often remarked to one another that if we cannot be said to live upon the Mall we cannot be said to live anywhere and taken what comfort may be had out of that.

★   ★   ★

The founders of Simla — may they dwell in beatitude forever — saw their golden chance and took it. Far in and far up they climbed to build it, and not being gods, but only men, they thought well to leave the more obvious forms of misery out of their survey plans. They brought with them many desirable things, not quite enough, but many; poverty and sorrow and age they left at the bottom of the hill. They barred out greed and ruin by forbidding speculation; they warned off the spectre of decrepitude by the "age limit" which sends you after fifty-five to whiten and perish elsewhere. This is an ordinance that many call divine, for want of a better word, but there ought to be a better word. They made it so expensive that the widow in her black takes the first ship to Balham, and so attractive that the widower promptly marries again. But they also arranged with Death that he should seldom show himself upon the Mall, so nobody has rue to wear, even with a difference. From ten to five we compose Blue Books, at least our husbands do; the rest of the time we gallop about on little country-bred ponies, and vigorously dance, even to fifty-four years, eleven months, and thirty days; and with full hearts and empty heads — and this is the consummation of bliss — congratulate ourselves. There are houses where they play games after dinner. I myself before I became the dryadess of a pencil-cedar, have played games after dinner, and felt as innocent and expansive as I did at nine.

Appendix C

"The Flippancy of Anglo-India," *Indian Daily News* (June 15, 1896)

It is difficult to guess to what extent a native of this country sojourning in England is susceptible of impression, beyond the material circumstances of life—the houses, shops, and music halls, the crowded thoroughfares, the spectacle of the Horse Guards, the redundancy of the hansom cab. If he has an eye to penetrate these things and examine the conditions behind them, and the people whom they in some degree express, he must experience a lively sense of contrast between the English at home and the same people as he has observed them in India. The difference would be a matter of fact and not of sentiments, and would not be affected by his own attitude toward them, or their's [sic] toward him. It goes without saying that the Indian finds the governing race agreeable at home, where his novelty pleases, and where the impression of his charming manners is not corrected by any brutal acquaintance with the characteristics that underly them. But contrasts broader and less personal are also plain, or might be to the Aryan perception: contrasts so palpable as to make more than a British "type" of the Englishman in exile, to make him, at all events, for the period of his life in the country, a differentiated individual moving in his somewhat circumscribed orbit, and responding to laws which mould him daily more and more the Anglo-Indian.

Nothing is more characteristic of English life than its seriousness—the platitude writes itself apologetically, claiming the necessity. We are serious at home in all we do, in work, play, religion, war, politics, literature, society, above all in the way we get our living. In many respects this is the result of Atlantic fogs—the Gulf stream is responsible for many a dull dinner, but in respect of the struggle for life it is directly to be accounted for by the competing pressure of a multitude of others all striving for the thing—the business, the clerkship we hold in our hands. In India—Anglo-India—the conditions are practically reversed.

It is true that the ex vacancy is coveted, the coming retirement—the other man's—sighted for, and often the just preferment perverted—by means not wholly pleasant to contemplate. But there is nothing vital in the struggle; food and shelter do not depend upon it; such things are secure. Leaving out the comparatively small number of capitalists, the merchants, brokers, trades-men, land-owning planters, and the smaller number of independent professional men found almost altogether in the Presidency towns, life goes in India upon props which give the creators thus supported no anxiety. Barring extraordinary incapacity or misbehaviour, fate cannot play him the ill turn of tossing him into the general human scramble to find his level there and prove his worth. The competitive examination is his godmother, and has endowed him with a comfortable purse for moderate exertion all his working day, and the reversion of a chimney-corner afterwards. If not the competition examination, the agreement signed in London; if not the Under-Secretary, the under-salesman, the merchant's assistant, the salaried tea planter. Permanence and affluence depend to some extent upon individual merit in these latter cases but the European occupant of a post of trust in this country holds it unmolested by the knowledge that dogs a man's labour at home, that should he quarrel with his task, or his task quarrel with him, to-morrow there will be found readily fifty to take his place. This would be reason enough for a light heart, but it is not the light heart alone that distinguishes the Anglo-Indian social body. That would be welcomed without criticism, and the air is full of criticism—self-criticism—in Anglo India. We exchange it, always excepting present company, at most dinner-tables; it is considered rather a refined and intellectual form of conversation. The emptiness, the vapidity, the poverty of social interests in this country are charges which we hurl at each other in all politeness constantly. To announce one's self aware of them seems a method of proving one's self their victim, and guiltless of participation. These things, joined to the light heart, result in the flippancy which might strike the observing Bengali returning from being rocked a while in the capacity of adopted child in the cradle of our race.

The condoning and explaining circumstances are not so often discussed. People talk of "official routine," and the number of thousand miles that lie between Bombay and London, and drag in by the horns that inevitable scape-goat, the climate. None of which are, doubtless, without their effect, but they only half account for the somewhat deplorable lightness of tone—co-existing with the dullest respectability—Mr. Kipling, that characterizes the Anglo-Indian community. To the artificial circumstance of pay and pension for ever sure, neither to be added, or subtracted from, to any appreciable extent by individual exertion, must be added all the indifference to the affairs of a country necessarily felt by those who can have no permanent part or lot in it. Even the business of governing, pervaded as it is by the intoxicating exercise of power and vast discretion, is robbed of half of its quality by its alien and temporary nature. It cannot be expected of the most enthusiastic Member of Council that his interest in any Indian bill affecting millions of our "fellow-subjects" from his conception of his duty will be as strong as the sentiment he feels toward the direction of a parochial matter at home. There is no running a hazard with public opinion, there are no risks, no chances, no approval or disapproval that counts to overthrow or his return to office. It is, indeed, a virtue if his work is not perfunctory since it can be inspected and rewarded only from overseas, and he cannot hope to see the fruit of it.

In our remoteness we are also far from the standards, the friction, the stimulus of life at home, and from the contemplation of the problems that perpetually beset the motherland, and are every man's burden. The realities of the existence we were born to, reach us in echoes that grow very faint in their way across the Indian Ocean. So, the male Anglo-Indian out of office is curiously like a bald-headed, moustached schoolboy out of school, while his female counterpart, neither bald-headed, moustached, nor in any way disagreeable, preserves still more remarks by the pleasing *enfantillage* which marks the pretty *débutanté*.

[This article has been attributed to Duncan by Thomas E. Tausky, *Sara Jeanette Duncan: Novelist of Empire*. Port Credit: P.D. Meany Publishers, 1980, 69.]

Appendix D: Contemporary Reviews

1. *Times Literary Supplement* 90 (Friday, October 2, 1903) 280

"The Pool in the Desert"

The globe-trotter in THE POOL IN THE DESERT (Methuen, 6s.), the new book by Mrs. Everard Cotes (Sara Jeannette Duncan), who observed, "I think you Anglo-Indians live in a kind of little paradise," must have been a singularly unintelligent person even for a globe-trotter. If we at home do not learn that Anglo-Indian life is no kind of paradise at all, it is not the fault of our novelists. They give it us from all points of view, and treated in all sorts of ways, of which Mrs. Cotes's is not the least skilful and interesting. Henry James is obvious in every line. You remember what happened in Mrs. Atherton's "The Californians" when "Henry James came." He is more of an active influence on that continent than in England, and they are right to make the very most of him. He is inimitable, but it is good to learn from him; and Mrs. Cotes, if she lacks what Henry James alone has, brings good things of her own into play — quick sympathies, warm blood, and a hearty laugh. The two longest of the four stories in this book tell of Simla — high, superior, official Simla — and of a few people in it whose "souls" (the word is objectionable, but saves periphrasis) have not been frittered away, or suffocated in gold lace, or killed through improper feeding, or starved. They are few, it would seem, and those so desperate that two of them — a middle-aged official and a woman of thirty — go quite off their heads when a young artist who can paint a little arrives. Are not our Anglo-Indian novelists a little apt to forget that, though doubtless things are focussed in India, the world is one? London and Paris can starve souls as well as Simla, for all the possible difference between the Simla Fine Arts Exhibition and the Academy or the Salon. Had the middle-aged official remained in London (and Mrs. Cotes allows that, when he had the chance, he soon threw it up), he would have found it just as difficult to haunt studios, smell paint, and chatter art. The tyranny of cliques is the same all the world over, and was there no nourishment for his soul in India, the country which invented it? A truer criticism on the life is to be found in the story called "A Mother in India," which is far the best of the four. It is admirably written, it deals with facts not fancies, and it handles the intimate tragedy of a situation that is only too common with a humour (the right sort, the sort with tears in it) which lifts it well on to the level of the best.

2. The Spectator (October 31, 1903)

The Pool in the Desert. By Sara Jeannette Duncan. (Methuen and Co. 6s.) — It is difficult to make up one's mind which of the stories in Mrs. Cotes's new book is the most uncomfortable and painful. In the story which gives its name to the collection the chief characters are two married women, intimate friends, and the catastrophe is that one falls in love with the son of the other. This is quite disagreeable enough; but the next story, "A Mother in India," is no more enlivening. Here mother and daughter are so hopelessly estranged by their separation during the girl's childhood that the mother enjoys laughing at her child's limitations and absurdities, just as she would at those of a stranger. The third story, which merely deals with the efforts of some Simla officials to conventionalise a young artist, is the most endurable. But what has Mrs. Cotes done with her inimitable gift of humour? Except for the third story, faintly outlined above, the whole book very nearly deserves the epithet "morbid," and this is an adjective which it is a grief as well as a surprise to have to mention in connection with any work of "Sara Jeannette Duncan."

3. The Critic

Cotes — The Pool in the Desert. By Mrs. Edward Cotes (Sara Jeannette Duncan). Appleton. $1.50.

Mrs. Cotes's tales are generally bright and readable. These four are particularly so, presenting the interesting view of the clever woman of the world who has caught the manner of her evident model, Kipling. Mrs. Cotes knows India well, — to be more definite, the ways and doings of the Anglo-Indian Colony. She gives us the throb of life as it is — in English society — in that eastern, anomalous empire; and, incidentally, picturesque and sometimes brilliant descriptions of the country itself. There is a notable one of the Taj in "A Mother in India," the best and most convincing of the four tales. The first, that names the book, is the shortest and slightest, but not the least vivid. The concluding story, with its dramatic — almost melodramatic — plot, its realistic picture of the little English world at Simla, and its love-tale running like a golden thread through it, we have read before in an English Christmas number, but were glad to meet it again.

4. The Athenæum 3967 (November 7, 1903)

The Pool in the Desert. By Mrs. Everard Cotes (Sara Jeannette Duncan). (Methuen.) — Mrs. Cotes has displayed in her recent works a more serious tendency than at the outset of her literary career, when she was known for a certain flippancy and brightness. These four stories confirm the impression that she desires to attack life with a grave face, as indeed it must be attacked on occasion. On the whole, there is a gain in power, for the sense of humour which characterized her earlier work is not altogether absent. The story of 'A Mother in India' is excellent, and serves to point a moral. The detachment of the mother from the daughter she has hardly ever seen since childhood is sincerely and vividly rendered. The four stories are all studies in situation, the situation usually being sexual. There are few writers who can draw women faithfully, and the women who do so, as a rule, adhere to one type. But Mrs. Cotes has a keen eye for the analysis of her own sex, and succeeds in depicting it in various phases. Nothing could be better than the portrait of Mrs. Innes in 'The Hesitation of Miss Anderson.' It is lifelike, it is convincing, and it is not so merciless as it might well have been. Miss Broughton can draw to perfection a woman whom she abominates. Mrs. Cotes does not seem to abominate any of her characters, which, of course, is a higher artistic attitude. But in the progress of her art Mrs. Cotes seems to be falling into the fault of imitation — a bad thing at any time, particularly so when the model is Mr. Henry James. We do not suppose that she has been consciously copying that master's formulas, but the deliberation of method, the occasional cryptic allusions, and the shyness of coming to close quarters, all suggest his influences. But in an age when the *conte* is cheap and nasty, serious work like this is acceptable.

5. New York Times (October 31, 1903)

In the Style of Henry James.
The Pool in the Desert. By Mrs. Everard Cotes, (Sara Jeannette Duncan.) In one volume. Pp. 318. 12mo. New York: D. Appleton & Co. $1.50
Mrs. Cotes's new volume takes its name from the first, and the shortest, of four stories of Anglo-Indian life, each a novelette rather

than the conventional short story. They are told with much cleverness and subtlety, in the elusive, fine-drawn style of the Henry James cult. Mrs. Cotes knows her world, and she makes her readers know it, too, taking them with her into the alluring, enervating atmosphere of the East — that India which has exercised so mysterious a fascination since the days of "The Lady of the Manor" and "Little Henry and His Bearer."

We think, however, that the Anglo-Indian ladies have cause to complain of the types Mrs. Cotes has presented. They are not at all "nice people." The Decalogue, which we Americans are said to leave at the Mississippi River, appears to be dropped overboard from the P. & O. liners. It is true the heroines do not actually hurl themselves into the abyss, but they are always on the verge — at least in two of the stories. "A Mother in India" and "An Impossible Ideal" steer clear of marital complications. The former gives a cynical picture of what motherhood means to an English officer's wife in India — an unwelcome fact in the beginning, separation and alienation as its sequelae. In "An Impossible Ideal," what seems a simple enough situation is made the most of in true Jamesian fashion, turned about, and dandled, and analyzed, until the ordinary reader is simply bewildered with its gyrations, and is reduced to open-mouthed wonder as to what the author would be at.

The stories are, however, constructed with much skill, and there is a literary quality about the book which gives it distinction; we read it with interest, and at times with delight, but we are unpleasantly conscious at the end that it has left rather "a bad taste in our mouths."

6. *The Academy and Literature* (October 3, 1903)

The Pool in the Desert
By Mrs. Everard Cotes (Sara Jeannette Duncan). (Methuen. 6s.)

Four notable short novels are a handsome allowance for a book that only bears the title of one of them and that one not the best of the bunch. "The Pool in the Desert" is a clever experiment in the style or rather the mannerism of Mr. Henry James. The subject is not inappropriate, for it is a study in incipient adultery which fails of development and ends in a renunciation when the paramount obstacle is removed. The scene is in India, as it is more or less in all the stories, and one is certainly touched by the middle-aged enchantress whose love for a man in his twenties so glorified her that, says the narrator, "I saw her through such a radiance that I could not be sure of seeing her at all." The interest gains by the friendship between this woman of forty and the mother of her lover, but appeal as the story may, we prefer the admirable study in parental relations which immediately follows it. "A Mother in India" forcibly presents a case that is really typical of family life in India: we mean the obligatory separation of child and parent. The soldier's wife of Mrs. Cotes' story is forced to commit her only child to the care of her husband's relations, and when she makes the little creature's acquaintance, it is more than the latter can bear without "hiding its face in the [aunt's] bosom that it knew." The timidity wears off, but the sense of estrangement persists, and the woman who has lived in stir and danger is ultimately companioned for life by a faultlessly priggish maiden, wearing none of that "look of wider seas and skies," with or without "the casual experienced glance, the touch of irony and of tolerance," which her mother attributed to Anglo-Indians. In "An Impossible Ideal" Mrs. Cotes refreshingly recounts the saving relapse into Bohemianism of an artist who was tempted to conquer the Philistines of Simla, and in her last story a jocular bigamist is too entangled in coincidence to be quite convincing. But there is movement and character throughout the volume, and a humour which, in the phrase "precipitous lap," contributes a new comic image to the literature of obesity.

Recommended Reading

Collu, Gabrielle. "Sara Jeannette Duncan: Portrait of a Colonizer/Colonized." *Textual Studies in Canada/Etudes Textuelles au Canada* 5 (1994): 22-31.

Birbalsingh, Frank. "Sara Jeannette Duncan's Indian Fiction." *World Literature Written in English* 16 (1977): 71-81.

Dean, Misao. *A Different Point of View: Sara Jeannette Duncan.* Montreal & Kingston: McGill-Queen's UP, 1991.

—. "The Paintbrush and the Scalpel: Sara Jeannette Duncan Representing India." *Canadian Literature* 132 (Spring 1992): 82-93.

—. "'You May Imagine My Feelings': Reading Sara Jeannette Duncan's Challenge to Narrative." In *Re(Dis)covering Our Foremothers: Nineteenth-Century Canadian Women Writers.* Ed. Lorraine McMullen. Ottawa: U of Ottawa P, 1990. 187-97.

Fowler, Marian. *Redney: A Life of Sara Jeannette Duncan.* Toronto: Anansi, 1983.

Gerson, Carole. "Wild Colonial Girls: New Women of the Empire, 1883-1901." *Journal of Commonwealth and Postcolonial Studies* 3:1 (Fall 1995): 61-77.

Nagarajan, S. "Sara Jeannette Duncan's Anglo-Indian Novels." *Journal of Commonwealth Literature* 12:1 (1977): 33-45.

Saunders, Rebecca. "Gender, Colonialism and Exile: Flora Annie Steel and Sara Jeannette Duncan." *Women's Writing in Exile.* Ed. Mary-Lynn Broe and Angela Ingram. Chapel Hill: U of North Carolina P, 1989.

Tausky, Thomas E. "Sara Jeannette Duncan and Her Works." In *Canadian Writers and Their Works.* Fiction Series, vol. 3. Ed. Robert Lecker, Jack David, and Ellen Quigley. Downsview: ECW, 1988. 23-100.

—. *Sara Jeannette Duncan: Novelist of Empire.* Port Credit: P.D. Meany, 1980.

—. *Sara Jeannette Duncan: Selected Journalism.* Ottawa: Tecumseh Press, 1978.

Zezulka, J.M. "Passionate Provincials: Imperialism, Regionalism, and Point of View." *Journal of Canadian Fiction* 22 (1978): 80-92.

—. "Duncan's Passage to India." *Canadian Literature* 73 (1977): 39-53.